# After the Peace

After hard times and odd jobs as a lone parent, FAY WELDON became one of the top advertising copywriters of her generation. She moved to TV drama (writing the pilot episode of the iconic series *Upstairs Downstairs*), then turned to novels – including classics like *The Life and Loves of a She Devil* and *The Cloning of Joanna May*. Her later sequence of novels about the Dilberne family, the Love and Inheritance trilogy and *Before the War*, draws to a close with this final instalment, *After the Peace*. Fay's been honoured as a CBE for services to literature, and is currently a Professor of Creative Writing at Bath Spa University.

# ALSO BY FAY WELDON

## FICTION

The Fat Woman's Joke
Down Among the Women
Female Friends
Remember Me
Little Sisters
Praxis
Puffball
The President's Child
The Life and Loves of a She Devil
The Shrapnel Academy
The Heart of the Country
The Hearts and Lives of Men
The Rules of Life
Leader of the Band
The Cloning of Joanna May
Darcy's Utopia
Growing Rich
Life Force
Affliction
Splitting
Worst Fears
Big Women
Rhode Island Blues
The Bulgari Connection
Mantrapped
She May Not Leave
The Spa Decamaron
The Stepmother's Diary
Chalcot Crescent

Kehua!
Habits of the House
Long Live the King
The New Countess
The Ted Dreams
Before The War
Death of a She Devil

## CHILDREN'S BOOKS

Wolf the Mechanical Dog
Party Puddle
Nobody Likes Me

## SHORT STORY COLLECTIONS

Watching Me, Watching You
Polaris
Moon Over Minneapolis
Wicked Women
A Hard Time to Be a Father
Nothing to Wear & Nowhere to Hide
Mischief

## NON-FICTION

Letters to Alice
Rebecca West
Sacred Cows
Godless in Eden
Auto da Fay
What Makes Women Happy
Why Will No-One Publish My Novel?

# After the Peace

## Fay Weldon

HEAD
of ZEUS

# After the Peace

*In the year 1979, the young Viscount Hedleigh, heir of the 8th Earl of Dilberne, drunk, in love and penniless, visited a sperm bank and earned £25 by selling his seed.*

*It was a very foolish thing to do.*

PART ONE

# PART ONE

## Rozzie Is Conceived

A whole lot of people were involved in Rozzie's conception. That was in 1999, some twenty years ago, when smartphones hardly existed. There were the initial four of us. One birth mother, pretty, hippie Xandra, aged thirty-nine. One very handsome – legal – father, Clive, aged thirty-six. There was one family friend to witness – that was me, Gwinny Rhyss, aged fifty-nine. And then, trapped inside the turkey baster, was the fourth: the sperm, the very essence of the young Viscount Sebastian Hedleigh.

There seems to be no firm use-by date for frozen sperm. Sebastian had been a stripling of twenty-two when he spent his seed, but was forty-two and by then the Earl of Dilberne when I finally injected Xandra's womb with the stuff. Clive had been the one who was going to do the plunging, but he lost his nerve at the last minute.

But we four were only the first of those responsible for Rozzie's existence – there were a whole lot more if you include the white-coated medical staff of the new Your Beautiful Baby Clinic in 1979 – in the unsupervised days when sperm donation was anonymous and a convenient commercial transaction, available to any casual passer-by who looked vaguely okay. No medical tests were required.

All the high flyers pictured in the YBBC brochure were involved in the birth one way or another, ten men and two women, in white coats and of various ages, lined up and brightly smiling, though a shifty-looking lot they seem to me in spite of their apparently excellent qualifications in genetic technology. But perhaps it's just the flares and the hair down to the shoulders.

You can find a copy of the original seventies prospectus of the YBBC online – I did. The place has long since closed. In 2005 anonymity of donors became illegal, and the supply of impoverished passers-by dried up, so the sperm banks did too. Flick through the pages and view the blank, outlined heads of available donors, rows and rows of them all the same: no names, no pack drill, no legal complications, just a brief caption beneath each silhouette citing occupation, eye colour, temperament and profession. Thus, donor No. 116349: '*6ft 1in, blue eyes, blond hair: BA (Oxon), action man, aristocrat.*' It was above these few words that my pencil circled and struck in January 1999.

We were all a long time getting there. It is my avowed intent to tell you how Rozzie came about. I have done my course in creative writing. I will do my best to be a reliable narrator. It was a long and arduous journey. Me, Gwinny Rhyss, of 23 Standard Road, NW5. My home.

## Men Have Art, Women Have Babies

That early staffing gender ratio is an interesting matter. The fertility business, and it's a very lucrative one, still seems to attract mostly men – envious, I daresay, of the female power to create. 'Men have art, but women have babies' was a common observation in my young days, and presented as an equivalence, a sop to any women envious of the male artist. As if by controlling and witnessing birth, men could own that too. And then, as domestic technology advanced, women had time and energy to go out to work and earn their independence, stopped worshipping the phallus and claimed art to be as much theirs as anyone else's.

Women no longer just had babies or looked pretty on a stage: now they had time to write and paint, compose, all sorts of things as well and be taken just as seriously as any man. And, to get things balanced again, men have been driven to get more and more involved with the technology of birth. One should not complain or bitch about that.

But by plunging the turkey baster on March 18th 1999, I had at least taken some part of the process back into female hands. I keep that brochure in mind as a memento of my courage and the wisdom of my choice.

Sebastian's theoretically anonymous sperm had been kept in various freezers since 1979. Xandra and Clive did not get married until 1986, after several years of living in sin – much to the distress of Xandra's mother. Perhaps the spirit of the sixties was carried in Sebastian's sperm, together with the subsequent disillusion that went with it. For him, the *All You Need is Love* theory of existence was fast being replaced by Sid Vicious's *My Way*. If Rozzie emerged into the world carrying all the baggage of four decades, and found the need to shuffle off the burden of the past it was hardly unreasonable.

'*Living in sin*' – Good Lord, to think we once thought like that!

## The Day Of The Plunger

'*Between the idea And the reality Between the notion And the act Falls the Shadow,*' Clive misquoted Eliot, as he sought to impregnate his wife with another man's sperm, turkey baster held high.

Clive had a ready fund of quotable lines, seeing himself as a great if misunderstood literary figure, when actually he was a spectacularly good-looking actor of the action man variety, who'd once enjoyed a successful career as a tenor in the world of West End musicals. But I could see his hand trembling. It was an elegant, sensitive hand, well creamed and beautifully manicured. It seemed the wrong moment to start an argument, even though the word is usually 'motion' not 'notion', thus making nonsense of the quote, but never mind – me, I blame printer error – as his wife lay there with her legs open. I let it go. 'And that shadow is doubt, Xandra,' Clive stage-whispered loudly, urgently. 'A great overwhelming doubt!' His brilliant blue eyes glittered, his curved lips quivered. 'I'm sorry, but I can't do this. You do it, Gwinny. You're the lucky one.' He lowered the plunger and handed it to me. 'Gwinny, will you please do the honours?' I took it into my rather red, slightly swollen, un-manicured hands.

'Oh please do hurry, Gwinny,' begged Xandra. 'Just do it, before I change my mind as well. Don't let the stuff get cold again!'

So it was that I, Lady Gwyneth Petrie of No. 23 Standard Road, NW5, otherwise known as Gwinny Rhyss of the same address, neighbour and witness to the life of Clive and Xandra Smithson next door at No. 24 – and having no children of her own – was the one who brought a new soul to life in the shape of Rozzie Smithson, destined to become the Lady Rosalind Montewan, born on New Year's Day, 2000. A Millennial, if ever there was one.

## The Moment Of Choice

Possible choices of suitable father, each captioned with a brief description of looks and temperament, appeared in blank silhouette on the 'Now choose your donor' pages of the Woolland Brilliant Baby Clinic's brochure. Would I have done better to have decided on '*5ft 11in, brown eyes, black hair: writer, thinker, healer*', rather than the '*6ft 1in, blue eyes, blond hair: BA (Oxon), action man, aristocrat*'? The blond aristocrat won.

I was born the daughter of a Welsh coal miner turned builder, so any innate grovelling to the upper classes, as the unkind few have suggested, was out of the question. Besides, I had learned the habits and failings of the aristocracy all too well in my earlier life to afford them undue respect.

No, being rather short myself, at 5ft 3in – back in the eighties an unfortunate *Daily Mail* headline about me read 'Pocket Cougar Venus Strikes Again' – I went for the extra two inches, and so ended up inadvertently choosing DNA which has been causing trouble for generations. Dilberne genes. The Dilberne family – peers since the reign of Henry VIII – has accumulated a lot of unfortunate DNA along the way, insisting, as they so often did, on marrying for love and not for property or land. Once unstable genes are introduced into a blood line, there's no getting rid of them: they keep resurfacing. Ask anyone who studies racing form or dog breeding.

But I may delude myself as to my own nature. Looking back, I fear my choice that day was motivated by a lack of self-worth, a poor self-image, rather than anything else – an absurd admiration for height. It was the extra inches that swung me. Stupid, stupid. If karma came back to bite me in the years that followed in the form of Rozzie herself, I could hardly be surprised.

Xandra and Clive declined to take on the responsibility of choice. Xandra claimed her eyes went blurry when she looked at the lists: Clive said, 'In that case leave it to Gwinny. She's the lucky one.' So out of guilt, I, Gwinny, obliged.

My finger dropped on '*action man, aristocrat*'. And that was that. A sloppy description in the first place, by some tired white-coated moron on duty at the 24/7 clinic the night of the deposit, hastily writing down the brief description the law required of sperm depositors at the time: height, race (defined by the colour of the eyes), education and profession. Sebastian probably said he had been a Captain of Cricket at Eton – the kind of thing young men were still proud of in 1979, the year Margaret Thatcher became Britain's first female Prime Minister, punk rocker Sid Vicious was found dead in New York and Mother Teresa won the Nobel Prize for Peace. Times have changed.

## Oh Yes, Gwinny Always Obliged

Just as when in 1999, Clive kept saying 'You do it, Gwinny! You're lucky,' leaving me to take up the syringe and glug the thawed and living Dilberne DNA into Xandra's vagina. At least we hoped it was living. It was sold to us at half price, being old stock: twenty years old, but it lived, and it produced our miraculous Rozzie.

Just as when in 2000, I named the baby Rosalind it had been 'You decide, Gwinny!' – Xandra being too exhausted and not sure she loved the baby (a difficult birth can create a delay in the bonding process) and Clive complaining there was too much choice, it gave him a headache. He'd hoped for a boy. Xandra had wanted a girl. So had I, very much so. I was not too fond of baby boys.

I liked Rosalind as a name, having been a great E. Nesbit reader when I was a child. I had adored *The Story of the Amulet* and *Five Children and It*. Rosalind sounded so hopeful, sweet and good and so it was that this name ended up on the birth certificate. Rosalind Melrose Smithson (the Melrose after Clive's deceased mother). As it turned out the name did not suit her in the least.

Far too Victorian for a Millennial. She was soon enough called 'Rozzie' anyway, which – ambitious, determined and ruthless – did not sound sweet and gentle at all.

So really I suppose all four of us, Xandra, Clive and me, not forgetting Lord Sebastian Dilberne, Rozzie's progenitor, deserved what we got. His Lordship, penniless and drunk as he was, should have walked home instead of selling his soul and his inheritance for a taxi fare home. Mind you, in those days twenty-five quid would have taken him almost all the way to Dilberne Court, the family seat in Sussex, not just the town house in Belgrave Square, such has been the devaluation of our currency.

I did not ask for this power over the Smithsons' lives. I suppose it was because I was a generation older than they were. I was a child of the 1940s, they of the 1960s: they respected me. I had money in the bank. They seemed to need me, and thought I was lucky, if a bit nuts. That everything always turned out right for me. Well, sometimes it did, sometimes it didn't.

The numbers in Standard Road run consecutively, not odd on one side, even on the other. I have no idea why. The Smithsons seemed a very pleasant young latter-day hippie couple, if on the hapless side, when they turned up with the estate agent. I'd not wanted No. 24 next door to lie empty, and to this end I had guaranteed their mortgage. In the same way people just drift apart we happened to just drift together. If we were in each other's pockets all the time it was because we found those pockets cosy, companionable and comfortable.

Or so I find it convenient to tell myself. It's true that when the Smithsons first moved in there were absurd rumours up and down Standard Road of troilism 'goings on' between No. 23 and No. 24: all total nonsense. Nothing sexual whatsoever ever went on between us.

We certainly were in and out of each other's houses a good deal throughout the nineties. Xandra needed feeding when she came home from her nursing shift. Clive had to be dragged away from writing his verse-novel, play or musical – sometimes *A Broken Chord*, sometimes *The Roar of Lament*, though occasionally it was a kind of multimedia opera, *Let's Get Out of Here!* He was good at titles, it was only the content and word-count that eluded him. And he was a rotten cook anyway. I'm what they call a good plain cook, that is to say better at feeding than concocting, better at fish fingers and chips than at a cheese soufflé, but no-one ever went hungry. I grew up with four ravenous wolves as younger brothers so I do know how to feed people. The neighbours went on puzzling and gossiping about what our relationship could possibly be… 'the nutty old lady with her yellow cycling leggings – once a whore always a whore – and that handsome young pair next door – well, him anyway, though she wasn't lasting so well, beginning to thicken up a bit in the middle in a double-chinnish sort of way – night shifts could do that to a girl (all those biscuits) which left him and the old bat together, and who paid whom for what? Troilists!'

A poison pen letter came through the letterbox to that effect but Clive Smithson laughed it off. 'Sticks and stones may hurt our bones, but words will never hurt me. Some nutter. Gwinny, do stop being so paranoiac!'

And he was right. It was only the once.

## The Other Man

The young Viscount Sebastian had been, as he eventually confessed, wildly intoxicated at the time of that one notable youthful ejaculation – there were to be thousands more in his lifetime, no doubt – but this was the first to bear fruit, and so was eventually to attract the concern of the Law Lords.

His Lordship was in love and on his uppers and extremely drunk – never a good combination – when he and his Bullingdon Club friends, having lost everything in their wallets gambling at the Clermont in Berkeley Square, were escorting their friend Monty back to his home in Regent's Park and happened to pass by the Your Beautiful Baby Clinic. Deposited sperm being still unattributable, trade was booming at the 'bank', which offered an all-night service. The young Sebastian, realising he could make £25 to pay for his taxi fare home to Belgrave Square, or even further, stepped inside. The chap in a white coat inside the open door made the quick assessment of appearance, race and temperament that was later to feature in the YBBC brochure, and guided him to a cubicle, handing over a selection of pornographic magazines. They were tame enough compared to today's porn sites, but more than sufficient for the comparatively innocent yet randy young Viscount. In and out within fifteen minutes. When he left a queue was already forming outside.

'It was a medical emergency,' Sebastian argued to his friends as they went on to Regent's Park. 'A necessity. Abstinence is bad for a young man's health, everyone knows. No-one else seems to value what I can offer. The lovely Veronica spurns it. Let the bank have it. Oh the spinning, the spilling, the spurning, the spurting of the spunk!'

At the time the Viscount was given to fantastical phrasing and fancied himself something of a belle-lettrist. Forty or so years later Monty was to quote this 'spilling, spurning, spurting spunk' to the judge in what became vulgarly known as the Dilberne Spillage Case, and caused great merriment in the land.

Sebastian was indeed being cruelly spurned by the Hon. Veronica Venice, a nineteen-year-old upper-class waif, who valued her virginity very much, not without reason. The upper classes have been breeding dogs, horses, wives and daughters for generations and know well enough that once a female of any species 'gets out' and procreates, it never afterwards reliably 'breeds true'. Nor do today's genetic scientists laugh the notion out of court; mitochondria in the womb lining do tend to linger and drift from receiving womb to receiving womb, via the phallus.

Only recently have our own royal family allowed non-virgins into the bloodline, and even back in the late eighties several of the nobility still saw an immaculate bride as the safer choice.

Veronica was not aiming directly for royalty – there were few available at the time – but a peerage is always nice. Who is to say what goes on in the head of a girl keen on self-advancement?

But really Sebastian should have known better.

## A Tricky Inheritance

On the good side, the bloodline of the lords and ladies of the Dilberne family does not date back to the age of the robber barons, but only to an artist-craftsman of Tudor times. It was in 1532 that one Hugh Hedleigh, master draper and Alderman of the City of London, became the first Earl of Dilberne and Montewan, for providing the monarch Henry VIII with six gold buttons decorated with blue enamelled hearts, together with the words *Amor Vincit Omnia* – love conquers all – to be worn at the King's ill-fated wedding to Anne Boleyn. Ill-fated for Anne, at least.

The coat of arms of the Dilbernes became an escutcheon with a laurel wreath around a lion rampant, a rose surrounded by a heart and a family motto, *Amor Vincit Omnia* – though it should have become obvious through the centuries that love, far from conquering all, simply causes a great deal of trouble. Through the centuries the Lords of Dilberne turned out to be a romantic and impulsive lot. They often married for love, and a lot of good it did them.

*'Love is all'*, we used to blithely sing when young, only little by

little coming to understand as so many Millennials do that in the end money, not love, is everything. Not *amor vincit omnia* so much as *pecunia vincit amor.*

And then Sebastian comes along towards the end of the twentieth century and can hardly be expected to resist the tendency to folly in his own inheritance. He is prone to impulsive gestures not just by temperament but by breeding. He should have borne his torment in patience. His seed was valuable: it carried with it status and possessions; he should have guarded it better for a suitable future destination, and not acted as if the Your Beautiful Baby Clinic was Onan's sister-in-law. At least he could, like Onan, have spilled it on the ground and thrown it away. Genesis 38:9: *'he spilled it on the ground, lest that he should give seed to his brother.'*

The legal and personal ramifications that might possibly ensue were far from his Lordship's mind. Sperm donation might have been technically anonymous but it was not going to be so difficult for his daughter to discover from whose loins she came and play it to her advantage.

Sebastian was born on June 27th. I, Gwinny, of course, have 'done' his star chart. The aristocracy may be richer and snootier than the rest of us, but they are as predisposed as the rest of us to the various blessings and calamities the stars preordain. So perhaps Sebastian is to be forgiven. It's just that Rozzie never would, never could, forgive. Being born with her sun in Capricorn, and her moon in Taurus in the ascendant, she was all too likely to bear grudges.

# The Moving Finger

Anyhow, there I was in March 1999 adding to family number by means of a turkey baster, Xandra on the bed with her navy polka-dotted skirt pulled up and rumpled and her legs apart, with Clive shielding his eyes in exaggerated horror as he watched. The turkey baster did glug rather ominously as I plunged in the very essence of what we later found out to be Sebastian. A turkey baster – in case you don't know – is a large plastic syringe which sucks up the juices in the pan in which a turkey is roasting and squirts it back over the breast to stop the skin drying out, so the bird emerges from the oven golden and splendid. Rather like Rozzie herself, come to think of it. She was the most beautiful baby.

But what was done on that day, was done. Too late to worry. As Xandra (born Sandra) closed her legs Clive quoted from FitzGerald's 1859 translation of *The Rubaiyat of Omar Khayyam* from 1100: *The moving finger writes, And having writ, Moves on: nor all thy piety and wit Shall lure it back to cancel half a line, Nor all thy tears wash out a word of it.*

Clive was a constant quoter. We all were, we pre-Millennials. We looked to the past for comfort and perhaps a little poetic wisdom to help us on our way. Millennials hardly ever quote: they seem to be in denial of anything pre-computer age, and look askance at us crumblies when we do it. They never learn anything 'by heart', as we used to call it. Perhaps they don't have hearts in the way we did? They'll burst into song, though, relying on a common current resonance, a common current understanding, just not old literature. Too elitist. Little girls will sing about letting it go, letting it go, turning away and slamming the door, because that's so now, but poetry is somehow suspect, an attempt to drag the young into the dusty, dangerous, privileged past.

And I must say even back then Clive's particular quoting habit could annoy. It felt over-theatrical – it wasn't as if we were at all sure the thawed stuff would work; it had been in the freezer for so long – and then he'd hidden his eyes and left the actual doing to me. He claimed the drama: he took the credit: I did the work. But what can you expect from an actor?

In the same way as my mother's generation used to quote the *Rubaiyat* for consolation, Khalil Gibran's *The Prophet* seemed to work for the next, all of us seeking Sufic wisdom from far away and long ago. As similar comfort-prose, I won't say banality, once Rozzie was born Clive became very fond of a particular quote from Gibran: *You are the bows from which your children as living arrows are sent forth.* He knew well enough that Rozzie wasn't his flesh and blood, but he was happiest in denial, preferring fiction to fact. Well, he's not the only one.

Both fathers, the legal one Clive and the birth one Sebastian, came to adore Rozzie, even though the emotion was not necessarily returned. She was, as Millennials might say, a touch Aspergery.

*My darlings, you give but little when you give of your possessions. It is when you give of yourself that you truly give* was another of the annoying Gibran quotes on which Clive was so keen. He would say it (indulgently, so we couldn't take offence) when leaving me or Xandra to pick up the tab at pub or restaurant. Had Clive not graced us with his presence, his beauty? Was not that worth more than vile money? He was almost pathologically stingy, as we see in the fact that even the sperm Xandra used was half price, being old stock.

He was lavish with words of love, but seldom with immediate cash. When it came to it, when paternal concern changed to a need for paternal activity he suffered from the same reluctance. He would rather watch the game on TV than get up and collect Rozzie from school. Too often that was left to me.

'Miss Rhyss, can you come round now and collect Rozzie? The father's not turned up and his phone seems to be off the hook.' And off I'd go, a signed-up and authorised proxy carer to collect pretty, charming, bright little Rozzie – gentle and sweet, an apparent child prodigy who in those days seldom cried and never complained.

Xandra was too busy at her life-and-death job up at the hospital for anyone to even think of trying to contact her. Besides, after the Millennium the hospital switchboard was always too busy to respond and mobiles had to be turned off near sensitive electronic equipment.

If one ever reproached Clive for not turning up when he said he would, he'd turn again to Gibran, always to me quite a puzzle: *'Yet the timeless in you is aware of life's timelessness, and knows that yesterday is but today's memory and tomorrow is today's dream.'*

I suppose nothing really changes as the generations try to justify themselves by fine words. In the same way that pert-bosomed Millennials now defend themselves, putting their trust in MeToo hashtags rather than the wordy philosophical ramblings of Eastern sages.

Oh, the guilt! How the past has caught up with us. How little we did to control the future. I should have stilled the moving finger that wrote while there was time, listened to my own misgivings. Xandra should not have been thrown by the thought of her relentless biological clock. Clive should have faced up to the fact that Rozzie was not his own, not preferred to be an adoring bad parent than not the parent at all, and should somehow have contained his own panicky meanness with money, time and affection. Should, should, should. Nor was I without fault.

Ovid got it right, way back when BC turned into AD: *Video meliora proboque, deteriora sequor*. I see the better way, and approve, but follow the worse. Whatever changed?

## A Matter Of Inheritance

This new science of genetics, feeding scraps of the frozen seed of the past into the present, must have caused quite a stir in the Bardo Thodol. This is the realm where, according to the *Tibetan Book of the Dead*, the souls of the unborn linger, waiting to choose their parentage. (Thus eventually, the belief was, that over a few million years, the scales of right and wrong would balance and a state of natural justice be achieved.) Sebastian, in his later years a member of the Buddhist Learning Centre, once told me he assumed Rozzie was the spirit of his great-great-grandmother Adela returned to bring about the fall of the House of Dilberne. But that, I imagine, was his guilt speaking. He should not have done what he did. Rozzie was his karma, not only for what he had done but for twelve generations of the Dilberne family working through him. She was the karma of all of us.

## Not In Our Stars But In Ourselves

Of course it's Gwinny (that's me) telling this tale: not some omniscient narrator. She just puts herself into the third person from time to time to get a more objective view of what went on; to at least attempt to see things from others' points of view, and so maintain impartiality and not put herself in as too much of a heroine. When writing in the first person it's all 'me, me, me' so one tends to absolve oneself from blame, while owing it to one's craft not to do so. Slips into partiality are all too easy. But here I am in the third person, speaking truth to power, in this case the narrator.

Let me warn you about Gwinny. She's something of a nutter. She will offer up the pattern of certain planets when people are born as an explanation of their personalities and habits. Instead of just describing the sperm-born Rozzie as having a paranoid personality disorder she will claim that the child's sun and moon are in a difficult relationship with one another due to the time of day and place where she was born – 'sun in Capricorn, moon in Taurus!' Which is obviously nutty and annoying to sensible people, though odd how so many use such metaphors in casual conversation:. *What star sign are you? A Leo? I'm a Virgo so we're bound to get on!* or *'Everything's going wrong, Mercury's gone retrograde yet again!'* and so forth.

Gwinny has been told that, evidenced by her strange beliefs, she suffers from a defensive paranoid personality disorder cluster complicated by a distorted thinking pattern. Which is why she'll believe in anything: not just astrology, but karma, telepathy, telekinesis, pricking of her thumbs and warnings from 'the other side' and even use Quantum theory – nothing has to be what it seems – to justify herself. She goes to fortune tellers. She drifts from one belief system to another in her 'search for answers'. If it's not the Welsh Catholic Christianity where she began, it's Buddhism and the *Tibetan Book of the Dead* and a kind of diffused animism in which karma plays a large part, and then eventually Hellenism – worship of lots of gods not just one, thus spreading her bets: polytheism not mono-theism, however much the latter is supposed to have advanced human civilisation.

Gwinny is fairly sure the Olympian Gods still move amongst us (she once encountered Apollo as the sun rose over Primrose Hill) often taking the form of our present-day celebrities in their louche attempts to further their sexual designs. Weinstein might be Zeus for all we know, ravishing Europa in the form of a bull, the better to conceive King Minos. David Icke might be Boreas, God of the cold North Wind, dismissing politicians as lizard forms, their tongues spitting poison. It's all a matter of metaphor.

And perhaps it was the Greek Goddess Flora who possessed me on that day in 1999 when Xandra and Clive implored me, 'Oh go on, Gwinny. *You* choose. You're so lucky!' – as we all three studied the instruction booklet the day the frozen sperm arrived in its cold pack through the letterbox. The original brochure, by the way, had been ever so well designed but they'd taken no trouble at all with this booklet. It was twelve badly printed pages, cheaply produced and hastily written. Why bother, I suppose, once they'd taken the money?

It was observably true I was lucky, most noticeably when it came to parking spaces: 'Hail Mary, full of grace,' I'd cross my fingers and mutter, 'let me find a parking space' – and lo! There would be one. That always impressed Xandra and Clive.

So it was that I, Gwinny Rhyss, of 23 Standard Road, NW5, the little terraced house where I'd been born, for thirteen years neighbour and witness to the life of the Smithsons next door at No. 24 – was to press the plunger and thus cause the soul of Rozzie to slip from the plane of the Bardo Thodol and into this alarming world of ours. Mind you, it was high time. Since the very day they'd moved in, since the day I'd guaranteed their mortgage, since the fabulous floral wedding (I paid for the flowers) on Hampstead Heath, the Smithson couple had been trying to become a family, not just a young couple. I could hear them next door trying; the walls were thin.

# Between The Notion And The Act Came The Wedding

My hope is that the reader will overlook Gwinny's occasional descent into schizotypal personality disorder, with a hint of paranoia, and see her as a troubled friend in need of help rather than an annoyance. Gwinny is the only narrator available who knows or can imagine the totality of this rather startling story about sperm banks, the druggy life, the guilt of the past and the revenge of the Millennials. And how, in some detail, and as the result of influences dating back some sixty years, Rozzie came to be born, one foot in the twentieth century, the other in the twenty-first.

Yet with what high hopes did Gwinny not embrace the Clive Smithson/Xandra Barker retro flower-power wedding in the June of 1986? Clive was twenty-three and Xandra twenty-six. High time to join the knot.

Much of the couple's twenties had slipped away in an acid and marijuana haze. Clive and Xandra had met when he was at drama school and she was studying to be a doctor, had been together for several visionary, rave-filled years, and let it be known that they were still tremendously in love. With this wedding they had declared their rejection of all that was past, a determination to live in newness of life in the next stage of their existence, drug-free, punk-piercing free, and finally settle down – boringly square though that might seem to some – to be adults and raise a family. Time, both agreed, to finally grow up. Clive was desperate to be fruitful and multiply, fill the earth and subdue it; and Xandra too, or so she said.

So much they publicly declared, even having a carpenter carve their resolve in antique rural script (rather ugly, as it turned out) onto a wooden board, to hang up by a nail on an old oak tree during the wedding party they planned for the first Midsummer's Day after they owned their own house. And now thanks to the nice lady next door at No. 23, they had it. A home of their own ready to move into at 24 Standard Road, NW5.

Not grand by NW3 reckoning or even NW1. NW3 had the heath and the wealth; Primrose Hill, NW1, just down the road, had a rare green space with trees, a children's sandpit and lots of artists, and was more exciting. Standard Road, NW5, a short brick terrace built by Victorian speculators for railway workers, was very much a poor relation. But for the Smithsons it was a start. And they'd have a Lady Gwyneth Petrie next door to add class, in other words Gwinny, the artist next door, who was rich enough to help them with their mortgage, and when the time came, help turn their fabulous flowery dream wedding into reality.

'*In fair round belly with good capon lin'd, with eyes severe and beard of formal cut, full of wise saws and modern instances,* that's us,' Clive had said – there is usually a Shakespeare quote for every occasion.

The sign now hangs in the kitchen of No. 24. Rozzie would read it fifteen years or so later – she was to be a bright child, reading when she was three – and could be seen on occasion staring at her pot-smoking, life-exhausted parents in dismay.

## Childhood Memories

Gwinny very much wanted the Smithsons' dream of happiness to come true. She had moved back into her childhood home a year back, and found it not quite what she had hoped. Used to big spaces, she found herself now confined to smaller rooms than she remembered. She had cleverly managed to buy No. 22 the other side, the better to 'break through' and so, she hoped, double the square footage available – only to find the neighbours were appealing to the Land Tribunal on some spurious ground or another, and work had to stop. The end-of-terrace property on Gwinny's other side, No. 24, was up for sale, but Gwinny could see that breaking through there would only run into the same difficulty. The neighbours were really not very nice at all, muttering, gossiping and pointing behind her back. A few remembered her in her teenage years. Those who remembered her as a child, when she was their little-girl midwife-helper, were all dead and gone.

'Rich bitch,' she heard someone say. And she once thought she heard 'whore!' behind her back but couldn't be sure. It might be her schizotypal personality disorder raising its ugly head, one had to be careful. But now the Smithsons were moving in and she wanted dull little Standard Road to ring again to the sound of childish laughter, the pitter-pat of little footsteps – only girlish ones this time, skipping and hopping and trilling – not the biffs and bangs, the shouts, curses and fireworks of Gwinny's four little brothers (little in birth order but not size), those tramplers of dreams, as they disturbed the peace of the street.

She had failed with her brothers, perhaps she would not fail this time? How she had longed for a little sister, though one by one, as a child herself, she had midwifed the boys' appearance into the world. Geraint, Owen, Trefor, David – all home births in the front room of the house she now lived in. She, Gwinny, the eldest child, the only girl, had witnessed those pink, sticky, enormous, overpowering male genitals as one by one her brothers emerged from the stretched rawness of their tiny mother, and despaired. She'd so wanted a sister. But it was not to be.

In April the Smithsons moved in, along with smart new furniture from Habitat and lots of books and saucepans, Gwinny was pleased to see, and no smell of dope. She'd paid for a thorough cleanse of the house and garden, and a few minor repairs as soon as the sale went through so the young couple wouldn't be faced with dirt, dust, spiders and strange smells when they arrived. She did it tactfully; nobody need know. She didn't want to be seen as an interfering busybody. She was rewarded by the young couple's smiling, cheerful, friendly faces, and indeed the sound of marital congress before the carpets were even down. The walls would need to be soundproofed but she could do that from her side. Surely the street would now cheer up.

The Smithsons had indeed turned over the new leaf they promised when Gwinny guaranteed their mortgage: they were settling down, starting a family, leaving the hectic life behind, just as Gwinny had, and going ahead with a wedding that was both celebrating the past and declaring their hope for the future. People were to talk about it for years.

## A Failure Of Nerve

And just in time. I'd been on the brink of moving somewhere more appropriate for a wealthy aspiring artist than Standard Road when Clive and Xandra Smithson turned up, and I knew by the pricking of my thumbs they were right for the house.

I'd even begun looking for a property in Cheyne Walk – a notoriously good address – all kinds of famous and arty people had lived here, from Whistler's mother to Dante Gabriel Rossetti, Holman Hunt to Thomas Carlyle and Mick Jagger, and I thought I would feel more at home there than I was in Standard Road. Fewer nasty remarks and whispers behind my back.

Sebastian was later to tell me the house I'd been looking at was where Sherwyn Sexton, his saintly grandmother Vivvie's husband, had kept his artist mistress back in the 1930s, but it seemed too garbled a version of events long past to take seriously. The really interesting thing was that the house next door was up for sale and valued at £9,000,000. It was being cleared and there was a whole row of skips outside. Sebastian stopped the car to scrabble through them and search for a bargain (the rich love bargains) and saw an old purple crushed-velvet sofa with its innards falling out, which Sebastian claimed was a valuable antique. We put it in the boot – lucky it was a Rolls – and ran off with it. He said his daughter Victoria would love it.

But the real point was that when I looked at the next-door house in Cheyne Walk in 1986 it was up for sale at a mere

£90,000. If I'd bought it I'd be really, *really* rich by now, but that wasn't to be. There's more to life than money. Well, it's what they say.

The Smithsons moved into No. 24 on April 5th — I remember the date because it was Agnetha Fältskog's birthday and I was a big Abba fan then.

## A Question Of Bonding

They planned the wedding for Midsummer's Day, Saturday, June 22nd. Just as well Xandra showed me the invitations before they went out; they had the day wrong. Midsummer that year was Friday June 21st. They had to decide whether to ditch the invitations and try again — they were very expensive and far too elaborate, I thought, all cut damask and silver foil (Clive's choice), indeed rather vulgar. So I advised ditching and starting again with the same stationer I used for my wedding to Lord Petrie, who could turn out cards at twice the quality and half the price. It was a very expensive mistake and the Smithsons were terrible at budgeting, so I got more involved with their wedding preparations; six weeks to go and 250 people invited — it was a real undertaking, but now being on a Friday rather than a Saturday, I had to explain, would cut down the numbers considerably. In the end 179 came. Only six people had come to my own small, private wedding.

It was in these six weeks that we three really bonded, Xandra, Clive and I, and were indeed in and out of each other's houses a lot, and green Harrods vans coming and going and causing congestion. Far from endearing me to the neighbours, as I had hoped, I had only inflamed their capacity to gossip. Though what exactly who was meant to be doing to whom was beyond my comprehension. I did my best to ignore the whispers and pointings down the street, my street, and Clive and Xandra seemed to be in blissful ignorance of anything untoward.

All in all the wedding ended up as quite an expensive business – though Clive was miserly in some respects, he could be lavish when it suited him – if only because he insisted on using Sandroyd & Hough in Mayfair to do the flowers that bedecked the trees, and not the local florist who would better understand what was required. But who cared. I had the money, they did not.

## The Fabulous Wedding

On May 12th, a week after the invitations had finally gone off – hand-engraved copperplate from Baddeley Brothers, silver edged and with tissue-lined envelopes – both tasteful and luxurious – Gwinny cycled all the way over to West Hampstead, greying hair flying in the wind, old legs in bright yellow leggings pumping away, to find the Hellenism Reborn Centre. Here facilities for burnt offerings to the Gods were available, and she made there a sacrifice to the female deities – Flora, Demeter and Persephone. In her bike basket she brought a careful mix of Simkins One's hair combings, white and ginger, brown and black (Simkins being Gwinny's calico cat) on which to lay a freshly baked honey-filled apple cake, three liquorice sticks, some finely chopped fresh turmeric, some lupin seeds for sprinkling and a couple of firelighters. All these went on to the dedicated grate and were burnt to ashes, which she powdered, mixed with retsina and took home to share with the Smithsons. They might well push their glasses away but the merest sip would suffice.

Gwinny was going through a decidedly Olympian polytheist phase at the time and it seemed the very least she could do, to ensure that the fruits of the Smithson union would be female. That, and asking for a verbal assurance that Clive and Xandra intended to have children, that the marriage would bear fruit, while signing the form which guaranteed their mortgage. This they happily did.

The wedding itself was a delight. 1986 was a tumultuous year – but then these days whenever is there a year that is not? The IRA were letting off bombs in London and all public waste paper bins had been removed; the Soviet Empire was suddenly beginning to collapse, and the technicians at Chernobyl were closing down their nuclear pile to see what would happen, but why worry, it was a gorgeous Midsummer's Day on Hampstead Heath.

Gwinny still has the wedding photos in her album, and an actual portrait of the lucky pair stored in her attic. It is not a particularly good portrait – Gwinny's paintings seldom are, and she is the first to admit it: but she trained at the Slade and has the spiel and the theory, and even a few fans – and when she offered the happy couple her portrait of them (three sittings and a couple of photos) as a wedding present and they suggested she keep it as a memento in her studio rather than have it grace their own walls, she quite understood. The new generations did not favour fauve canvases weighed down with layer upon layer of expensive oil paint, preferring thin watercolours and delicate lines in the same way they preferred a salmon mousse to roast beef and Yorkshire pudding.

What a fabulous retro-predigital-hippie-punk occasion the wedding on Hampstead Heath had been! It was the last gasp of the Age of Aquarius. Many who were present still believed that peace would rule the universe and that love would direct the stars, and retained a lingering belief that druggy altered consciousness would yet save mankind, or coming up fast on the inside, personkind.

Oh yes, it was a wonderful Midsummer's Day! Sun shone and birds sang. Music played and people danced with all the hip-hop energy of the e-generation, and all troubles fell away as everyone remembered what it was to be young and rejoiced that they still were, or young enough, as the band played anything and everything that you could dance to and remember the words, whether the acid romanticism of the Beatles, the stoned classicism of the Grateful Dead, the smacked-out nihilism of punk and all stations in between. The band, the DreamyScreamers – electric bass, drums, guitar and amplified lute – played on a wooden platform over green, green grass on a flower-bedecked stage.

The sky was blue, strange expensive glorious flowers inter-weaved the trees, M&S catered so no-one was hungry and Oddbins so no-one was quite sober – cannabis fumes curled heavenwards and joined in with the scent of flowers so no-one could be gloomy. Everyone had dressed up at their best in honour of the happy couple, and look! Gwinny had abandoned her usual T-shirt, cycling leggings and beret for a Doric chiton in white linen with a gold chain belt. How they danced and smiled and hugged ecstatically upon the soft green sward, and if anyone looked up at the blue, blue sky and feared the radiation drifting over from Chernobyl, what wet blankets they were!

Clive was ever so tall and handsome in a white suit and green satin tie but a spectacular Mohican, which he ceremoniously shaved off when the cake (a Mocha from Louis' Patisserie in the High Road) was cut: Xandra had arranged a pretty brown curly wig over her hitherto bald scalp, removed the nose ring which had caused such a nasty infection in the past, and now, wide-eyed and petite, was floaty and flowery in a flowing chiffon floral dress – more sixties than mid-eighties perhaps, but who cared? If some copulations went on in the bushes and a few ended up in pregnancies, all to the good. It was that sort of occasion. Gwinny was sure she glimpsed Flora herself amongst the dancers, tall and gracious, gowned in white muslin, one breast exposed, in a floral headband and carrying a horn of Greek flowers – though it might have been a bunch of exotic blooms of the kind Sandroyd & Hough provided. But when Gwinny looked again she was gone.

Xandra's mother Anna Barker was there in formal mother-of-the-bride wear, pale green silk suit with wide shoulders and wide-brimmed white designer hat with ribbons and bows from Dickens and Jones, for her an unusual extravagance. She smiled bravely through the party, though she let it be known the whole thing was a wicked waste, and why her daughter wasted her time on these peculiar people she had no idea. She paid the £35.30 for the civil wedding in the Camden Register Office which followed and so made the Smithson union legal. She was relieved that the living in sin era had come to an end, and Clive was finally going to make an honest woman of her daughter, and with any luck herself a grandmother not to bastards, that terrible old word, but to legitimate children.

Gwinny paid £3,352 for the flowers: three times as much as she had bargained for, but Sandroyd & Hough turned out to be a very expensive florist. Not that she begrudged it.

## Degrees Of Separation

Alas, Anna Barker is to outrun her luck and have her fatal stroke three years before Rozzie was born, in 1997. (1997. Albania almost collapses: 2,000 reported deaths. More trouble in the Congo: many more unreported deaths. In the UK a man with a friendly guitar sweeps to power and 'things can only get better'.) Xandra is greatly grieved and Clive less so, remembering her mostly as the person who failed to guarantee the Smithson mortgage so Gwinny had to step in. The expected baby has not yet arrived and the nursery is soon used as a junk room.

Anna, had she lived, would have been pleased to know about the sperm bank, and that her granddaughter was not to inherit the genes of Clive, a man she had always mistrusted, but those of an aristocrat and a Dilberne at that.

As it happened, back in 1895, Anna's grandmother Elsie, a simple Sussex girl, had gone into service at Dilberne Court as a parlourmaid. She was sixteen; a good post for a bright girl, a life in service being a far better option than working on the land, and the Dilbernes being known as good employers.

The young heir apparent of the house, Arthur, Viscount Hedleigh, was eighteen and had a roving eye. Youth calls to youth, and he did Elsie wrong, visiting her up in the maids' attic, as later he was to visit the lady's maid Grace of blessed memory. Elsie, young and foolish, was flattered and pleased by the attention, and might even have induced that attention with a flick of a leg and a frilly apron, for Arthur was a good-looking lad. But if we look back at the past with the eyes of the present we will see that considering the power-relations between the two – poor shivering maid, rich swaggering aristocrat – it was unforgiveable.

Elsie was very soon pregnant, since young girls a hundred years ago were kept in ignorance of contraceptive practices. But the Dilbernes, being a kinder family than many, didn't throw Elsie out but chose to believe the father was Albert Barker, one of the young gamekeepers as she herself attested, sent her home to have the baby, leave it with her mother and return to work. Which she did, and Arthur kept out of Elsie's way.

Gwinny believes – schizotypal personality disorder again showing – that family patterns return and return. We go on reliving our families' pasts, even if it takes a sperm bank to do it. Up there in the Bardo Thodol those who decide seem determined to get all the stray Dilberne family members together again. Xandra has Dilberne DNA down the unofficial line, in order to reunite Rozzie back with the main branch.

It is more comforting, Gwinny thinks, to see some kind of mysterious plan up in the heavens, than to contemplate the total randomness of our couplings. Better a conspiracy, any day, than chaos.

Later Elsie was to marry Albert Barker, and he accepted the baby as his own. Just as Gwinny's stepfather Aidan had accepted her, Clive accepted Rozzie. Gwinny herself, Gwen's child, ends up living next door to Xandra, and the oddest things happen to bring that about. 'What a coincidence!' we cry, when this, that or the other happens, but of course it's not. The little wheels of fate spin and spin, the big wheels revolve slowly but inexorably on. Only occasionally do we get to notice the gearings.

Many a hidden coupling went on in those large estates. They do say Mrs Thatcher's mother was a young maid up at the local great house, knocked up by a neighbouring lordship in 1925, but who saw her right, and married her off to the local grocer, so she ended up with DNA which made her fit to govern, however eccentrically.

Gwinny helped Xandra sort out Anna's possessions after her

death and they came across a silver-rimmed cut-glass bowl of considerable value, given to Xandra's great-grandmother Elsie, so Barker family legend had it, by none other than Lady Adela Ripple herself (as a bribe to keep quiet about some scandal or other, possibly concerning Elsie's own parentage). Adela Ripple herself was of the true Dilberne blood line, and had gone down in Dilberne history, as Sebastian was later to tell Gwinny, as a lewd and ruthless but very beautiful and seductive person. Born 1884, died 1944, she was grandmother to Mallory – now living in Dilberne Court, in her nineties. Which does make Rozzie the more likely to be a Dilberne on both sides, if so diluted by other blood lines it hardly counts. Except perhaps in the Bardo Thodol.

Secret sexual acts have singular reverberations throughout the universe: secrets are so seldom kept. Women always tell, mid-row or mid-divorce. *'I slept with him and you didn't even notice. And he was much better than you, I can tell you!'* And men as well. *'I slept with her, of course I did, why are you surprised, you frigid bitch?'* – and then everyone suffers; he, she, him, her, but most especially the children. The Gods themselves take notice.

Up in the Bardo Thodol non-substantial ears prick up. Adela Ripple stirs in her slumber and comes out to cause further damage. Sperm bank fathering no doubt creates more complexities as well as opportunities in the timeless, spaceless realms of the Bardo Thodol, where souls queue to choose their destiny, the parents to whom they will be born. Christian doctrine of course frowns at the spilling of sperm, but perhaps storing it in a test tube is a lesser offence. Perhaps Onan in the

Book of Genesis was more sinful than Sebastian Hedleigh in the late twentieth century AD.

The story being that Onan was told by his father Judah to look after his deceased younger brother by providing his widow with children, as was normal practice at the time, but Onan wriggled out of the obligation by spilling his seed. A disappointment to everyone but apparently also to Jehovah, who slew him for his pains. Sebastian earned £25 for his, and it was sharing not spilling. Times have changed but Gods still see everything, which no doubt is why they're so unpopular. They offend the right to privacy, such an issue these days.

See Psalm 139, from the King James Bible: '*O Lord, thou hast searched me, and known me. Thou knowest my downsitting and mine uprising, thou understandest my thought afar off. Thou compassest my path and my lying down, and art acquainted with all my ways. For there is not a word in my tongue, but, lo, O Lord, thou knowest it altogether. Thou hast beset me behind and before, and laid thine hand upon me.*' Sounds like Facebook to me. Ouch! No body space either – tough for Millennials.

## Lost Souls

Gwinny herself, or I, Gwinny, if you prefer, could be described as a faith tourist, as others are described as conspiracy tourists, drifting from one mad conviction to another. How pointless and time-wasting it was to wander through those misty realms of the Bardo Thodol where time does not exist, wondering why the soul of the child of young Lord Arthur of Dilberne and parlourmaid Elsie Barker back in 1895, should have surfaced again a hundred or so years later in the form of the great-great-grandniece of the then current Lord Dilberne. Who is to say why Rozzie chose the womb of Xandra Smithson (née Barker) to grow in, plus the DNA of that particular test tube for a father, and not that of the '*5ft 11in writer, thinker, healer*' where Gwinny's discorporate finger so nearly fell, only to draw back? Perhaps Rozzie is right and chance rules all. It is difficult to believe that every one-night stand at the back of a pub can evoke so much attention.

As a property owner in the twenty-first century Gwinny probably saw the outer face of any religion as very little different from the outer face of any municipal planning department. When time comes for a public consultation, decisions will have been made in advance behind the public's back. The more 'openness' is declared, the more secrecy descends. Free choice just does not happen. Souls do not choose their parentage – that's a Tibetan delusion. The helpless souls follow already settled directives just like the rest of us, and go where they are sent.

Surely Adela was not sent back to try again on her convoluted path to Nirvana, only to become a Millennial for whom the past was an irrelevancy. For them the moving finger just writes on and on: a TV serial rather than a TV series: why bother to look for a conclusion? There is none.

## After The Ball Is Over, After The Dancers Have Gone

After the civil marriage signing that followed in Camden Register Office and made the union legal, Gwinny retired to her room and took off her Doric chiton that she'd worn in honour of Goddess Flora, in the expectation that she would bless and make the young couple fertile, and turned on the news, as we over forty-fives so often do, as our sexual energies abate and leave a vacuum behind into which virtuous indignation tends to pour. The news makes excellent fuel for it.

As it happened the news was about Chernobyl, the Soviet nuclear power plant which had exploded on April 26th spreading radiation far and wide and giving Gwinny ample cause for outrage. Two months after the accident news was still filtering through. Finnish and Danish sources were reporting alarmingly high levels of radiation; nor was the news from Britain good. A nuclear cloud floated over the whole continent, and over England too, except for Somerset, which was miraculously spared, or so the local council claimed.

'No, no sign of it here.' If you couldn't see it, hear it, smell it, what danger could there be? The Cold War Geiger counters were rusty and dusty: if they started twitching and peeping at the back of the cupboard there was no-one to see or hear.

'Plant operators had made several mistakes, creating a poisonous and unstable environment in the reactor core,' said the BBC. The operators had gone ahead anyway, hoping for the best, and the cooling water boiled and turned to steam, and then the control rods got bent in the heat and couldn't be slid back into the pile – no-one had thought of that at the time – and one way and another there were a couple of explosions in the reactor, which released radioactive smoke into the atmosphere: estimated at 400 times the volume of that from the atom bomb on Hiroshima.

The world had come to Hampstead Heath that day: you can't see it and you can't hear it, but now the world is truly global, thought Gwinny, and nothing from now on would ever be safe, or was that only because now you knew too much about what was going on in the rest of the world?

The Ukraine – who'd ever head of the Ukraine? A half-life – what was a half-life? Things that were not subject to immediate decay – that did not just fade away like everything else, so one couldn't eat Welsh mutton for the rest of one's life? But the panic of the half-life was short, a month or two; people forgot and life went on. The Welsh hill farmers would just have to change their ways, which were pretty rustic at the best of times and needed to change and whoever ate mutton anyway, rancid stringy stuff, and nothing compared to what had happened to the Welsh miners a year back.

## The Dreaded Sounds Of Silence

The TV went on in No. 24 that day and Gwinny heard about it; how she heard all about it! As soon as the happy pair returned home, before even any sounds of delighted marital congress,

Clive switched on the TV, a Mitsubishi 26-inch stereo, the latest thing. Clive liked 'latest things'. The sounds got fuller and the screens got wider for the next twenty years with never a gap for quiet between. Clive liked the TV on loud: he found the sounds of the outside world reassuring. He needed it, he said: it helped the depression of silence from creeping in and over-whelming him. He even approved of universal Muzak. It filled in the cracks.

'I like noise,' Clive says. 'It makes me know I'm relevant. People boo and cheer and then I know I'm alive. If I don't have the background I might just disappear. Some people worry about exploding. I fear I'll do the opposite; I'll implode.'

Besides, as later on he once explained to Gwinny, he needed TV and talk radio to keep in touch with what was going on in the outside world, didn't he? To keep up with the zeitgeist? He was after all a novelist, as well as an actor. Or was he a playwright or a librettist? There was a nice lesbian girl in Soho who sometimes helped him with the music: he brought her round for a meal once and she was perfectly pleasant and obviously lesbian (you could tell from the haircut and the jeans, so Xandra could stop worrying).

Xandra preferred silence and space to think; if she was on night shift especially so, but Clive took little notice of what he called 'Xandra's sleep thing': 'Surely when a whole ward is asleep, that's the time to snatch a nap, not when I'm up and awake.'

Clive had private health insurance dating from the time he was

Joseph in *Joseph and the Amazing Technicolor Dreamcoat* so all his vocal cord ops and procedures were covered and he had little concept of what life in a public ward was like.

As for Clive's tell-tale squeak, it was the reason his career had failed. His vocal cords were shot to hell. His nearest and dearest, even Clive himself, had almost ceased noticing it, but when the tiny strained noise first came from the glorious hulk of the rest of him, strangers had to stop themselves from laughing and sometimes failed, and then how he hated and despised them and cursed them and their children, so even Xandra flagged in her devotion.

It had happened gradually – nodules, then actual polyps, developed on his vocal cords. Clive, always so vague about medical matters, thought that too much showbiz cocaine when young was at fault and the voice would recover in time, but it just hadn't. Xandra, more knowledgeable about medical matters, thought the high notes at the end of the *Close Every Door* number, in *Dreamcoat,* sung when Clive was only seventeen, had done the initial damage. Young voices need to be protected from strain. But *Close Every Door* had always drawn such rapturous cheers from the young audience – so much passion and sincerity! – that Clive had delivered the entire song at Mario Lanza volume. Xandra had begged management to take the song down a key or two – something, anything – but she was a mere Benjamin's wife in the show and dispensable, as Clive was not, and so had been ignored. The show must go on!

Microscopic laryngeal surgery can work very well, and as jobs had begun to dry up Clive had overcome his initial fear and distrust of doctors and submitted to the procedure. Alas, in four per cent of cases surgery fails to work. Clive was one of the four per cent, perhaps because he didn't stick to the important post-op whispering rule. He always found it difficult to believe that rules were meant for him as well as other people. And what with the perforated and split septum not only the leading roles dried up – over time the minor roles too. It was as well, as time went on, that Xandra was gaining higher and higher qualifications in what Clive called 'the bedpan business' and so earning more and more.

Clive, understandably, avoided talk-light music programmes on the radio but loved the news, especially the sudden bangs and crashes, the sound of shattering glass and the wail of ambulances. He couldn't explain why – perhaps it all just seemed so conveniently far away. So long as it stayed over there all was well here. Xandra sometimes wondered what effect the background of constant noise might have on Rozzie, but not enough to do anything about it. One can get used to anything.

## Needless Swelling Of The Population

But just as H-bomb tests and the Cold War had haunted Xandra and Clive's early life, just as V-1s had haunted Gwinny's (the sound had cut out overhead and one had fallen at the end of Standard Road so the foundations of Nos. 23 and 24 were shaken and had required underpinning), the clouds drifting over from the Ukraine haunted the wedding day. Though at least these were not intentional but accidental, the result of human folly and not human venom, still they had their effect.

The talk that year was all 'Who wants to bring a child into a world like this? The world is overpopulated anyway – five billion, they say!' A billion in those days seemed the most incomprehensible number. These days it takes a trillion to impress us.

Perhaps the Smithsons havered even on their wedding day in their desire to bear fruit and multiply? Perhaps they kept up appearances for Gwinny's sake, designating the first-floor back room as a nursery and painting and decorating accordingly? Or was that just part of the paranoid personality disorder, the pervasive, long-standing suspiciousness and generalised mis-trust of others Gwinny had been told she suffered from? She did wonder.

Having a baby was not exactly a trendy thing to do, and Xandra and Clive had lived by trendiness since adolescence and might well have more difficulty getting it out of their systems than they anticipated. The birth rate was falling fast as the sheer expense of child care became a factor. No longer just *'Shall we, shan't we?'* but *'How can we afford to?'* Keeping the newborn in your bottom drawer as Gwinny's mother Gwen used to would bring social services round in a flash. Though many were taking up marriage instead of drugs to solve their problems, procreation was hardly the point of cohabiting permanently. Not any longer. It was beginning to be more about two working people getting on together and sharing the rent, and Xandra was doing very nicely thank you. So Gwinny could sympathise.

Gwinny tried not to hear too much about what was going on in No. 24's marital bed but it seemed to have more to do with athletics than procreation, which did annoy Gwinny just a little.

# PART TWO

## A Case History

Let me tell you a little about myself. Well, quite a lot, actually. Not that I want to make this a misery memoir. In some ways I'm blessed, and with Capricorn strong in my chart the older I get the better my life is. But there have been quite a few bumps on the way. The circumstances of one's birth mould us all, of course: just as the rather extraordinary manner of Rozzie's birth affects her, and why I spend so much time considering her background and the particular energies the decades have brought which have created our new Millennium. We live in a nation where violent events circle round us but seldom intrude into our private lives: so far – I fear the noose tightens and no amount of wishful thinking will save Millennials from the chaos that threatens. The bullet blasts away the flower in the barrel, soft snowflakes turn quickly into the trampled mud of the battlefield. But enough of all that. I want to talk about me.

## Me, Me, Me #MeToo

Gwinny had been born in No. 23 Standard Road, Kentish Town, North London, the eldest child of five and the only girl. Her father Aidan Rhyss, a jobbing builder, had come to NW5 in the late thirties the better to make a decent living. Times had been hard in Wales but now there was work to be had in London where war preparations were already under way. Air raid shelters had to be built, blackout curtains fitted. Belsize Park Underground was being adapted for the storage of Government documents. Aidan was a good tunneller; Belsize Park, NW3, is just around the corner from Kentish Town so that was where Aidan, along with quite a few others from the Rhondda Valley and thereabouts, set up shop.

But London was a strange and distant place, and not wishing to come alone, Aidan had brought a new wife with him. This was Gwen, a pretty sixteen-year-old runaway made pregnant not by Aidan but by an opportunistic stranger, whether by rape or just a surfeit of politeness and sheer ignorance on her part Gwen never made quite clear.

'I didn't know what he was after but I didn't want to offend,' she'd say in her lovely soft Welsh lilt. Aidan, a kind and generous man, had taken her in. She was a smart hard-working girl, thrown out by virtuous Catholic parents from her home in the Rhondda Valley for fear she'd corrupt the rest of the family, and she was living on the streets.

Whichever or whoever it was – as Gwen was to describe it to her daughter, one day when she had taken a little too much drink – a tall, dark stranger had knocked on Gwen's door when her parents were out. She had politely offered him a cup of tea, and thinking nothing of the strange activities he seemed to want – being innocent of the facts of life, and not wanting to offend – had done as he suggested. He then disappeared down the garden path never to be seen again, leaving Gwen no longer a virgin and with a bun in the oven. And Aidan had taken her in and now counted her as one of the family, and Gwinny should be grateful and always treat him as her father.

Gwinny, trying to determine why she was so different from the rest of the family, being small, delicate and fairy-like while all the others seemed to lumber and hulk, preferred to believe she had been switched at birth and was really a princess.

## But No Place Like Home

Aidan had money enough saved to buy the little two-up, two-down terraced house in Standard Road, built cheaply in the 1870s. Each house was designed for four families or twenty or so single men. For heating there were two little coal-burning fireplaces, one upstairs, and one downstairs.

Now, with pregnant Gwen installed and Gwinny on the way, Aidan ripped cracked linoleum from the floors and replaced it with new; stripped torn wallpaper from the walls, re-plastered, painted and even built an extension out at the back to serve as kitchen and in time an indoor bathroom to replace the WC in the back garden – the better to set about 'building his family', as seventy years later the Woolland Clinic was to describe this time-honoured process.

So Gwinny was born in June 1939 to the sound of much hammering and the smell of damp plaster in the smaller of the two-ups, the birth attended by a midwife from round the corner, who dropped cigarette ash 'down there', or so Gwen complained.

There was still no bathroom, no hot water – only a single cold tap in the kitchen when they moved in: so water had to be boiled for birth, bath and nappy washing. General warmth in the winter months was dependent on coal kept in a sack in the hall, carried in the scuttle to be burnt in one of the little fireplaces. Soon there was also an upright oil stove, a smart green 'Aladdin' with a smoky wick which always needed trimming; it could be moved from room to room if you could stand the fumes, the coughing and the spluttering.

But it was Aidan's home and he loved it. And Gwen said she did, though she always pined for the valleys that had thrown her out and disinherited her, that being human nature, and took a little too much drink by way of consolation.

And Gwinny loved it too or she would surely not have determined to move back into it in later years, when she could well have chosen somewhere far more salubrious. This pathetic property, if you are interested in this kind of thing, is now worth more than one and a half million, and rising.

Wealth can be measured, they say, by the number of taps you have in your home. A nice house in the suburbs will have eight or ten (remember bath and shower) plus one for the garden hose (a single mixer tap counts as two); the most miserable studio flat in the city will manage at least six. Sink: two. Wash basin: two. Bath or shower: two. If there's a real shower and not an attachment: two more. These days, what with the posh loft extension, and the hoped-for breakthrough to No. 22 – though only basic work has been done, thwarted as she has been by legal arguments from envious neighbours – Gwinny has a count of thirty-two. This obsessive tap-counting behaviour may be nothing to speak of clinically, but is a mild outward manifestation of an inner anxiety personality disorder, of which Gwinny knows she must beware. Just sometimes deep breathing doesn't help and she succumbs.

## Gwinny And The Brothers

Anyway, by the end of the forties Aidan, who'd kept busy putting up again what bombs had knocked down – the V-1 on the sweet factory at the other end of Standard Road had blown in a lot of windows – could afford to bring the outside loo inside, and plumb and wire No. 23 to contemporary standards, admittedly not very high in 1946. Even by the time she was three Gwinny would toddle along behind her father whom she adored, offering spanners and paintbrushes as required, even pasting up wallpaper, and was much annoyed when her mother called out from the bedroom that she was giving birth to a baby. That was a shock. No-one had warned Gwinny in case so doing stirred up some disturbing conversation about the birds and the bees. In a society without access to contraception any talk at all about sex was discouraged. Girls needed to be kept innocent. Gwen pushed the boat out a little when she was tipsy but Aidan frowned upon 'loose talk'.

Gwinny remembers crying and trying to stop her father leaving the flour-and-water pasting job half-done and responding to the moans and groans coming from the marital bedroom. She'd wrapped her arms round Aidan's legs to stop him from going and had to be shaken off. So of course the paste had dried out by the time he returned. Too late to call the local midwife. She remembers the boiling kettle, and watching aghast as the baby emerged from the bloody red gap in her mother's centre, first a perfectly tidy if smeary bald head, then the cord, then the great untidy wrinkled balls, out of all proportion to everything else, flopping everywhere. That was Geraint.

And after that, by the end of the war, Owen, Trefor and David had arrived in swift succession, all home births, all boys, like the swing of some disastrous Foucault's pendulum in her life. Every time the oversized, wrinkled, floppy balls squeezed out, first the heads and then the organs of their own procreation – though with David the bum came first, he being a breach birth – Gwinny felt the future close in on her, while Dadda rejoiced in the next room and said, 'Thank God, a boy!'

Gwinny had witnessed girl newborns – 'our little midwife,' the neighbours would say, 'only waist high and always such a help!' And girl babies had such neat little pink folds where their legs met. She longed to have a little girl of her own.

It seemed strange to her when faces fell when she said, 'It's a girl.' Everyone else always wanted boys.

## The Cinderella Years

So here was little Gwinny, busy as Cinderella, washing nappies and trimming the wick of the Aladdin heater, looking after boys and never allowed to go out with her Dadda in the van. Even when she was nine and the nappies stopped her mother Gwen had to have her cups of tea brought up to her. At least there was now an electric kettle. Gwen was delicate, and frequently bedbound. The doctor said after Owen's birth that she should go carefully, but Aidan said doctors knew nothing and anyway contraception was against God's will, Gwen was perfectly healthy and pretty as a picture, just a little too fond of the drink. Hadn't he turned her home into a palace? And he was a man after all, and had a man's needs. So Trefor and David came along in swift succession.

When Gwinny was ten, and Geraint seven, Geraint spat at Gwinny when she told him to clean his own muddy boots, and told her that she was a bastard, not part of the family at all, only fit to be their maidservant. She was to clean the boots at once or he'd beat the living daylights out of her. She cleaned the boots, but when she next saw Dadda she asked him if it was true about her being a bastard. Dadda took his belt to Geraint – which he hardly ever did – and said Gwinny had his name, she was a Rhyss like the rest of them, so she was his daughter.

But it didn't end there because her mother got upset at Dadda using his belt on Geraint, her favourite. After that she began telling Gwinny about the stranger coming to the door. Not that Gwinny minded all that much, because she'd already decided about being switched at birth. If her real father was a stranger at the door then he was obviously a passing prince. All the same she rather went off her mother, and her father too. One of them must be telling lies, and if it was her mother then her mother was in a state of mortal, not even venial, sin.

And of course now she was in trouble with Geraint for telling tales. Life was clearly never going to be simple. But she was doing well at St Patrick's Primary, her convent school, and they said she'd get into Camden Girls where there was an entrance exam if she worked hard enough at Maths.

Gwinny tried teaching her younger brothers, but they seemed incapable of stringing two words together, no matter how hard she slapped them. All four boys had trouble reading and writing at all. They weren't under a spell and it wasn't catching – dyslexia is 70 per cent a genetic condition, as later generations would discover – but in the forties and fifties such children were dismissed as mentally retarded, and not encouraged to turn up at school for fear of holding others back.

So the Rhyss boys were at home a lot, deriding Gwinny's attempts to teach them, developing uncouth eating habits, spurning knives and forks, eating fish and chips from the chippie in Kentish Town with greasy fingers and then wiping them on their corduroy shorts. Or eating spam fritters, their favourite, off the table without plates when their father could be bothered to fry any. All the while Gwen cut the crusts off her elegant tomato or fish paste sandwiches and nibbled at them delicately – she had very little appetite herself and coughed and swayed round rather a lot. The boys didn't worry about being illiterate, and as they got older used sweethearts and wives to do any necessary reading and writing.

One way and another it was increasingly left to Gwinny to do the housework and laundry – still no washing machine – and more and more she resented it. She stopped being a good little girl, was rude to the singing teacher, fell out with the art teacher, and failed to hand in her homework; she bunked out of school to follow Lonnie Donegan and Chris Barber whenever they appeared round London, played a comb for a skiffle band, and had a run-in with the truant officer.

She was jeered at by her brothers, who tore up her drawings and drowned out her singing with football chants, told her she was turning out a bad girl like her mother, and pulled her pigtails until tears came into her eyes, when they would jokingly grab her and slobberingly kiss her better. They were giants of boys, massive, all four of them. She hated them. David was a bit better than the others but not much. At least he used a knife and fork.

When her mother forbade her to go to the Ballad and Blues Club yet again to listen to Ewan MacColl, and then to the Norrington Awards at the Drury Lane theatre ('not for the likes of us'), and her dad said that rock and roll was the work of the Devil and that a single advance ticket for Bill Haley's world tour at one pound four shillings was not just ridiculous but immoral, and it was high time she stopped lounging about and annoying her brothers, got a job and learned what money was worth – she knew it was time to leave. The next day was her birthday. She was going to be sixteen.

That night she packed her mother's best leather suitcase – she tried Geraint's rucksack but it was far heavier even than the suitcase – stole four pounds three and six from her father's pay packet, opened her brothers' piggy banks with the can opener and stole a total of thirteen pounds, eight shillings and fourpence – the brothers ran a nice little business dealing in cigarette cards at the school they seldom went to – released her plentiful fair hair from its pigtails, smeared on Max Factor lipstick in a greasy scarlet streak too wide in places for her lips (she couldn't get to the mirror without waking the house) and spent the night on a bench on Primrose Hill: not far from home but at least not there. That was in June 1955. There was a full moon. She used her suitcase for a pillow and spread a coat over her legs. Lisle stockings are quite warm anyway. She slept well, fortunately unmolested.

Not that there were many molesters on the hill in those days. By day the occasional flasher would turn up and try to intimidate school children playing happily, unsupervised, on the hill. Gwinny for one had no clear vision of what this ridiculous purple swollen stick was for, other than it was forbidden. But you just had to stare and point and cry 'Seen better than that at home', whereupon the flasher would slink away abashed and you could get back to whatever you were doing. But that was then and this is now.

## A Lesson Well Learned

As my Dadda had predicted, I very soon went to the bad. I got pregnant the very day I ran away, gave up the baby, and then, homeless and distraught, moved into various houses of ill fame, where my looks, a natural intelligence and a kind and uncomplaining nature served me in good stead. By the time I was in my early forties I'd received two big inheritances – not spectacular sums – one million or so in 1981 and a lot from another source, plus another title, in 1984. All that was not so much luck as hard work and good judgement. Being a trophy wife is not easy. It's a competitive and insecure business; and does not necessarily bring happiness with it. My luck seems to be more about parking spaces than anything else and the occasional burnt offering to Aphrodite.

This is simple enough to do. You wear a rose crystal pendant round your neck, light your frankincense twig – you can now get them on Amazon for a fiver – write a sincere poem to an imagined lover on a sheet of typing paper, place a lock of your hair on that (you're meant to add honey but this gets so sticky I leave it out), sprinkle rose petals and a little salt water (tears are best, but if you can't manage these for laughing, buy some contact lens solution from the chemist – it's saline after all – remember the conch shell on which she rose from the sea). Roll the contents up in the paper to make a little packet, and then burn it in the sink – in a microwave-proof bowl to be on the safe side. I've always found it works but it's still only my sample of one. Don't put too much trust in it. Because it works for me doesn't mean it will work for you. And I am an unreliable narrator.

I'd been discovered as a 'model' in my late teens, ended up as a *grande horizantale* in Paris in my twenties, returned to London and dangled my legs in fashionable bars for a time, had been lucky enough to land an old rich lord who died aged ninety-two when I was in my early forties. And just as well, for I was beginning to suffer from early onset rheumatoid arthritis in my extremities – not badly, but enough to swell, curl and redden my fingers and toes – which rather wrecked my potential in a market where youth, gaiety and physical perfection are so much in demand. His family took me to court and got nowhere. I suppose I was lucky in the judge. 'She loved him and looked after him,' he said, 'that is all there is to it.' He banged his gavel and I was a million better off. But it was true. I had been very fond of old Bunny.

His best friend Lordy Peterloo was my pet name for Lord Petrie of Mainsworth, who took me on after the funeral; Bunny having left me to him in his 'wishes', so I warmed his Lordship's even older bones and not much more for four years. I really cared for him too; his family wanted him to die before he spent all his money and I didn't like that, so I married him. I spent those years finally taking my O and A levels (the exams which had taken over from School Cert. and Matric), then a degree in Eng. Lit., always useful in the trophy mistress business. 'Good conversationalist' goes along with no holidays, no children, no apparent bust or buttock surgery, excellent table manners as qualifications for this very hard-working profession.

Then he too died and left me £1,550,000 along with a title, which I suppose was lucky enough, there being others who'd had some claims on his assets, including four young pole dancers from Stringfellow's. And as I could see I was not now the vision of loveliness I once had been, it seemed wiser to give up and retire. If the host of younger punters now arriving on the scene were to be satisfied, long, perfect crimson enamelled nails on straight fingers needed to creep up the pole. A stray bent arthritic finger creeping up smacked too much of mortality. Youth calls to youth. The computer age had arrived and money had become easier for the young to amass. They could afford quality and insisted on it. No point any longer in naked bosoms peeking out from behind that exhausting pole. Mine were no longer pert. I was no longer the kind to lure important and titled persons to my side – my giggle of adoration rang too false. I was a second-division trophy mistress and must face it, not the first-division kind who end up with top rock and rollers or Heads of State, and when finished with get simply handed on, not cast adrift. The same as happens to old nannies as they outlive their usefulness.

So retire: be satisfied with the occasional honourable mention and your well-deserved gains.

## Back To Where I Began

And then my father, the master builder, died and left me the little house in Standard Road, NW5, where I'd been born and bred. This was very much to the rage of my four large brothers. I might be the eldest child but I was a bastard child, my mother's by-blow and not one of the real family. I had no right to the inheritance, and that as a bad girl who'd brought shame upon the neighbourhood and not been seen for thirty years it was outrageous to come back and demand anything at all. The house was morally theirs, not mine. I was a born whore, had even been seen 'touting my wares' on Primrose Hill the very day I ran away – a foul calumny – and wasn't fit to lick the family boots I used to clean for them.

I'd been rather taken aback by their vehemence, which some-what echoed Rozzie when at the age of twenty she told Victoria Hedleigh, then aged thirty-three, that as the elder child Rozzie had the legal right to inherit; and Lady Victoria retorted that Rozzie might have the right DNA but she was still not of the right blood line, being a blackmailing tart of loose virtue and legally a bastard, not of any prestigious inheritance.

They're all such great hypocrites, the Dilbernes! Like her great-great-aunt Rosina, a well-known lesbian, author of 1904's scandalous *The Sexual Manners and Traditions of Australian Aboriginals*. Sebastian gave me a copy of the book to read, which was where I read about the great Bandicoot, who peopled the world by lifting his arms when he woke from sleep and letting thousands of the little people run out of his armpits, which is why we have Australians. Rosina hated Australia – I think she was something of a satirist. Victoria is a lesbian, her father tells me, but no satirist. She takes nothing lightly.

My brothers had been raised as good Catholics though their own behaviour had scarcely been any better than mine. They'd all gone whoring, within marriage or without. I had always seen myself as a good girl who just happened to fall in love with men nearing the end of their lives; though of course, as I see now, 'falling in love' is open to many interpretations especially in my profession. But once my mother (so profoundly respectable in spite of her own confessed history) had predeceased him, it seemed that my father had felt able to forgive me. He left me the home in which for the first fifteen years of my life I had laboured so hard. How could I not rejoice?

## A Morning On Primrose Hill

The morning of the day after Gwinny ran away from home in June 1955 dawned bright and beautiful. (1955 – the year Ruth Ellis was hanged, the war in Vietnam began, the Warsaw Pact was signed... and I, Gwinny Rhyss, lost my virginity.) Gwinny woke to bird song and a bright new morning dawning: the sinking moon still in the sky, grey and enormous in the west, as the sun rose in the east and the grass became very green and the sky very blue. She sat up. Her muscles ached a little but not too much. She was on her favourite bench near the top of the hill, in a circle of trees, with a view over all of London. The air was soft against her skin and quivered with expectation and delight. She rejoiced, though quite why she was not sure, remembering that she was a thief, a runaway, an ingrate.

'Maiden Mary, meek and mild, take oh take me for thy child', she mouthed, appealing to a familiar deity for help, as no doubt her mother had before her – much good it did her – and then, for no other reason than it was what she had been brought up to do, she began to repeat her Hail Marys: 'Hail Mary full of grace the Lord is with thee blessed art thou amongst women and blessed is the fruit of thy womb JESUS.' Because the priest at the confessional required an appropriate number of Hail Marys as penance for various sins, and you might have to say it a hundred times, the emphasis fell on JESUS. She thought she should do a thousand to be on the safe side.

But after ten she stopped and fell quiet. The air around her had stilled and there seemed to have been some kind of shift in reality. The air was being sucked from her lungs. The trees seemed to be bending as if they were bowing down. The hills did that in the psalms, and the valleys did too. This was no longer the familiar park where she played with her friends. But perhaps places always looked like this in the early mornings, everything the same but different.

The sun suddenly glanced through the trees and dazzled her; now everything was white and shiny, brighter and brighter in reverence as something approached; and her ears were opened and now she could hear faint notes of music, some wind instrument plinking and plonking, but getting louder and louder by the minute, and now a slow thud, thud getting heavier with each footstep as the leviathan came near: but wasn't the leviathan a sea monster? She was in some kind of sacred grove where there was not even a difference between sea and land; she had seen such a picture in a library book: had she disturbed some sacred rite? She had no business here, it was all too strong for her; she got up and ran, suitcase banging against her legs. And as she ran even the daisies beneath her feet seemed touched by a kind of brilliance, the glory of the Lord, and every blade of grass exalted.

She made for the WC outside the workmen's café in Regent's Park Road to scrub up and redraw her lipstick more accurately. There was a good mirror. Lipstick proved she had joined the adult world: she may have used it rather liberally. Then she went in and ordered a full English breakfast. She was rich, after all. Nearly twenty pounds. It would see her through and more till she had a job. Eggs and bacon, sausage, black pudding, baked beans, and HP sauce on the table. The place was busy. She was the only woman there so she got a few curious looks. These people might think she was a bad girl, up to no good.

There was Charlie Plaister, a plumber friend of her father's, calling in for a cup of tea, which was rather a worry. But he didn't seem to recognise her. Why would he? Her hair was down, not in its normal pigtails so no-one could pull them, her lips were thick with scarlet lipstick and she'd opened her blouse a bit so she didn't have the high-buttoned good-Catholic look people were used to. Her parents might call the police to find her; they might not. They might think good riddance to bad rubbish and just let her go.

She would send a letter to tell them not to worry, that she was all right. She was going to join a folk band and be a singer – her voice was good enough. She'd been Mary in the school nativity play: Aidan and Gwen hadn't even come along, but everyone else told her how beautifully she sang. She'd send back the money she'd stolen as soon as she was earning.

Once restored, she took the bus to as near as she could get to the Theatre Royal, Drury Lane, where she joined the queue of screaming fans, already forming for the first night of the Norrington Awards and joined in the general hysteria and this would be the night she lost her virginity.

## A New Dawn

I do not forget the exultation of that early morning. I remember every detail. How well I slept, how fresh the air, the sudden clarity of colour, the startling sculptured perfection of the daisies, how the air grew still as the sacred grove formed round me, as if the air had been emptied from my lungs, and how the terror of the unknown had made me run. It took a time to fade; even over breakfast the peculiar clarity of the slices of black, black pudding on the white, white plate remained. Indeed, it was not until I took acid that I'd known anything like it, and even that trip was a vulgarised, godless experience, unlike this. I'd had some kind of mystical experience, I suppose, the kind Einstein himself spoke of – he'd experienced one in his youth – when one feels as if one has been touched by some kind of higher or greater truth or power and one never forgets it. The early Church Fathers used to argue prodigiously over whether these experiences were sent from God or Satan, but nobody doubted their existence.

That long-ago experience of mine on the day I ran away certainly didn't give me any kind of Einsteinian brain power, just a sense of disappointment because nothing ever since has seemed quite real, just a shadow of what it's meant to be, could be.

I daresay one of the real reasons I'm back in Standard Road is that it's less than a mile from Primrose Hill, not just to spite my brothers. I do go up there sometimes even now, but it seems a perfectly ordinary place, only the trees are a little taller nearly seventy years on, and the grass and daisies trodden down and litter-strewn by the tourists who climb the hill for the view over London, and the crowds who traipse up there to see the fireworks on November 5th or to watch eclipses of the sun and moon in company. My bench is long gone but at least there's a quote from William Blake now engraved on a stone wall which reads: '*I have conversed with the spiritual sun. I saw him on Primrose Hill.*'

So I daresay it was Apollo himself, the Sun God, who visited; he can blind you. It was his lyre that I heard, a cosmic pling-plonging, far too like the kind you hear when Sky News is waiting for something awful to happen, and irritates you to hell with its soporific almost-music. Awful, awful. But nothing's perfect.

I saw Apollo's statue while visiting ruined Pompeii from the Marina di Stabia on old Bunny's splendid yacht – called *Gwyneth* after me; those were the days! And my! He was attractive, sunlit, young, beautiful, all coiled-up energy, and after days of Bunny something of a relief, if only in the imagination. Bunny was sweet but quite an effort.

Apollo sometimes comes back in dreams, I find, when in sleep you're almost in a strange new lover's arms – though you can't quite yet discern his face, but all those sexy feelings have come surging back in the dream, only then everything vanishes away and one wakes, disappointed. The lover's face, as I then try to recall the dream, resolves itself into Apollo's, a metaphor, I suppose, for all things one has ever desired in a man, and not, come to think of it, unlike Clive's. Oh dear. But still a shadow.

And though I paint and paint my portraits in brighter and brighter colours, fauve paint layered on fauve paint (I love Derain's portraits), which can disconcert clients, I know, but I daresay my time in the sun will come. All I can manage still seems a shadow of what I intend – the clarity and truth of what I glimpsed that morning in the numenistic grove and later, in a slice of overcooked black pudding in a workmen's café. (Rozzie once asked me what was the strange black circle with the brown dots in the corner of one of my unsold portraits, and I replied 'blood pudding' – quite rightly, black pudding being made from oatmeal and pig's blood – and she looked at me very oddly.)

Apollo, like Zeus, like all the Gods, can change form, though Zeus mostly did so in pursuit of his lustful ambitions – a swan, an eagle, a bull were as nothing – but I do think it might well have been Apollo with his lyre who turned up at Drury Lane that night in the form of the folk singer with the dirty toes.

Another dreadful thought occurs to me. Clive might indeed be my son, taken away from me and adopted, perhaps even by the car dealer. But no, the dates don't tally. Thank God. There's too long a gap. People have been known to tell terrible whoppers when it comes to age, mind you, but if indeed Clive is noble Apollo's ignoble son, then I must add incest to my crimes and I'd rather not do that. He said he was fifteen when he might have been eighteen and abashed to be found a virgin at so old an age. Gwen might have had many reasons to fudge the date of my birth. But no, enough is enough.

So I moved back to the house where I was born and restarted my life as a respectable woman, no longer a source of shame but a spinstery portrait painter – always my ambition – having finally finished the art course at the Slade which I had long since abandoned.

But if you're lucky in life you're unlucky in love. I have ended up with no husband, no children of my own, and no family other than the faux-family Smithsons. If I was 'lucky' in choosing Sebastian to be Rozzie's father, or unlucky, you, my reader, must decide. I was certainly to spend a great deal of time and energy dealing with the consequences.

Mind you, considering the slovenliness of the Your Beautiful Baby Clinic, Rozzie was certainly lucky in being born at all. God knows what might not have happened in the phial as it lay there. Twenty whole years! Sure they say sperm, once frozen, lasts for ever, but how can anyone know? And supposing it's thawed by accident and then refrozen; what about power cuts?

Whatever, it lived, it worked – the main problem was that no-one liked to tell Rozzie she was a sperm bank baby. The same way no-one liked to tell my mother Gwen about the birds and bees. Just as no-one told me I wasn't Aidan's child until I was ten and then it was a brutal telling. I suspect it was one of the reasons I ended up at too young an age if not on the streets, at least in some very clean, comfortable and well-run brothels, treated rather like a delicate race horse.

## The Neighbours Move In

The Smithsons moved into No. 24 the year after I'd moved back in next door. That was in 1986, when they got married and resolved, just as I had done, to settle down and live a better life; and we became close. They bought the property for £95,000 and are still in it, Xandra on the edge of retirement, and Clive still waiting for his big break, for his ship to come in, even though it came and went when he was seventeen and played Joseph in *Dreamcoat*. My father had bought the property for £250. These days No. 23 is worth 2,000 per cent more. Xandra and Clive signed it over to Rozzie one day when they were feeling particularly guilty. Parents can do this so long as they then live on for at least seven years. So while Rozzie owned the roof over their heads she could at any time have decided to throw them out. She did not, but liked to keep the threat hanging there.

I have become quite a figure in Camden Town, I am told, an elderly woman cycling through the back roads (cycling keeps rheumatoid arthritis at bay) grey hair flying behind, paint-stained denim jacket, bright yellow socks, narrow calves pumping away, head down into the wind. An old hippie with a tale to tell in a world gone wrong.

It was in the twenty years before Lord Sebastian spent his sperm that we most spoke of love, and when I reckon it was that the bad karma of our present days started to build. It was that careless, stupid, smug Aquarius generation of mine, with its hymns to hair, drugs, equality, freedom, that led to what we have now and the poor, baffled, indignant, work-deprived, renting-not-owning Millennials. *All you need is love*, we sang. Ho, ho, ho. Stick a flower up the barrel of the gun, and trust to luck.

## A Confessional

And now I suppose I have to tell you something which may help you understand this strange relationship between Clive and myself. And I am not even sure that it did happen, just possibly happened much earlier, before even Xandra was part of our lives, but you might see it as significant, as I try and keep you in the picture as to our lives and loves. It doesn't reflect very well on me, I'm sorry to say.

It happened, or would have happened if it had, in 1978, back when we were strangers. 1978: the year in which inflation had fallen to 8.3 per cent; Mr Callaghan-the-forgotten was Prime Minister, the one between Mr Heath-of-the-Five-Day-Week-and-the-power-cuts and Mrs Thatcher-of-the-*Belgrano*-and-the-selling-off-of-the-family-silver fame; the year Julie Covington still sang *Don't Cry for Me Argentina*; Xandra's mother bought one of the new microwave ovens; and Clive's mother took Clive, a lad of fifteen, to see *Star Wars*.

I reckon the latter gave Clive a love of heroics which never left him. He himself was a half-way house between Harrison Ford, with a dollop of Frank Sinatra thrown in, and his mother kept telling him so, not without reason.

Anyway it was 1978. I was thirty-nine and a professional courtesan. That was before I went on, very prudently, for age-related medical reasons, to leave the sleep-your-way-to-the-top game (and game it was; a gamble; you won some, you lost some) and settle down as an ordinary person. I was never in the very top echelons of harlotry, you must understand, the A-list is for taller girls than me: B- or C-lists are rather a relief to leave. You never quite know who you'll meet, or how they'll conduct themselves.

I do sometimes wonder as I pedal down Camden High Street on my sturdy ex-police bike – wicker grocery basket in front, this skinny-legged old woman in a bright yellow sweater for visibility, flowing grey hair sticking out from under my beret, no helmet for me, no way! – what people would think if they realised how rich and strange my life had been. Though this of course can be said of many old people (though most, unlike me, prefer not to attract any attention). Some may suspect, but no-one knows.

The Clive of fifteen I encountered in 1978 was the most beautiful boy, almost girlish, dark curly shiny hair, black-fringed blue eyes, a smooth chin, not yet with enough testosterone for stubble. He told me his first name. He didn't mention his second name. I was quite a looker myself in those days, I must say, though my looks went off quickly – the ever lurking arthritis helps no-one. That, as much as sheer exhibitionism, is why these days I try to keep cycling: they say constant movement staves off the aches.

I was doing a favour in London for Madame Clothilde, the high-end Parisian Madame. Yes, for a time I was as fancy as that: I could charge a lot, though Madame certainly took a good rake-off, and the lifestyle is extremely expensive. You have to look good for dinner at the Dorchester, be ready for a yacht trip to the Antibes or a shoot in Scotland at a moment's notice. It requires a large wardrobe and the very best face creams.

Clive's father, a top-of-the-range car dealer, was one of Madame Clothilde's lesser clients, and had brought his son along to lose his virginity. Traditional fathers still did that kind of thing in those days, as anyone who ever went to a louche nightclub will testify, especially if the sons looked a little feminine, were too close to their mothers, and so in danger of turning out gay, and this Clive was just so *lovely*, tentative but sweet. I did what I could. It was over in an hour. He was more than a willing collaborator, but very shy.

At least I think it was Clive: that was certainly his name, but whether it was the same Clive as the one who lives next door I can't be sure. One Clive amongst so many, and for all I know he gave me a false name anyway! People are very sparing with names when doing what they'd rather was not made public.

The grown-up Clive certainly doesn't make any connection – all that was well behind me by the time I guaranteed the Smithsons' mortgage in 1986.

And how could he recognise me? I was no longer the call-girl type, blonde, high busted and long legged whom he'd spent an hour with years ago, just a gaunt and mousy make-up-free cycling neighbour when the estate agent came round in an effort to get No. 24 off the market.

The house had stood empty for some five years and attracted nothing but damp and dust, and only a few likely buyers, and even they'd all pulled out. Until Xandra and Clive turned up and I began to wonder whether this was the same Clive as I'd encountered eight years back.

## The Return Of The Warrior Queen

As you know, I was born and brought up in No. 23 until I was fifteen when I got cheesed off with my family, and ran off in search of greener fields for a future of my own making, not theirs. That was in 1955, the year of Bill Haley's *Rock Around the Clock* and Lonnie Donegan's *Rock Island Line*. I was a serious fan. I'd wanted to do art at school and Aidan and Gwen wanted me to be some kind of domestic drudge: that was all they thought of me. I didn't belong to them anyway: I belonged to my real father, who was perhaps out there somewhere looking for me, Gwen having taken me with her when she ran off with Aidan who didn't want me anyway. As I say, I was fifteen.

So when I moved back in in 1985 as Lady Petrie, having inherited No. 23 – my third inheritance, and the most memorable, being from my father – I was shocked back into common sense. I had tried him to the limits of endurance yet he had forgiven me. I would start again where I had left off; I had taken the wrong path, but now I would take the right. I would give up my old depraved ways, and I would go his way instead: steady, reliable, even-tempered, long-suffering, noble Aidan.

I had No. 23 cleared out, repainted and mended and moved back in. See me as a Claire Zachanassian, the heroine of the Friedrich Dürrenmatt play, *The Visit*, who returns as a wealthy widow to the village where she was born to seek her revenge.

That was certainly the way my four brothers saw me, but I left them alone. I did not seek them out. Silence can be the best revenge. My brothers hoped to contest the will on the grounds that I, having broken my father's heart by the disgrace I brought upon the family's name, shouldn't be the one to inherit, but they had no case. And I had a good local lawyer, who knew on what side his bread was buttered.

My brothers still live in North London, successful artisans; builders and plumbers all. They do not visit me nor I them. If any of the wives pass me in Sainsbury's they cut me dead, pointedly drawing away from me as if any actual contact might pollute them. I have no doubt they stir up trouble up and down Standard Road, but I leave it alone. Unlike Claire, revenge is not in my nature. I fear the Tar Baby too much. The Tar Baby is a doll made of tar and turpentine, used by the villainous Br'er

Fox to entrap Br'er Rabbit. The more you fight it the closer you stick. My father would read me the Uncle Remus stories when I was a child and they made a great impression. Good intentions come back and bite you. Best not to get entangled.

All mixed inextricably in my mind with memories of Lead-belly's *Gallows Tree*, and somebody's *Hangman* – '*Oh, hangman stay thy hand, and stay it for a while, for I fancy I see my true love a-coming across that yonder stile*'. But somehow the true love never turned up for me, and MacColl's *Prickly Bush* – '*Once you get into the prickly bush you'll never get out any more*' – made more sense for me.

And now I struggled to get out of the prickly bush, too delighted with this opportunity to start my life anew than seek more revenge. I had too much to get on with. By then I had realised I was an artist at heart: all that *grande horizontale* stuff had been my *violon d'Ingres*. The painter Ingres was sure his real life's work was to play the violin, but he was no good at it it. Visitors, coming in droves to buy his very successful paintings, used to block their ears when they heard him play and beg him to get back to his easel.

My real role in life is to paint people as they really are, not how they'd like to be, translated into abstract form by the medium of paint. I sense their souls. Alas, not everyone has the courage to face what they really are. But then art is not to do with popularity, is it? The true artist community despises those who seek commercial success. Art must be for Art's sake!

Living in the same street as you were born does have its disadvantages. People know too much about you and uncalled-for rumours do get about – in my case mostly propagated by my brothers, who still live in the neighbourhood and cannot forgive me for having inherited a home they feel is rightfully theirs. Some people are just petty and evil. Their motivation was always to drive me out, and after a couple of years they nearly succeeded.

'More men go into that house then ever come out of it,' I over-heard the old trout from No. 17 say. I'm pretty sure she was the one who helped deliver Geraint in a shower of cigarette ash, but I was beginning to feel a tad paranoiac. I might have been wrong.

'High time she took herself elsewhere if she thinks herself so grand.' That was No. 21. I didn't think myself grand. I wasn't grand. I was just going back to my roots. To which surely one is entitled? But the postman had brought a letter addressed to Lady Petrie and that had put the cat amongst the pigeons. Escaping the past can be a real problem.

No. 23 was always a bit dank and dreary, though I'd done my best by putting in damp courses and having the square of a back garden landscaped by a genius young designer, who removed all the nasty, worn-out old Victorian soil (my brothers would piss out the back window when the toilet was occupied, events which I remembered all too well) and replaced it with much-needed hygienic and sterilised earth.

All this was very good for property prices in Standard Road, and you would have thought people would have been grateful up and down the street, but no, it was just more of the 'who does she think she is?' jibes, and once a turd came through the new letterbox. But my activities must have stirred up the Gods because they came to my rescue.

## Intervention By The Gods

A new For Sale sign went up outside No. 24. Activity begets activity, activity begets profit. The asking price went up £5,000 to reflect the comparative grandeur of its newly painted neighbour; the For Sale sign itself seemed rooted more firmly in the earth. (The way to sell a flagging lipstick brand is to double the price, not halve it. It's the magic that sells, not the coloured grease itself.) And it was when the For Sale sign went up that I stopped the Cheyne Walk negotiations – though that decision still nags away at me. £900,000 then, £9,000,000 now! (Surely I could have rented out No. 23?) But so many of our yesterdays are littered with houses we should have bought but didn't! Lamentation is to no avail. *The moving finger writes...* etc.

When the new For Sale board stood straight and upright over No. 24 I had the strangest, strongest pricking of the thumbs feeling. *'By the pricking of my thumbs, something wicked this way comes'*, though these days 'wicked' is used for something really good as well as really bad. One just can't tell which it's going to be, just that something remarkable is about to happen in one's life.

And by this odd spooky breathless kind of understanding, this pricking of the thumbs, I understood that I was not intended for Cheyne Walk, it would be dangerous to proceed. So I didn't. I know it sounds nonsense but I'm like that. I do get these kind of prophetic gut feelings from time to time; it's a trembling feeling, an inner excitement, and a conviction that something life-changing is about to happen. And not of one's own volition, which is why it's so spooky.

It's different from the feeling I get when Mercury, my ruling planet, goes retrograde. It happens two or three times a year – a special kind of irritated, fed-up mood, a shadow that passes over one's normal spirits and good cheer. I run to Google to look it up, and yes, Mercury's gone retrograde – at least that's what it looks like from Earth, though it's really an optical illusion – and you know that for the next few weeks nothing is going to go right: the Hellenic God Hermes, messenger of the Gods, known in Rome as Mercury, the God of communication, is up to his tricks, good and bad. Thieves flourish, con-men succeed, gangs rejoice, crime reaches new heights, cheques bounce, messages go astray, friends take offence, contracts don't get signed, shows are cancelled, emails simply vanish. At least I am forewarned, and take extra care while it's going on and then the day comes and suddenly Mercury is back to his customary cheerful self again, and communication is back to normal.

The God Mercury is presented as a handsome teenager in the Greek statues, an intern, with winged feet for speed, and a moody, slightly untrustworthy look. I don't see why we insist on having one God – having a whole pantheon makes more sense to me. The kind of people you meet around but more so – not unlike the celebrities we have today, celebrated for just being them, not for anything they've done or achieved.

Anyway, Mercury went retrograde just after the new For Sale sign went up, so nothing happened for a month or two – there was the normal retrograde delay in getting papers together, I suppose; there was quite a housing glut at the time so demand was slow. No. 24 was a cheap house in a cheap area in an unfortunately named road – it would have done better as Maple Drive or Milton Road – anything but 'Standard', which denied any possible peculiarity – and it had suffered the V-1 bomb damage in the war. I remember cowering in my bed as a four-year-old and hoping the engine wouldn't cut out, but it did. One of one's first major disappointments. Another one being that while I was dithering about whether or not to buy the Cheyne Walk property someone else snapped it up. I could have kicked myself, and my thumbs altogether stopped pricking.

But then all of a sudden the Smithsons, or rather Clive Smithson and Xandra Barker – they were not yet married – were standing outside on the pavement looking up at the house. The estate agent was making a bad job of fake enthusiasm. He was blasé and bored and evidently thought they were wasting his time. Mercury in a sulk. And me, my thumbs were pricking like billy oh again.

Not just one but two Tar Babies had entered my life – Clive and Xandra. I had stooped out of care and concern to rescue the young couple from the prickly bush and got entangled, and years later I still am. And the two became three, and now there's Rozzie, Tar Baby *par excellence*.

## The Wheels Of Fate

I was wheeling my bike out of No. 23 when I saw this little huddle on the pavement under the For Sale sign. The woman seemed perfectly normal, if you disregarded the ring through her nose – young, neither plain nor pretty, and sensibly dressed, as if she had better things to do than worry about how she looked. The nose looked a little swollen and red and my guess was that she'd been having a hard time trying to remove the ring before the viewing appointment and had failed. I'm a jeans and T-shirt kind of person but I do notice these things.

The man was a different matter, tall and exceptionally good-looking in a matinée idol kind of way. Mid-twenties, expensive clothes and tailored black leather jacket – one could sense the muscles as he moved – and the latest Nikes in the very latest style on his feet. He moved with a grace you seldom see in men. 'How did she ever manage to catch him?' I remember thinking. Thick dark hair and amazingly blue eyes with long black eyelashes – a young Terence Stamp. And then it struck me.

I felt the shock of recognition without realising quite what I was recognising – the shocking blue eyes, the thick fringe of eyelashes, the perfect nose and the lovely lips. It had been a long time ago. And hadn't he kept his eyes closed while I was busy stealing his virginity, and modestly lowered afterwards?

This person did not seem in the least modest: rather, he looked the sort to throw his weight about. No, this was probably not the same person at all. My defensive paranoid personality disorder was showing again. I stopped my bike on the edge of the pavement and fiddled around with my wicker basket and listened and looked.

My thumbs were pricking. I was breathless: a kind of catch in the throat but not unpleasant. It wasn't a something-in-the-future feeling either, it was right here in front of me. A Goddess, or even a God, swooping down amongst mortals to reward or punish. You felt it in the disturbance of the air as somehow it was being sucked from your lungs. Immensely exciting but also dangerous – one never knows quite how the Gods will react to things. Or even what has drawn them in. They're whimsical.

'It's not just a house, it feels like a home,' Xandra was enthusing. I could see she was really quite cute, large soft blue eyes, a retroussé nose and an appealing, charming manner. Pity about the nose: it gave her a frivolous air when actually she was a rather serious, almost humourless person. 'There's even a garden. We could live here, start over, get married and raise our family here. It's cheap and it's just right. Our darling little home! I feel it in my bones. Oh, Clive, do let's!'

So his name was Clive. Modest stripling lads turned into men. He was indeed the same person as the boy whose virginity I'd taken. I was right. That raised a practical worry. Had I broken some law? Girls were protected by age of consent law: but boys? I realised I had no idea. It had hardly seemed relevant at the time.

But then 'It's a bit dark and damp and terracy and the rooms are too small' came from the beautifully curved, sensuous lips in a voice that was risible. It was a hoarse, broken, Miss Piggy squeak which came and went, so unlike anything one would have expected that all first impressions had to be spiked. I was wrong. He might be called Clive but never, ever my Clive. I was having to stop myself giggling. The estate agent was having difficulty keeping his face straight.

And this Clive couldn't finish there, he felt obliged to squeak more, in the form of a quote. '*A house is made of walls and beams; a home is built with love and dreams,*' this Greek god squeaked. 'I think I dream of something a little grander, Xandra, if you'll forgive me.' He was reproachful.

'A grand house needs a grand income,' said Xandra, primly. She could be very prim. She didn't seem in the least troubled by the voice. 'But until that happens this is just right. I can get a job at the Hampstead Hospital up the road, there's a good school round the corner, it's a quiet street and safe enough for a child to play in.' Oh, she had such normal ambitions!

'But we'd have to get a big mortgage. Simpler to stay where we are and go on renting.'

'If we buy, Mama will guarantee a mortgage, she said she would. She'd love to get us properly settled. It's not you she hates, it's my living in sin. Oh please, Clive, let's do it! This is a real home, not just any old rented place.'

'*Behind every successful man lies a surprised mother-in-law,*' squeaked Clive/one or was it Clive/two? 'Of course she hates me. I'm an out-of-work actor and if there's anything worse it's one who's in work.'

'It's perfectly possible that these streets will go up in value,' said the agent, 'walking distance from the centre, and easy to run.'

'Or down,' squeaked Clive/two. 'Dismal and dilapidated never changes.' This was not the kind of sentiment which Clive/one would utter. It couldn't possibly be the original one. But then I dithered and thought back to that incident long ago, so short yet stored in my memory – so much beauty, grace and innocence erupting into that rather grisly, money-making world I then inhabited – and I wondered.

The *cris de jouissance* men make come in all shapes and sizes, a fact that always fascinated Madame Clothilde; had Clive/one's been of the squeaky variety? Perhaps this new voice was the same, just hadn't ever broken due to some medical condition? Could this happen? At what age did men's voices break anyway? I had no idea. I thought back to Ernest Lough singing 'O, for the Wings of a Dove' in that high pure, beautiful voice, on my mother's favourite 78 record of the ten she owned. I thought back to my four brothers who had once shattered the peace of the street as they raced up and down it, and all I could remember was shouts and yells. I had so few good memories of my childhood. And yet here I was, back again, lured by some invisible string, my past rearing up to meet me.

I realised I couldn't go on fiddling with my bicycle basket indefinitely, without beginning to look foolish.

'I bet it will go up, and it's a really good buy.' Xandra was hopping about on her little ballet-type shoes.

'A titled lady lives next door. An area on the very brink of breakthrough, and these small terrace houses will certainly always more than keep their price.' Then he yawned. They were wasting his time. He'd given up hope of any possible sale – an excitable girl without proper shoes, far too flimsy for the weather – and an out-of-work actor? He'd never get a mortgage even with a guarantee. The agent wanted to get back to his tea and to selling more salubrious properties up in Hampstead.

Perhaps it wasn't just the pricking of my thumbs, but the way I was feeling that day – over-emotional and all stirred up because I'd just had a letter (those were the days: letters not emails!) from another old flame of the Madame Clothilde days, which made me want to conclude that Clive/one and Clive/two were indeed one and the same and I needed them next door in order to make amends. If I had spoiled his life with too early a sexual encounter, I would make it up to him. I really wanted this pair living next to me. I could feel in my thumbs that they were the allies I needed.

Was it actual recognition or subliminal guilt? I suppose I will never really know, and I certainly never mentioned the possibility to either of them during our years of acquaintance. All I really know is that I laid the bicycle down on the pavement outside No. 23 as if I had given up hope of ever fixing the basket, and said, 'Oh do please be my neighbour. It's such a friendly road and the houses are so convenient and easy to manage!'

And thus we made our acquaintance, and when the time came and Xandra's mother Anna refused to guarantee their mortgage, I was the one who stepped into the breach. No problem for me. I had lots of money. I said how nice it was to have young people in Standard Road – we were all growing so old – and hoped they wanted to have children and they said it was their dream and ambition.

*'They are the sons and daughters of Life's longing for itself* – Gibran,' Clive was to quote later, even as Mr Ipswich my solicitor looked on and I signed.

I have to admit another thread ran through my thinking. Clive/ two was Ganymede grown up, and I could think of nothing nicer than having him living next door. I could put up with his voice. I could put up with Xandra.

I told you I was an unreliable narrator.

## A Certain Loss

I sometimes wonder if there can be something mystical about losing one's virginity? It certainly propels one into a different stage in one's life: more important even than losing one's handbag, though that can seem dire indeed.

I lost mine in 1955 to the most divine folk singer, backstage at the Theatre Royal, Drury Lane. It was my sixteenth birthday. It was an awards show and the winner that year was *The Dawn of My Very First Love*. I too believed there would be happiness and joy ever after, as girls could in 1955. Divorce was rare: young female sexual hysteria was not. I was a fan not a groupie. I screamed and shouted at all the best shows, and was overjoyed to be picked by this handsome young bearded sandal-wearing, dirty-toed singer and taken behind the stage. I believed, as one could in those days, that love and sex were the same thing. It was very quick, and did hurt – but oh! those eyelashes, the perfect black curve against the smooth young cheek – or perhaps I get confused and misremember? At any rate I thought sex and love equated. He looked like Ganymede to me. I hoped and hoped he'd left me pregnant, and so he had. If he's still alive and doesn't have dementia he'll be worrying about historical sexual abuse, or should be.

Whatever was going on in my life, I have trained myself to look out for beauty where beauty is to be found. I am, after all, a painter. I found it first in the folk singer. What if his name too was Clive? What a hoot that would be! (The Gods are all about irony, and as I say, what really goes on in the Bardo Thodol heaven alone knows.) But I don't think so. He looked more like a Fred, just with a nice voice and this young, bouncy skin.

The next morning he did not even recognise me as he got on

the tour bus – I was outside it waving. I was at a gawky stage at the time, to which I was to return. I noticed his toes were perfectly clean – the grime had been nothing but a folksy affectation. I was stupid: I deserved no better.

But like Eos – who sacrificed her virginity to Ares, Aphrodite's consort, thus rousing her to anger – I was henceforth condemned to lust only after god-like men, while being perpetually lusted after by inferior mortals. Well, it was good for business, if not for my heart.

Perhaps Aphrodite lifted the curse when I took Clive's virginity, he being so god-like in his youth. An eye for an eye, a tooth for a tooth, give one, take another. Eos had earned her release. Nonsense, I know: but better to feel that I had balanced some kind of psychic scales than carry guilt round with me for ever. And certainly, in the unfeeling world I inhabited at the time, I at last seemed able to feel a genuine affection for my very elderly, now deceased, husbands, if not exactly love, and certainly never lust. But at least it was not all self-interest on my part. I earned my first two inheritances, though I daresay scarcely deserving the third, having upset my brothers so much, and not perhaps being the nicest, kindest, big sister in the world. But I was always top-totty-call-girling, something done in comfort and with grace rather than street-walking, though my brothers are too dumb to tell the difference; all they understand is imprecations. Foul words of dismissal and insult.

But I took sex seriously; I never stopped; to me it was a sacrament, a heavenly gift to be passed from one human being to another, the ultimate sharing of the gift of life, as well as a means of earning a living. I was Aphrodite's honoured slave.

## The Love Of Beauty

Beautiful men do exist. Beauty falls like a cloak over some people, a rare gift from a fairy godmother; they're born with it; mostly women, sometimes men. It lasts a lifetime. Both Clives had it, Rozzie too, I never did. What I had in the Madame Clothilde days was good looks, slim legs, even teeth, a nice voice, a sexy manner and a lot of energy, but not the magic gift of beauty itself.

I recognise beauty when I see it. Odd thing about Clive: himself the epitome of beauty, he fails to recognise it in anything else. He and Xandra rely on IKEA for taste guidance, but seem always to go for the worst not the best on offer. The sofa he chooses is always going to be garish and ugly; if a lamp, it will be expensive but useless; if a bunch of flowers, old stock – though Clive did sometimes bring expensive bunches home, in silent apology I always thought, for something in all probability going on behind Xandra's back. Clive's father the car salesman was a great brothel-goer, after all, and I suspect it's an inheritable tendency. Not necessarily all bad: extra-marital sex saves a lot of marriages. But I would say that, wouldn't I.

When Rozzie came along Clive didn't even recognise her as a beauty. But she too had been blessed at birth. But where Clive was all strong skin colour, like the virile young Adonis, Rozzie was the most delicate of pinks, a Botticelli Venus rising from the sea.

'For God's sake, girl!' Clive said once, when Rozzie was on her way out to her chess club dressed in drab denim jeans and jacket. 'Brighten yourself up – you're thirteen. Quite old enough for a little lipstick.'

Rozzie needed nothing to ornament her then or later. Aphrodite had been present at her birth. She was all symmetry – even when and if she was scowling. If anyone had been there at Clive's birth it would have been Adonis. Clive was not above an eyebrow pencil or a spot of lip-liner; at least I saw them in the bathroom of No. 24 and Xandra didn't use either.

I'd always worried because Rozzie was told nothing about her 'birth circumstances', as Xandra and Clive referred to the turkey plunger business; the books all said introduce the subject early, but Clive saw no reason to do so.

'*When ignorance is bliss it's folly to be wise,*' he was fond of misquoting if ever I brought the subject up.

Xandra would just say, 'Don't let's talk about it, please, Gwinny. It upsets Clive, and there's more than enough to cope with as it is. Different generations deal with things differently. It's a new world.' And once she played the age card. 'I daresay things were very different in your day, Gwinny. You were alive in the last war. But genetic technology is now a part of life. No-one is going to get upset.'

Which was about the most stupid thing I ever heard her say. But then she and Clive didn't use condoms. Perhaps with every intimate encounter they passed stupidity between them in the form of soothing hormones. There had to be some excuse, so I allowed them this, understanding and forgiving being still my motto.

But disclosure of the truth had to happen sometime. I remembered how shocked I'd been to discover my father was not my father. When Clive then said, 'Of course such good looks as Rozzie's got she's inherited from me, not you, Xandra, ha-ha,' and Xandra made no objection, but laughed as if she found this amusing, I realised that they had all but forgotten the turkey basting.

On the occasion of Clive's lipstick advice I was about to bring the conversation round to inheritance and sperm banks as tactfully as I could. But the terrorist murder of Fusilier Lee Rigby was on TV and Clive turned the sound up. It was the latest Panasonic TX-P50GT60B, 50-inch plasma screen, so there wasn't much conversation after that.

## Trying To Forgive And Forget

For Gwinny the understanding-and-forgiving crunch didn't come until her father's funeral. She had had enough spare time during her stint with Lord Petrie for a certain amount of self-improvement; she'd educated herself, taken college exams, taken art and creative courses but most importantly been twice weekly to the most expensive and fashionable psychotherapist in town, a Mr Marco Lyonstone. She'd even taken Marco with her on board *Gwyneth* so she wouldn't miss sessions whenever they went abroad. Lord Petrie hadn't minded: indeed, if he ever noticed! When old Bunny had passed me over to Lord Petrie he included *Gwyneth* in the bargain.

Marco had abandoned Freudian analysis for the softer, kinder shores of Jungian psychotherapy. The difference, he said, was that the analyst works through silence, not saying a thing other than a very occasional query, followed by a doubtful/surprised/ censorious rise of the eyebrows, but lays the patient down on a couch and waits – often for well-paid years – for the patient to get tired of listening to the stream of their own nonsense and to cure themselves (or not).

The psychotherapist, on the other hand, is on your side the moment you walk through the door, explains how everyone else is to blame and the best thing you can do is 'break the ties that bind'. Once you've done that, you're theirs for life.

The latter's a more fun job, Marco would say, stretching his rather good tanned and oiled body out on deck as he sunbathed and told me what to do, think and feel.

My problem was suppressed rage, he told me, which explained the bouts of depression which occasionally affected me. The answer was not to let the rage out but to learn to forgive. 'To understand is to forgive' was his watchword one therapist-hour – fifty minutes actually: twice a week for three years. He even wrote a self-help book on the subject and very well it sold, too – he was not poor. It was advice I tried to follow – until the day of my father's funeral when I realised just how crazy that advice was, and how it leads to the apologising, therapeutic world we live in today.

*'You were abused in childhood yourself, so a suspended sentence and an apology to the victim, please,'* says the Judge. *'Sorry people died,'* says the Minister of State, *'but there were so many overlooked cases I couldn't keep up. I'm only human.'* The bank/social media/diesel engine/mesh implant scandals. *'So, so sorry to our customers for this breach of trust!'* says the CEO, tears in his eyes. Apologise, and you don't go to prison. *'Knifed your mother because she deserved to die, did you? Social services must have failed to pick up your mental health issues. They owe you an apology.'* How we are obliged to forgive one another!

This therapeutic, apologetic, victim-oriented, impractical, team-, not leader-led twenty-first-century world we lot left the Millennials to cope with is of our making. No wonder Rozzie wants us to apologise for bringing her up the way we did. She blames the four of us indiscriminately for her creation; we, the half-baked ones – me, Clive, Xandra and Sebastian, Lord Dilberne. Personally I blame Rozzie herself; she obviously chose to come to four parents rather than the normal two when she was up in the Bardo Thodol. Not that Rozzie, she, the arch Millennial, the crude reductionist – in dictionary terms 'a person who analyses and describes a complex phenomenon in terms of its simple or fundamental constituents' – has any time for that old *Tibetan Book of the Dead* stuff.

## Not Fit

Rozzie once said to me – she was in full excoriating mode; we had just been interviewed by the Judicial Committee of the Privy Council as to her right to the Dilberne title – that my claim to be a fit person to bring up children was hardly valid. On reflection I can see that Rozzie was right. I was not fit. I had lied through my teeth to the court, insisting I was mentally stable and not the whole cluster of personality disorders I realise constitutes me. They'd seen through me when I addressed the judge as Themis, Goddess of Justice. I saw members of the court look at one another, as if to say 'another nutter'.

When I am under stress the distorted thinking disorder can get out of control. Rozzie had made her usual good impression. I had not: my fault.

People often blame their parents for ruining their lives – and it's good to find someone to blame, for whose life turns out the way we dreamed when we were small? – but these days I blame my male siblings. I've long since forgiven my parents who no doubt did the best they could in the light of their own natures and, I may say, lack of education; but I don't forgive my loutish brothers, Geraint, Owen, Trefor and David.

I will go into the third person here as I try to look at my relationship with them coolly. I can see I may be being unreasonable. I realise I live under a cloud of personality disorders. It becomes difficult to find the 'real me'. Marco says there is no such thing as the real self; we just move from one personality disorder to another, but then, being irreligious, he has no sense of soul, as I do. I go on looking for it.

But from the sacred to the mundane. Let us look in on the scene in the office in Mornington Crescent in 1985 when my father's will is being read.

## A Matter Of DNA

1985... a good year: Live Aid, inflation not too bad, Madonna in all our heads, the Aids epidemic almost under control, and for once we're not officially at war with anyone so we can concentrate on developing our own small family battles.

The family solicitor – Sam Ipswich from Norwich, how could one forget it? – is reading the will. Sam Ipswich has been Aidan's solicitor for a few years, dealing with small matters of bounced cheques, leaking pipes, insurance claims, building contracts, overdue monies and so forth. Aidan, as did Sam himself, has a reputation as an honest and reliable individual, who did what he said he would if he possibly could. The same cannot be said of Aidan's sons, who have on occasion come to Sam's attention, not always in the best way, in cases of fraud and general flakiness.

Heaven knows what unhappy combination of Aidan and Gwen's genes led to this awfulness. None of their children were spared. Only Gwinny, inheriting a different DNA from her father, who although a hit-and-run lover, must have been a prince amongst men, came out of it well. Some bright young medical student with a social conscience, perhaps, coming to the mines to study working conditions and seeking comfort a long way from home. When she thought about it, which was quite often in her dreams, the medical student turned into a philosophy lecturer or a famous writer, but always with the coal dust smeared on the handsome, strong-jawed Apollo face though with her own eyes, her own sensuous mouth. The dream would stir a quite inappropriate thrill of desire. But fortunately she would always wake before anything serious happened.

But I must return, please, to the reading of the will and the present tense, free from any tendentious comment from me, me, me too, determined as I am to maintain through thick and thin that I'm a victim.

## Death Of A Good Plain Man

Aidan Rhyss has died suddenly in his bed in No. 23, widowed and alone and in his eighties, but still a regular congregant at the Roman Catholic Church of Our Lady up at St Margaret's Road, walking briskly up the hill to mass on Sundays and Wednesdays, apparently sound in wind and limb. His four sons have long ago left home though all remain local boys, married with families, engaged in the building trades, and would occasionally drop by to see how the old man was getting on and ask his advice on some obscure building problem – how to underpin a 400-year-old wall, how to raise a tile roof in one go.

Sam Ipswich knows from a birth certificate he found once amongst the old man's papers that there used to be an older daughter, not seen or heard of for many years, but rumoured locally to have gone to the bad. So when Lady Petrie contacts him (the death was reported in the local paper, the *Ham & High*) he asks her to come along to hear the will read. The date of the funeral has been postponed until after the required autopsy, which could take weeks, even months, but the old fellow is well frozen up at the hospital mortuary so the delay is of no consequence. The old fellow obviously died of natural causes, but was just doctor shy, as so many of these old fellows are. Lady Petrie offers to pay for all costs, which is good of her since Sam would probably have trouble getting the brothers to cough up.

The brothers have been in touch. Sam understands that they are eager to hear the will read. They expect to inherit some fortune which does not exist, or at the very least a share from the sale of the house, itself no use to them since they themselves have moved either up to Hampstead or more shrewdly up to Primrose Hill – now fast moving up in the gentrification stakes – there to pursue their regular careers in building and plumbing, clasping their boring little children and wives (in that order: all are great sentimentalists) to their philistine bosoms. They are artisan slaves to the arty folk who were moving into the area. It has not occurred to them that the big sister who vanished back in 1955 when they were children, never to be seen or heard of again, will resurface. Nor does Sam tell them in advance; he is under no obligation to do so.

Sam does not look forward to the meeting. Siblings, especially brothers, tend to behave very badly after a parent dies. They steal, cheat and plunder, have rows and quarrel and sometimes never make up, and no-one seems quite sane for at least six months after the deceased has been laid to rest, when they sheepishly reassemble and embrace one another.

Sam, who is a nice guy, thinks that grown-up children are more to be pitied than blamed. It is not greed so much as unconscious sibling rivalry, he will argue, as all compete to be the one most loved, the one most deserving of parental attention. *'I was the favourite, so I deserve the most! Fuck you!', 'I was the one who was breast-fed longest, so obviously I was the one most valued.'* And the Ming Dynasty vase is smuggled out, and the Georgian silver salver disappears and *'I'm sure the Japanese golf clubs were in the attic, well, where are they now?'* And the blame game begins.

But here they all are, crowded into Sam's small law-book-lined office in Mornington Crescent on a really hot day, one Volvo 760, one Leyland Sherpa and one Transit van parked outside. All four of them are six-footers and wide too with bellies going before; wriggling on chairs they overflow, sweaty and fussed – and already perching on the desk when they arrive, elegant legs swinging, in a bright green suit with very square shoulder pads, and on apparently good terms with Sam, is a slim woman beyond her first youth but still a looker, introduced as Lady Gwyneth Petrie, née Gwyneth Rhyss.

'Thank you, Sam,' says Gwinny into the ensuing silence. 'Hi, Geraint, Owen, Trefor and David. Yes, Gwinny herself, your big sister. Remember me?'

Geraint is the first to recover. 'Oh, the bad penny. Yonks ago. Stole everything there was to be stolen, and ran off to whore on Primrose Hill. What are you doing here? You're not one of our fucking family. Mummy's little bastard. Dad took you in out of pity. Not that the old grouch ever showed any to me. Him and his belt! Want to see my bum? Still scarred. These days he'd be in prison.' That sets the scene.

'Respect, please, Geraint. Gwyneth was properly adopted by your good father back in 1939,' Sam Ipswich – or is it Norwich? – intervenes. He's a brave man. 'Lady Petrie is legally Mr Rhyss's oldest child.'

Geraint snorts and falls silent, as sudden worry replaces bluster. Big runaway sister back here because she's been left something in the will? Could it be? Not that the old fool had much to leave, only a few sticks of furniture, some rusty old vintage tools, and of course the house. Geraint has assumed that if any of the others get any of the house he might want to buy them out and they'd let him.

'You! You're the one who opened my piggy bank with a tin opener,' says Owen to Gwinny. He's on his feet, red face sweating, pointing, enraged. 'Bitch! I fucking needed that money.'

Lady Petrie idly swings an elegant leg. 'When I was thirteen and you were nine, who lied for you when you were stealing bikes and the police came after you? I did.' Owen puffs and huffs and falls quiet. He's always been a kleptomaniac.

'Mr Norwich here says whenever you leave his office his toilet rolls go with you,' says Gwinny. She might have slapped him a bit hard, she'd admitted to Mr Norwich, but Owen would steal the nappy pins from under your nose while you were changing him.

'Don't you bad mouth my big brother. Stuck-up little tart!' puts in Trefor. 'Mum always said that's what you were. And lover boy's name is fucking Ipswich not Norwich.' She'd had to wash Trefor's nappies with cold water: and he'd taken longer to get potty trained than any of them.

Trefor looks daggers at Sam, taking out his notebook and making a note: it was clearly going to be horse's-head-in-the-bed time soon.

Geraint laughs and says, 'Not too good at your geography then, Lady Whorish Muck. Bastard Ipswich, as he is widely known in the vicinity, is a con-man and a fucking liar. See any poor old man and he'll rip him off. Undue influence if you ask me. Ask anyone.'

Sam refrains from reacting. He reflects that to work as a sole solicitor amongst the needy is not the kind of higher service to humanity he had believed in when he started out. Better to have joined the police instead of the law and sent more people to prison, rather than toiling away keeping them out of it.

And then David, the leanest and most intelligent of them, the one Gwinny has almost been fond of, the one who came bum first into the world, ripping his mother apart, says, 'You killed our mother. Broke her heart when you left. Stole her purse and crept off to become a whore.'

'Come back as Lady Muck,' puts in Owen. 'I wonder what swill you swam in? First stop Primrose Hill.' Gwinny had told Sam Ipswich she'd toil all the way to the sandpit in the playground so Owen could throw sand in rich children's eyes, and work out which bikes were worth stealing.

'I didn't ever whore on Primrose Hill,' says Gwinny. 'I can tell you that much.'

'That's a lie!' says Geraint. 'Charlie Plaister saw you the night you left, out of your mind on drugs with a boob hanging out. You're a disgrace to the family, drove poor Dad to his grave with the shame of it. You broke his heart.'

'That's right,' says Owen, 'That's why we didn't send the police after you when you vanished. He saw you next morning in the caff too. You were on the game even then. You brought disgrace to our family name. Mum tried to beat the evil out of you but she didn't try hard enough. Weak as a kitten, poor Mum.'

'I don't see why you're even in this room,' says Geraint. 'We're a decent law-abiding family here and you're nothing to do with us, born out of wedlock to whoever and whatever, a slut and a whore. And if my father has left you a penny, I'll fight the will to my last breath, won't I, Sam. You know me.'

'Indeed I do, Geraint,' says Sam Ipswich. 'And that's quite

enough from all of you. To save further ado, I can tell you that Aidan Rhyss, in memory of the great service his eldest daughter rendered to her mother in her infirmity, and to you boys in your growing years, and as a token of Aidan's lasting affection and admiration, has left to his eldest daughter, Lady Gwyneth Petrie, the property and contents of No. 23 Standard Road, NW5. David gets his vintage tools and Geraint the contents of his savings book, circa £200, towards the purchase of candles to be lit every Sunday for the souls of Aidan and his beloved wife Gwen.'

'There'll be no candles lit by me,' says Geraint, into the stunned silence. 'Poxy old bastard. Not a tiny bit of gratitude. After all I did for him. I'll contest the will.'

'Perhaps had you visited more…?' says Sam. There is a silence, then mayhem ensues and all four of them, making no doubt for the pub, bump bums, stomachs and fists in the small hot room as they compete for a too narrow door. Gwinny locks herself in the loo for safety, as they swear and spit. She can't remember such a sudden eruption of noise and activity since police raided Madame Clothilde's twenty years back, and that time too she'd had to lock herself into a far more salubrious loo until the invaders had been paid off. Here everything is peeling and spidery and the toilet rolls have gone – presumably to Owen, who would have secreted them about his lavish person.

She can hear Sam reciting a list of possible grounds for contesting a will as the noise abates and the room clears.

'*Reasons for contesting a will: lack of knowledge and approval; undue influence; fraudulent wills and forged wills; and rectification and construction claims.* None apply. It won't get them very far,' says Sam as Gwinny steps out of the loo.

'Can I move into the property now?' Gwinny asks Sam.

'Give me a week,' says Sam, 'and it's all yours. I'll get in the clearance people from the council. They'll do it for a tenner out of hours, and sell off what they can.'

Lady Petrie flings her arms round Sam Ipswich and comforts him in the only way she knows. He seems accustomed to it, and doesn't stop her, though he has a perfectly nice wife at home.

## Understanding And Forgiving

God, I'm awful. Anyway, after the will reading I tried to make it up to my brothers – so much is owed to family – but they remained obdurate, and I'm afraid told even more personal secrets, especially mine, up and down the street. If such came to Clive and Xandra's ears after they moved in they made no mention of it. Xandra was so often out at work, and Clive, sofa-bound, writing his novel on his word-processor and listening to the TV, they didn't have much connection with the street. They themselves had few relatives who might be curious about the new useful neighbour next door.

Clive was an orphan. His car salesman father had died in a

car crash while taking Clive's mother out for a spin in a new delivery and pushing the car to its limits, showing off. Both were killed. The accident had made the news, largely because the car being tested – a brand-new design Bentley Melrose, a performance car – was seen as ratings fodder.

Clive was only fifteen, and at his desk studying Thomas Hardy's *The Convergence of the Twain*, when his headmaster came in and tactlessly broke the death of his parents to Clive in front of the class. He cried, and the embarrassment was even worse than the news.

He then actually saw on the news that evening a clip of the car crash in which his parents had died – the posh Bentley nothing but a crumpled heap of metal and splintered glass – and he could swear he saw his mother's white leg protruding from the wreckage, or perhaps he imagined it? The young Clive was rather relieved his father was no more – the Madame Clothilde visit having confused him as to where his loyalties lay – but devastated to find his mother gone. It was too early in technology's history for him to be able to freeze the broadcast at the metal-and-leg shot and make sure. Later in his life Clive complained to Gwinny it had got mixed up with the Thomas Hardy poem about the *Titanic* and the iceberg:

> *Over the mirrors meant*
> *To glass the opulent*
> *The sea-worm crawls – grotesque, slimed, dumb, indifferent.*

*Jewels in joy designed*
*To ravish the sensuous mind*
*Lie lightless, all their sparkles bleared and black and blind.*

Perhaps that memory was why Clive kept reciting poetry when anything particularly bothered him?

## A New World And A New Start

I was grateful to Sam Ipswich, but decided enough was enough. He had a wife at home, and a wise woman obeys the fifty-mile rule – no illicit entanglements other than far from home – and Sam lived a mere three miles round the corner and when it came to it was no Greek God. But he was a good straightforward competent lawyer, and a loyal rather than an expensive ally. We occasionally shared a joke together and sometimes a little more. I was, besides, determined to live an uncomplicated and even celibate life. Too late now to have a baby, but how I'd like to have another chance at bringing up a family. I didn't do too well the first time round, judging by results.

I moved out of the Dorchester and into my new/old home, resolved to suck the juice out of my childhood in the way a child sucks the juice of an orange, first pushing the finger into a hole made in the skin, then putting the fruit to the mouth and squeezing. It pleases the palate and quenches one's thirst but one must expect the mouth to get a little sore. No. 23 throbbed to the sound of builders and renovators but all was not plain sailing. Like life improvement, house improvement seldom is.

And all that time the essence of his Lordship lay there in a frozen phial, already eight years old, waiting, getting older and older year by year while its thoughtless but legal owner went on to inherit the earldom when his father Oliver died, his mother Lucy becoming the Dowager Countess, and Sebastian marrying the lovely Hon. Veronica Venice in June 1986 (the same month, coincidentally, that Clive and Xandra were married) who then became the new Countess of Dilberne (how her mother-in-law Lucy hated the demotion, how Lady Veronica hated Lucy). In May 1987 Veronica gave birth to the Hon. Victoria Hedleigh – who as a girl, under the law as it was then, was never going to inherit. Little Victoria's sun being in Taurus the Bull, she did not easily forgive or forget, let alone understand. She was almost thirteen years older than Rozzie. Both girls had their moon in Aries and their Saturn in the ascendant, and were bound to go head to head.

Sorry about this lapse into schizotypal personality disorder, but a flight into astrology is hard to resist. I know well enough, rationally, the absurdity of believing, as Western astrologers do, that people can be divided into twelve personality types according to where the sun is every month, but Indian astrologers (who at least divide us into 365) won't let you get married, take a job, or sign a contract without consulting them. They can't all be charlatans, can they?

If only it didn't seem to work it would be so easy and certainly convenient to dismiss the whole thing as arrant nonsense. But since my sixteenth birthday when I – sweet sixteen and never been kissed – awoke on a bench on Primrose Hill as the sun rose, I have believed in a lot of things that others don't. That was the day I came of age, met heaven and met hell.

In 1956 (the Suez Crisis, the Hungarian Uprising, Anthony Eden as Prime Minister. *Refrain* wins the very first Eurovision Song Contest) my baby is born. But that's a buried memory I try not to think about. Whew! I mean, enough is enough. Though I have always found events, like personality disorders, do tend to cluster.

Between the reading of the will and the wedding came the funeral and the wake. *'Between the idea And the reality Between the m(n?)otion And the act Falls the Shadow'*. If the funeral was the idea, the Shadow was the wake, when reality crushed all Gwinny's hopes of a return to 'normal family life'. Her understanding-and-forgiving mood came to an abrupt end.

## You Can Forgive But Can You Forget?

It was only with the funeral that I had finally realised how wrong Marco was. That 'understand and condemn' is a much healthier approach to life than 'understand and forgive'. Let me tell you about this funeral.

The row over the reading of the will was bad enough, but once the coroner had released the body (it took more than six months, so busy were the forensic labs, and coroners being in such short supply), having found nothing suspicious, then the funeral could go ahead. I paid top whack at Golders Green cemetery

– the least I could do – and asked the brothers round for the wake. I thought, I hoped, they would have become used to Dad favouring me the bad girl above them, the respectable ones who had followed in his professional footsteps. I was wrong.

I had spent the six months cleaning and decorating No. 23, having found that when it came to it the 'out of hours for a tenner' council house clearance people actually did a fiver's worth of work. So I set to myself, scrubbing and swilling as I had in my early days – the same floors, the same stairs, and in so doing exorcised much of the stains of the past, for now I was doing it willingly, out of love and affection, not under duress.

Odd, I thought, that the bedroom of any old man has the same feeling as the next, no matter what their income, Lord Petrie or Aidan Rhyss, rich or poor – an air of depletion, a sad sparseness as they wait for death.

You can do a lot of thinking while cleaning. I thought of my friend Tess back in the home for unmarried mothers who hanged herself when they took her baby away for adoption and left her howling and her dress stained with milk. I came back from prayers and found her hanging from a hook in our dormitory. She was dead but her breasts were still dripping with milk.

Her handbag had seemed lively enough when she was alive: poke your finger into its leather and it bounced back, resilient. As soon as she had gone the energy drained out of her bag too. I had to go through her few pathetic belongings – the nuns didn't want to get too close to a suicide – and there was no life left in her bag either. She had taken it with her, or it had volunteered to go. It too was a fresh corpse, limp, flabby and desperately sad. I poked my finger into the leather and it just stretched and split. I was sixteen, she was seventeen. I walked out of *The Sound of Music* when it came my way ten years later. *Sixteen Going on Seventeen*: I could never abide that song.

Buried memories. Life can turn out so differently from one's expectations. I daresay that's why I have all these odd beliefs. That there's more to life than meets the eye. It's not a personality disorder – it's just simple experience of what happens on the ground, in the world we live in, not the scientific version.

When I stripped Aidan's bed his nylon sheets had the same limp look and feel of departed energy as Lord Petrie's 100 per cent Egyptian cotton. I noticed that the analogue alarm clock by Aidan's bed was the same make (the London Clock Company) as the one by old Bunny's, except Bunny's was rather jewel encrusted and a gift from some Sultan or other while Aidan's came from Woolworth's. I expect the same derelict feel went with King David's room, or tent – it being 1000 BC – when he lay with Abishag the Shunammite in his old age, but didn't shag her.

Just call me Abishag. Except I was by no means a virgin. I just lay in Lord Petrie's bosom and gave him heat. Same principle: 1 Kings 1–4:

> *Now King David was old and stricken in years; and they covered him with clothes, but he gat no heat. Wherefore his servants said*

*unto him, Let there be sought for my lord the king a young virgin: and let her stand before the king, and let her cherish him, and let her lie in thy bosom, that my lord the king may get heat. So they sought for a fair damsel throughout all the coasts of Israel, and found Abishag a Shunammite, and brought her to the king. And the damsel was very fair, and cherished the king, and ministered to him: but the king knew her not.*

No, poor old bugger; Viagra hadn't yet been invented.

But I digress. The funeral went as normal funerals do. The brothers had wanted a 'simple', in other words a pauper's, funeral in an unblessed lot, but I paid for the best Golders Green would do in conjunction with St Christopher's Church. I slipped away early to finish preparations for the wake, which I had organised at No. 23.

I'd dug out the oil portrait of my father I'd done when I was fourteen – a splendid piece – from a dusty old cupboard where it had been relegated, presumably since I ran away, my name never to be mentioned again. I dusted it of spiders and cobwebs and put it back where it had originally hung in the front hall, in pride of place. I was head of the family, after all. I took down all the photos of the boys' sporting triumphs – the soccer team, the Boxing Club, the Rhyll Road choir, the karate team – they were yellowed and faded, and needed to be taken down.

I put on the kettle, opened the wine and uncovered the sandwiches and bits I had taken the trouble to make by hand – during the Lord Petrie days I had been consulting Constance Spry's cookery book, so there were breaded chicken drumsticks and cheese and pineapple (fresh pineapple, not tinned) on sticks for the older folk, and tiny cream profiteroles for those not on diets.

I'd even rushed down to Woolworth's in Kentish Town Road to buy a couple of extra-large teapots. About thirty people from the church, the pub, the local Welsh Male Voice Choir turned up. Sam Ipswich, now my solicitor, came along and a scattering of neighbours looked in – Dad had kept himself very much to himself in the end. If they seemed to look at me a trifle curiously, why! curiosity is a natural thing, and one must not give in to the paranoiac tendency.

Marco always warned me about that. 'You have a paranoiac personality disorder,' he would say. 'A generalised mistrust of others. You live in fear, suspecting a conspiracy against you. You invent strange religions to protect you; you even create Hellenic Gods to come to your rescue. Why else do you see me as Mercury?' What a reductionist the man was – though very good-looking, I must say, as he lay well oiled and sunbathing on the deck of *Gwyneth*.

All kinds of people were there at Dadda's wake, even the man who read the gas meter who just happened to be passing by, everyone except Aidan's sons or even grandchildren. It was embarrassing. People were beginning to drift away – the con- dolences given, memories of the oldster exchanged, all the elegant food eaten and the drink finished – when the four

Rhyss boys and their appurtenances suddenly crowded in. They had seen fit to stop off at the pub on the way to drown their sorrows, and a massive, moving, noisy, half-drunken lot they were.

The smell of alcohol and cheap scent wafted in with them; the men in too tight black funeral-and-wedding suits. Shiny black fabric strained over protuberant bellies and caught the light. I'm an artist so I notice these things. And their womenfolk! Increasing weight was clearly a problem for the whole Rhyss family (except thank God me: I inherited from my real father, the handsome medical student).

The mountainous wives all wore bulky fur coats, padded shoulders and wide-brimmed black hats which clashed together and so caused shrieks of laughter and/or dismay – so blowsy, so noisy! Crowding in with them came a host of spotty, lumbering lads and lasses, dragged along against their will and showing it. They went round draining the dregs of other people's sherry glasses. I do not forget the sudden shattering of the peace of my decorous, well-planned gathering: this vulgar Rubensesque invasion.

Trefor of the nappies looked at my portrait of our father in his prime, laughed and said, 'Well, you didn't know the old bugger very well, did you! Put it back in the cupboard where it bloody belongs.'

'Give it to me and I'll put it in my paint-stripper tank,' said Geraint, the one who'd labelled me a bastard all those years ago, and he pretended to vomit. I'd loved Dadda even though he wasn't really my dad. He'd read me stories when I was a child. My mother was always 'too busy'.

And Owen of the stolen bike said, 'Whoever did that painting couldn't tell one end of a fucking brush from another,' which hurt, though I knew he only understood house painting.

And David of whom I had been slightly fond looked round my nice clean and white-painted living room, what he could see of it for guests, and said, 'Very spick and span for a massage parlour. Scrubbed fucking heartless. Mum always said you were a scrubber at heart.' How they all chortled at the joke.

I could tell they'd been working themselves up into a frenzy at the pub about me having the house and not them. But it was no excuse: they were hard to forgive. I tried. But Geraint's wife Sylvia drew her skirt away so as not to touch me as I passed, and hissed 'bitch' at me, at least I think she did, and Owen's blowsy mistress whispered loudly: 'Hush, Sylvie, don't! She'll hear.'

They tipped the last of the sherry down their throats and demanded 'proper drink', and finding none, sent one of the wives back to the pub for whisky, beer, crisps, porky scratchings and pickled eggs. While they waited, cursing her the while, they made themselves comfortable, settling down to roll joints and spill ash and grind cigarette ends into the polished floors.

Mr Ipswich had been about to leave when they arrived but he stayed to look after me. He was kindness itself, a quiet, gentle, firm man, and quite good-looking in a bespectacled kind of way.

And then David, the only unmarried one of the brothers – I think he was gay – asked me from out of a cloud of dope smoke why I had not gone to my mother's funeral and I said no-one told me she had died and he said, 'Well, it was you who cast us off, not the other way round. You fucking broke her heart, you know. She said you had bad blood from the tramp who raped her.'

Well, I wasn't going to argue, was I, explain what kind of wonderful man my father was, not some brutish oaf of a rapist, and fed up with their jeers and sneers and bad language, not to mention the smell of drink and cheap scent which had wafted in with them, I threw them all out of my house, my home.

'Get out of here!' I shouted, altogether losing my cool and I imagine my posh accent. 'I'm not made of fucking wood. No. 23 is mine, not yours. I'm fucking fed up with the whole shitty lot of you. Get out and stay out!'

And they just looked at each other and then me and someone muttered, 'Language!' (that was a laugh) and someone else, 'Sensitive little pussycat, isn't she, considering,' and they went off to the pub, no doubt. Mr Ipswich held the door open – all the other guests had long since escaped – and slammed it behind them.

'Check your toilet rolls,' he said. 'Owen will have them for sure.' And so he had. He'd have taken the light bulbs if he could.

I'd see the brothers out and about sometimes with their kids and sweethearts and whores, but they'd cut me dead, and I them. They were out of my life and my consciousness. I was free to do as I liked. I thanked Mr Ipswich in the only way I knew, and like the Smithsons next door, *'resolved to put my old ways behind me, having truly and earnestly repented of my sins, and was in love and charity with my neighbours, and intending to lead a new life'* (C. of E. *Book of Common Prayer*) and was celibate thereafter, I swear.

## Getting On With The Neighbours

The neighbours wouldn't speak to me for a bit, it's true, and they certainly resented me. The local girl made good is expected to move elsewhere, not just move back in. A few even dropped by at the wake, but apparently sneered at the sandwiches – accustomed as they were to ham or tuna doorsteps – mine being altogether too posh and dainty. With all the hammering and the scaffolding and the white vans coming and going and then my discarding of the brothers, local boys – the news quickly got about – and hadn't I walked out as a teenager and gone on the streets and so broken my poor hard-working mother's heart, and now put on airs and talked posh – nothing was ever forgotten or forgiven on their part – so why should I be any different? I got so fed up with it I almost chickened out.

Indeed, as you know, I was on the brink of moving somewhere less dear to my sentimental heart and more appropriate to an aspiring painter than was Standard Road, and had begun looking for an expensive property on the Embankment, where the sweet Thames runs softly by, as the poet Edmund Spenser wrote in 1596 shortly before his house got torched in the Nine Years War in Ireland. If ever I mention the house I nearly bought in Cheyne Walk, Clive quotes Spenser's very long poem, the better to annoy:

> Walked forth to ease my pain
> Along the shore of silver streaming Thames,
> Whose rutty bank, the which his river hems,
> Was painted all with variable flowers,
> And all the meads adorned with dainty gems,
> Fit to deck maidens' bowers,
> And crown their paramours,
> Against the bridal day, which is not long:
> Sweet Thames, run softly, till I end my song.

I'd been in the middle of negotiations when the For Sale sign went up outside No. 24 Standard Road, and my thumbs started pricking and I withdrew from the negotiations and that was that! And so my bridal day never came. Just as well, no doubt.

When the Smithsons moved in the troilism whispers soon began and carried on for a bit – well, quite a while – a whole fifteen years was to go by until Rozzie came toddling out into the street and called me Gran, for some other scandal erupted and I daresay they soon forgot about the troilism after the Smithsons had been established at No. 24 in 'newness of life' for a time. The fabulous wedding had been and gone and now we all had to settle down and wait for Flora to do her stuff. But as I say, life seldom turns out the way one expects it to.

Flora took her time about it and we had to wait until March 1999 for her to come up with the goods. And all the time his Lordship lay in his frozen state in store as the Your Beautiful Baby Clinic went out of business and the Woolland Clinic took its place. Supposing there had been a power cut: supposing his Lordship had been thawed and refrozen and lost his virility in the interim? As it was he was offered at half price because of his anonymous provenance. And Clive could never ignore a bargain. For once he paid, not me. But the sample survived all and took root, and Rozzie wriggled and kicked her way into life thanks to me, as the hands of the clock moved from midnight to just one minute past midnight, and the Millennium Bug failed to clock in. Computer software was not expected by many to survive after January 1st 2000. However, it did. The robotic stuff did not even blink.

Victoria Hedleigh was born nearly thirteen years earlier, and so was expected to inherit after her father's death, since the law of progeniture was soon to be changed, now that gender was what a person chose to be, not what others assumed. If Dilberne family history suggested that Victoria was a re-run of the bluestocking and lesbian Rosina (1883–1939), just as Rozzie was of the adventuress Rosina's cousin Adela (1884–1944), so be it. Let those in the Bardo Thodol sort it out.

There it goes again – the schizotypal personality! Sorry.

Can it really be nearly four decades since the glorious wedding on the Heath? Well, time passes quickly if you're having fun, even if it's not exactly fun, just what one gets accustomed to.

We had grown together, Clive and Xandra Smithson at No. 24, the eccentric Lady Petrie at No. 23. Like plants we have fused together to become inosculated, a somatic hybrid, as Rozzie was to describe us, not unkindly.

Of those thirty years or so the first thirteen were spent waiting for the Goddess Flora to come through with the promises she made on the day of the wedding when I sacrificed to the female deities to ensure a girl child. I didn't mention that I added a gold ring to the flames to placate the God Mercury – as it happened my wedding ring from Lord Petrie, which caused such angst amongst his relatives. The ring didn't burn, of course, but I later rescued it from the ashes, and have it by me to this day. No doubt Mercury, God of intelligence and wit, played a part when they were sorting things out in the Bardo Thodol and Rozzie eventually came down, beautiful little prodigy that she was.

It was in those waiting, childless thirteen years that Xandra climbed patiently towards the top of her NHS career ladder, Clive battled with his voice and professional problems (and if I may say so his own vanity) and I established myself as a talented portrait painter in my studio in the loft extension. They were not wasted years. In the second decade Flora relented and let Rozzie come whizzing in from the Bardo Thodol via myself and the turkey baster, and we coped with her IQ test rating, 140 and counting. And in the third decade we coped with the reality of Rozzie, Millennial, elder child of Sebastian, Lord Dilberne.

In retrospect the first ten years of the new Millennium were heaven: the second were more or less hell. And it was all our fault that it happened. Silence is not golden, ignorance is not bliss when it comes to deceiving a child about their real parentage. Rozzie did not forgive.

Goddess Flora can curse as well as bless; on the surface she is all things lovely and pleasant, but in her shadow side harpies linger, those beautiful, dangerous, destructive, ravenous bird ladies of Olympia, one of them I fancy these days with the face of Lady Adela Riddle.

And perhaps as Rozzie came to woman's estate, with the first drop of blood the harpies showed Flora's shadow face: cold, clever, greedy and rational. That day at the West Hampstead Hellenism Reborn Centre I should have added mint to the sacrifice. I forgot. Perhaps the gold wedding ring was a mistake – gold is associated with Mercury, God of the intellect and quick thinking. He never got on too well with Flora.

Mea culpa. (So much of a woman's life is mea culpa.)

# PART THREE

## Three's Company, Four's A Crowd

I've already explained that it's Gwinny telling this tale, not some omniscient narrator, and how she feels happier shifting into the third person should she feel embarrassed or distressed. In the third person she can get a more objective view of what actually went on. She can look at herself with a little less of the me, me, me, which in the first person one can hardly avoid. It's just that occasionally, like now, impartiality slips. I have, she has, something to confess.

I told you that when the Smithsons moved in the rest of Standard Road gossiped themselves into a frenzy about perceived troilism, and only ceased when years later little Rozzie staggered down the street at sixteen months calling me Gran. Then the rumours finally stopped and it was all semi-apologetic: *'Silly old us, they're not perverts after all, she's his mother not his lover.'* We did not advise them of their misapprehension, merely encouraged Rozzie to call me Gran more often. Rozzie, after all, had no grandparents of her own, all were in their graves and spinning or not as their natures dictated.

As 'Clive's nutty mother' I made sense to the neighbours, the mythical one who had started life in Standard Road, run off and gone to the bad, only to return as a wealthy widow with an illegitimate child, without even the sense to move anywhere upmarket.

The worst anyone could do was pity Xandra for having such an interfering mother-in-law – 'Poor Xandra, what a fate!' I was now the evil mother-in-law, bossy and controlling, but no longer a sexual deviant. It was a kind of promotion.

But I avoid the point. I am meant to be coming clean. I implied earlier that there was never latterly anything sexual between me and Clive but I lied.

There was one small incident but only one in all our thirty-something years or so of togetherness. We were normally very careful not to touch one another unnecessarily, of course, as a mother sometimes is with a favourite son, or a father with a daughter, in case something brewing unconsciously suddenly explodes.

Anyone who is familiar with making homemade wine will understand. Pressure builds unseen and unthought of. Then bang goes the glass demijohn, and shards of glass are every-where, sticking out of the plaster in the walls, all over the floor and swimming in oceans of red sticky sweet stuff, and with any luck not piercing your skin or your carotid artery, which can be fatal, I believe.

That single sexual incident Gwinny speaks of – how she does wander off; nervous, probably – was in January 1999 (Kosovo war: Nostradamus predicts it will cause massive landslips but it doesn't), a whole thirteen years after she and the Smithsons first become neighbours. It was the night after Clive went back to the Woolland Clinic, there to receive the diagnosis – mumps in adolescence; not a living sperm in sight; just these concentrated, heavy-duty, feel-good hormones – verdict: infertility, but a life full of adoring women. That was the very night when Clive's voice came back full throated and glorious after years of squeaks and bleats, and he opened the front door and embraced me, and it turned into a kiss, and tongues were involved and then a totally unexpected sudden bending over and leaning back like a practised couple. I could only hope the neighbours weren't watching through the windows. They would have added incest to their list of sins.

Look, it was a very emotional moment for both of us. I was sixty and should have known better. I paid their mortgage, built their loft, paid a few direct debits, was Lady Petrie to his wife's mere Mrs, and so was in a position of power over Clive which I should not have exploited. But it was in no way harassment, which I suppose Xandra might have claimed had the matter ever reached public attention or come up in a divorce. Few secrets are ever kept between couples for long. Adulterers beware.

It's just sometimes I find the old call-girl habit of first touch and immediate response does resurface easily, even years later. It's what stops clients feeling embarrassed and nervous and not knowing quite how to proceed, which is more common than you might suppose. Let the pro make the first tactile approach, and make it quick. The oldest habits die slowest.

Neither of us ever mentioned the incident again. It was clearly inappropriate between long-term neighbours. And it hadn't happened before and it hasn't happened since. Just the once – if we forget that other incident back in 1978 which might or might not have happened. I am very fond of Xandra. And look, I have somehow drifted into the first person. Confession, as any Catholic will tell you, eases the mind greatly.

## Waiting, Waiting, Waiting

For a whole decade the Smithsons did nothing to prevent a baby being conceived. But still no-one worried – other than Gwinny, of course. 'Give it time,' the putative parents thought. 'Give it time. We're so young!'

The nineties turned out to be such a busy, even entertaining decade. Passed like a flash. Margaret Thatcher turned to John Major, turned to Tony Blair. Many at that glorious wedding party didn't after all achieve redemption but became clubbers, and the Smithsons tried to stay out of it, not always successfully, as the soul boys, jazz funkateers, rare groove heads, electro poppers and the still sometimes apologetic seekers after gay culture made their pitches for the future – and fashions in altered mind-states swept the land in a series of tsunamis and retreated, leaving a fair proportion of wrecked and broken minds behind. But not theirs.

Isms came and went, political correctness rose and fell and rose again, and hate crime became a matter for the police. It was the

Age of Therapism. Satanic Ritual Abuse was replaced by False Memory Syndrome (if you were fat your father had abused you) and a more generalised therapy, the talking cure, became the answer to every ill – depression, broken marriage, migraine, headache, amputation, a massacre in the playground, IRA attack, any natural disasters, volcanoes, earthquakes, hurricanes – talk it all out, don't brave it all out; always remember, never forget, always apologise. Scrape and scrape away at the old scar tissue – that's the only way to heal a psychic wound, end a trauma. And house prices went up and up and life expectancy with it.

And all through that decade I waited for Flora to come through with the baby girl she'd promised. I busied myself with this and that: it was not time wasted. I had my painting to get on with. I occasionally broke my vow of celibacy, and nothing passes time quicker than the thrill of the occasional affair, but nothing serious.

And then there were the Smithsons to look after. They needed me. Xandra moved slowly but surely up her NHS career ladder in a job she loved, Clive pursued his singing career – he'd once played the lead in *Joseph and the Amazing Technicolor Dreamcoat* and let no-one forget it – learning poetry and writing the greatest verse-novel the world had ever known. If only he could find a middle, let alone an end.

Ten years in which endless dinners were eaten out; friends made and unmade, drifted on, disappeared or died; parties dressed up for and recovered from – myself always an honoured guest:

an older generation than theirs but no-one seemed to mind – I was young at heart, wasn't I? – and a baby vaguely tried for, but every twenty-nine days – Xandra was always very punctual – the drip, drip, drip of blood, as all that pleasure came to nothing. And time passed and time passed.

## The Childless Years

It was true that sometimes Gwinny felt vaguely persecuted, like the lonely circling satellite planet to a central Smithson sun, the one who has the spare key to the house and never loses it, the one who can be called upon when any difficulty looms. But then she had put herself in this position. And no doubt for their part the Smithsons felt it too: the sheer weight of gratitude, of being obliged. Gwinny next door, the portrait painter, artist, wild child with wilder hair, with her odd religions and strange beliefs, and her degree in English Literature (who took in the *New Scientist*, delivered weekly, compared to Xandra's *Vogue*, delivered monthly), wife to no-one, mother to none, so always available for a chat and a chore, to share a joint (after the glow of the wedding had faded), to let in the cat, open the door for the dishwasher man, take over when either of the Smithsons was off sick or in trouble, the one who had paid their mortgage, to whom they had to feel indebted. Maddening. Worst of all, who was obviously, year after year, waiting for Xandra to fall pregnant, but so seldom mentioned it. There'd be patches of coolness between the next-doors but they soon recovered. Gwinny would find a gentleman friend; Clive would get a part, Xandra yet another promotion; the sun would shine again.

Clive worried about his health quite a lot, almost to the point of hypochondria, though what with the ongoing mystery of his vocal cords that was hardly surprising. At least BUPA paid for all that, thanks to that insurance policy still active from the *Dreamcoat* days. So through the childless years there were occasional trips to A&E with mysterious aches and pains which normally turned out to be false alarms – indigestion not heartache, sore throat not laryngitis, a cold in the nose not the Hong Kong flu – and Gwinny would run him up to the hospital and wait for him. If Xandra had a minute she'd run down from Intensive Care to be with her husband. Whom she loved, no doubt about it. She, like her husband, was highly sexed.

Every family needs a neighbour like Gwinny – the one who takes you in from the storm if your electricity goes off, your central heating shuts down (in her attic she has emergency oil lamps and an old Aladdin heater), pays your mortgage because she likes to give more than receive, and has your roof mended along with her own out of sheer goodness of heart, takes the husband in to Emergency and the cat to the vet, and presumably, should you decide to have a baby, might very well end up doing quite a lot of the minding, while you got on with your career.

Clive might not have the makings of the best father in the world, but there would always be Gwinny next door to help. When the time came, just not quite yet. Drip, drip, drip, as Flora turned away her face – though every mid-month Gwinny made a little excursion on her bike up to the Hellenism Reborn Centre with appropriate offerings for burning.

## I Had Sinned

And so it was that I acted as the Smithsons' nurse/provider/ guardian angel through their childless years: none of this seemed onerous to me, just natural. I had the time, the money and the inclination. Why not? I had no family of my own, having broken all contact with my four huge horrid brothers, and I served as a kind of all-purpose mother for both Clive and Xandra.

And if every now and then I felt the non-appearance of a baby was a punishment for past sins, giving up my own baby for adoption as I had when I was sixteen, I tried not to let it surface. I'd had no choice. They'd snatched my little girl Anthea away at six weeks old, time enough for me to have bonded, for the milk to be in full flow, and handed her to people as anonymous as Lord Sebastian when he spurted out his sperm, crying, as later reported by Monty in the Dilberne Spillage Case, 'Oh the spilling, the spurning, the spurting of the spunk!'

It was 1956. I was sixteen years old, a Catholic girl who thought she had sinned, and had no way of supporting myself, let alone a child as well. There were no state benefits, only National Assistance, which offered help to male bread-winners (women's wages were seen as pin money) but certainly not to unmarried mothers, and Charity, which can be very cold indeed. In my case the very conditional comfort of strangers of the kind the nuns offered in the Sacred Heart Home for Fallen Girls, Paddington, and think myself lucky. (They'd changed the name from 'Fallen Girls' to 'Mothers and Babies' but the ethos was the same. You were a disgrace to society.) I had to choose between an orphanage and adoption for my bastard child. There was no way I could keep it myself. I chose adoption, being promised a nice middle-class Catholic family. And that was the last I heard of Anthea, carried off at six weeks old in another woman's arms.

I do try to forget. All I know about her is that she was born on Monday 26th March at 3.15 a.m. At least I can do her horoscope and work out what she is likely to be doing. I think she is probably a model like me, though being a sun in Aries will be taller than me, Jupiter being so well aspected in her chart. And the quasi Apollo who fathered her and disappeared on the tour bus was handsome enough, God knows, he being the one with the dirty toes. I daresay this is why I put so much trust in astrology: it's not exactly a personality defect so much as a means of spiritual survival.

But then of course for all I know she may be dead by now: sixty-seven years since she was born. She might not even have survived infancy. They snatched her from my breast before I had finished feeding her. Her new parents had a train to catch. The one nice nun in the place told me not to worry, the parents had seemed perfectly pleasant and respectable and had been given a bottle of expressed breast milk to take home with them.

'Whose milk?' I'd asked, startled. I've not forgotten that.

'No idea,' she'd replied. 'We pool it.'

Perhaps some of it came from Tess, I've always hoped so. Some of the other girls had quite nasty diseases. Tess was perfectly healthy, a lovely, rosy, happy girl, and made so much milk I envied her. She dripped it all over the place. And then she went and hanged herself. Drip, drip.

## Last-Minute Panic

Well, forget all that. That was then, this is now, or at least further on in history. I write this in my eighty-fourth year, looking back from 2023, and these being the days of the morning-after pill you can reasonably replace the world 'fallen' with the words 'thoroughly stupid'. That's the Millennials' view for you, and we can see it as progress.

But back, or forward, whichever you like (you're the reader, you choose) to 1995. What with one thing and another and Xandra found herself nearing forty with a baby in her head but not in the real world – and she began to worry. She had a charming, civilised, well-run household. She was a nurse, after all, and had pretty soon learned to keep things neat, clean and ship-shape. Gwinny hadn't been much help in this respect, tending to go for artistic chaos, the sort who lets the dishes pile up in the sink while thinking of higher things. Xandra even had a room initially reserved for a nursery, and still referred to as that, even though Clive now used it as somewhere peaceful to write, set up as an office with its own TV – albeit an old 26-inch Toshiba CF26C30 – and if Clive could be eased out of it was all ready and waiting for the baby. Finding space for the baby was the first thing Xandra had done when they moved in. Could it really be all that time ago?

Xandra could see she could no longer leave it to chance. Clive grumbled, but moved his office and TV to the new conservatory extension (Gwinny paid).

Xandra repainted the nursery in Dulux White Delicious, pink but not noticeably so. As fashions in baby wallpaper changed over a decade from pastel sweet to rich red to purple power – even once to black – she had kept up. She liked to decorate every two years.

Clive really liked the black – he was certain the baby (what baby?) would be a boy. 'None of your girly floral nonsense,' he'd say. Xandra, who would much prefer a girl, had stayed dumb.

Possess the image, possess the reality: sympathetic magic. Xandra hung a mobile featuring pretty little ducklings from the ceiling. Then she bought a cot. But still it didn't happen. And before she knew it, Xandra's time clock was now ticking 'now or never, now or never'. Everything was in place: her career was well settled and there was a job waiting for her when she went back to it, in about a month, perhaps. She'd forgotten any qualms about the morality of bringing a baby into an over-crowded world, and by 1996 had even lost faith in the efficacy of white magic. Still no baby. And she wanted one.

'Forget about over-population, the civil war in Afghanistan, the new one in Chechnya,' she urged Clive. 'The world needs babies like ours. What about me, me, me? And what about us?' she added prudently.

'You could always think about adoption,' I said. 'It's a morally sound choice. Help a child who already exists.' Clive rose to the bait at once.

'Adoption!' he cried. Never in a month of Sundays. You never know what you might get!'

'Oh Gwinny, how little you know me! I want Clive's baby, not any old baby. I love my husband. Clive's baby. There has to be something created between us to honour that love. Clive, loving each other the way we do, there must be a baby, half me, half you! I want *us* to go on into the future.'

Now Clive was busily engaged learning Coleridge's *Rime of the Ancient Mariner* by heart and I think it was only coincidence that he quoted imperfectly '*Instead of a cross an albatross about my neck was hung*', before leaning forward and taking Xandra's hand and saying, 'Half me, half you? What a lovely idea. And so it shall be.'

Actually I do know Xandra fairly well, if only because the walls between Nos. 23 and 24 are so thin one might as well be living with her. I knew the Smithsons' ups and their downs, their ins and their outs, as it were, and I can make a pretty good guess at what was going on in Xandra's mind and have no qualms about reporting it. Though as they say on the news websites '*These thoughts and opinions do not necessarily coincide with those of the broadcaster*', that is to say me, now in omniscient narrator mode. The Writers' Huddle – the Kentish Town group of aspirant novelists I meet with once a week since I started writing this story – some are even published – says this is okay. I was rather hurt, I must say, when Xandra said, 'How little you know me!' It's the other way round.

## Having It All

This, Xandra was thinking, was NHS Britain, not some dark savage place far away, and she Xandra was entitled to a year's maternity leave even though she didn't intend to take it. With her savings they could manage quite easily until she got back to work, which would be within the month, and Clive was at home a lot; she could probably persuade him to do the house-husbanding so there wouldn't be child care to pay. Clive would like that, and the trendy mummies at the school gate would adore him and he would be happy adoring them back – in a theoretical way, of course; Clive loved her and would never betray her – and there was always Gwinny to help, she was as good as a spare grandmother, so wasn't it not just their right but a positive duty to have a baby who would save the world, rather than the multitude who could only add to its burdens? Couldn't they just concentrate on actually having a baby?

And Clive, surprisingly, said yes. He was happy enough to concentrate. Xandra had never worked in a maternity ward – she was an Intensive Care specialist – but had access to all relevant material. Clive had his friends in the Soho theatrical pub where he occasionally had a drink or two. I kept out of it. I found myself more prudish than the Smithsons, coming as I did from an earlier generation. My father would not have believed his ears.

The missionary position if you want a girl, doggy if you don't (Clive wanted a boy, Xandra a girl; they took turns; no more anal sex, unless they weakened). No tight underpants for Clive, no coffee, no more smoking, rationed alcohol for both of them, as much sex as possible, forget fertility watch; it only made couples anxious and spoils the pleasure.

And sex was a truly masterly performance on Clive's part. Gwinny heard it nightly. The wall between the two adjacent bedrooms was thin. But it had seemed to Gwinny that it did occasionally conclude in an inappropriate place if what you were after was a baby. More particularly it seemed to Gwinny that this happened in the few days when Xandra was at her most fertile. Perhaps Clive confused safe days with risky days. Or perhaps one or other of them were not quite as keen on swelling their family as they pretended? They certainly lusted after one another, but love? And what was the difference between love and lust anyway?

Clive had this albatross (unconscious guilt, presumably) hanging round his neck – what was this all about? Xandra certainly had a rock (caution, and a need for practicality) weighing her down. He acted before he thought, she thought before she acted. He was certainly the more fun. But when both spoke of 'love', were they talking about remotely the same thing?

Gwinny still owned one of those little Catholic birth control monitors (left over from her previous life) that told you which days of your cycle were safe and which were not, though for her it lacked any practical purpose. She kept it, she supposed, for sentimental reasons, in the same way women keep their wedding dress long after they can fit into it. Such monitors were far from fail-safe, as Gwinny knew to her cost. Reliance on it, when once she had, resulted in an abortion. Aristotle thought that ensoulment – when the soul enters into the body – didn't happen for some three months, but she'd left it too late and it had to be done at four months when the foetus had quickened; which was when, come to think of it, she'd got interested in the *Tibetan Book of the Dead* and the Bardo Thodol. The Buddhists allowed a cap or IUD as a barrier to prevent the sperm getting to the egg, but once conception had occurred they wouldn't allow the destruction of life at any stage. She became sure this little scrap of discarded life still lingered there in the Bardo, waiting to choose someone better. If Gwinny could ever become pregnant again, she might even be given a second chance and get the terminated one back again. Odder things happened.

Gwinny, by the way, hates the very word 'abortion', that torn and bloody grievous thing. 'Termination' was much more polite, safe and clean, as if a contract is under discussion.

But the more you wanted a baby, judging by the Smithsons, albatrosses and rocks round both their necks, the harder it was to get one and the more un-loving felt the activity. And worrying about not having a baby was what stopped you not having one. It was all a total nightmare.

Coleridge, by the way, obviously took the albatross for a much smaller sea bird, for example a petrel, or so the critics say. But a dead petrel would also get rather smelly and disgusting. I think Coleridge just liked the sound of '*instead of a cross, the Albatross*' so much he ignored the fact that it made no sense. I got into trouble at school for saying as much, though Rozzie said it was a perfectly reasonable supposition. Rozzie had an eidetic memory, and once she had looked over the poem, at the age of four, could quote from it by memory. It took ages for the adult Clive to learn all 150 or so stanzas. Have patience, we will get to Rozzie presently. Just see me as the wedding guest: '*He* (the Ancient Mariner – me, that is) *holds him with his glittering eye – The Wedding-Guest stood still, And listens like a three years' child. The Mariner hath his will*' – as I tell this tale of how a *fin de siècle* turned into a *début de siècle* with the birth of Rozzie, the original, *echte* Millennial, born on January 1st 2000, a second after midnight struck.

## Suspicion Dawns

Since Xandra had had two terminations in her teens and Clive said he had never to the best of his knowledge made a girl pregnant – '*I always kept my head when all about me were losing theirs and blaming it on me*': Clive often misquoted from Kipling's *If* – it seemed to Gwinny that Clive might very well be the one to blame for Xandra's failure to conceive. Not 'blame' of course – apologies all round – say, rather, 'responsibility'. The trouble was, put it nicely, that Clive failed to appreciate that though things could go wrong with 'women's insides', as he called them, his were outside and obviously in totally good working order. How could they be otherwise? They were his. They were perfect. They rose and fell to order. Everything about him was perfect, you only had to look in a mirror to see. Except his vocal cords, which you couldn't see, and that was a regrettable matter of youthful cocaine and bad advice from his singing coach when he was seventeen, the one who had told him not to shy away from the high notes of *Close Every Door*.

Xandra thought perhaps it was time to see a fertility expert, but the NHS only offered treatment to under thirty-fives, so she was already too old for that, and going private meant unnecessary expense. Clive wouldn't approve of such a thing. She hesitated to argue the matter out with Clive: perhaps he was right, she was worrying unnecessarily, but the worry began niggling away more and more. She was in a quandary and when she was in a quandary she usually left it to Gwinny to sort out. Gwinny was obviously in favour of a baby and would know when the right time came to approach Clive.

Sometimes Xandra thought that Gwinny was closer to Clive than she was, apart from the sex, of course, in spite of her being so old. Indeed, Xandra wondered sometimes if she was being used almost as a surrogate mother for Gwinny's child.

## Doubting The Goddess

And I too had begun to doubt Flora and worry about Xandra's biological clock, thirty-eight years old, and already the odds of her having a Down's baby were beginning to creep up. I'd been down to West Hampstead and made a few more orisons this time to Demeter as well, Goddess of the harvest and the cycle of birth and death, and could have sworn she smiled at me, but the smoke was quite heavy in valerian, banana peel scrapings, oatmeal and passion fruit so I did not put too much credence in the experience, and Xandra went on drip, drip, dripping every four weeks on the dot. And still Flora did not come through with the goods. Perhaps I had annoyed her by sharing with Demeter – they could be rivals? Mea culpa, again.

Then I realised just how wry Demeter's smile had been, or at any rate my perception of it, and how if she was saying anything it was 'meet me half-way, buy a ticket', and it occurred to me that a visit to an IVF clinic for the pair of them was in order.

Xandra was fertile enough – she had had two early terminations: she'd told me how much she regretted the suffering this had caused her mother. (It was usually Anna who suffered, I'd noticed, not Xandra, Anna being something of a narcissistic mother – defined as *'a parent who is exclusively and possessively close to her child and may be especially envious of, and threatened by, their child's growing independence'*, so Xandra's fertility was not in doubt. But Clive?

Clive had got to thirty-five without producing any progeny I knew about, though he had an active sex life and a not necessarily exclusive relationship with Xandra, though he was always very careful to keep his adventures to himself and not upset her. It was unusual for any man to be so lucky for so long. The fault might very well lie with Clive, though Clive would be outraged by the very idea.

I had very rarely brought the subject up: it tended to raise hackles if I did. They were perfectly entitled to change their minds about bringing a baby into the world. Because I had quite lightly mentioned once or twice that I hoped they'd start a family as I signed the mortgage guarantee, did not mean they had to go ahead and do it.

Having a baby was an expensive business and certainly not very fashionable. Couples these days valued the childless life, and the longer they had it the more they liked it. Romantic holidays, consumer durables, electronic must-haves, meals out in fancy restaurants, freedom and future itself – giving up all that in order to turn two into three, and the third a yawling, squalling monster who never slept? Now that was a real sacrifice, not just a burnt offering that could be put in a basket attached to your bicycle handles.

I was well aware that the new digital life would be inimical to sharing with a mewling, puking very non-digital infant. Okay when the kids turned into teenagers and could go shopping (preferably on Amazon) or watch football with you (table footie, perhaps?) and then look after you in your old age (A.I. robots were coming along fast), would the advantages show, but the years in between were too much like hard work to be endured. 'The future' was such a misty concept to most – you'd be dead before it happened, anyway.

One only had to look round the office at anyone who'd had a baby in the last couple of years, and see that the fathers could hardly keep awake and had fallen behind in the promotion stakes, and the mothers looked old and strained and annoyed everyone, arriving late and leaving early if they were there at all. It was no advertisement for parenthood.

Yet the young couple had been so sure that they meant to have children! If occasionally through the nineties I'd tried to bring up the subject, and asked about the pitter-pat of little feet (a kind of joke between the three of us, if a rather nervy one) they'd laugh and say first they were 'waiting until the house was finished', and then it was 'we have to wait before Xandra is settled in her so-called career' (Clive always referred to it as 'so-called'), and then it was something or other about maternity leave and timing, and then once an admittance they were trying like billy oh, but nothing seemed to be happening. But lots of time. 'No hurry,' they'd say. 'No worries. Everything inside Xandra works like clockwork, and Clive works pretty well too.'

'*A guy's gotta do what a man's gotta do,*' he misquoted John Wayne, creating a vision of him in cowboy gear leaping upon Xandra at all possible times of day or night, or so he claimed, and I'd no reason to think it wasn't true. It also rather reminded me of my father saying after Owen's birth that he 'was a man, after all, and had a man's needs' and went on to produce Trefor and David. 'Of course we want a baby. I love Xandra to bits. It's just a matter of time. God knows I'm doing my best,' Clive said. 'It's just – sometimes I get these migraines.'

He kept best practice for Xandra's sake; if trying for a baby meant floppy underpants so be it. The alcohol and cigarette ban was good for weight and complexion, though surely applied to women only. More like a feminist plot to make men suffer, like insisting the father was there at the birth to witness 'what he had done', as if women hadn't enjoyed it too and known the possible consequences. And he was not, he asserted, at all neurotic when it came to sex. The more the better. It helped him write.

But the time came when any pitter-pat mention began to evoke an almost hostile reaction from Clive.

'Just because you helped out with our wedding doesn't mean we have to live our lives according to you,' he snapped at me. 'We live as we want, you live as you want.' (He seemed to have forgotten about the mortgage guarantee.) 'So for God's sake go easy on the pitter-pat.'

'Not that we're not grateful for all that you do for us, Gwinny,' Xandra had put in hastily, but otherwise she just sat there looking pretty, and determined not to challenge Clive in anything at all.

And then when Clive said to me 'Funny about these migraines, they just seem to come at the wrong time,' I remembered Marco saying there's no such thing as an accident when it comes to illness and I wondered if Clive actually wanted a baby as much as Xandra did.

Life was going along quite nicely for him, after all. There were a few lip-synching openings nowadays, so he could at least act being a singer when he wasn't actually singing, though he mostly had to keep quiet about it. He didn't get fame or much money, but he looked good on a stage and girls, or at any rate middle-aged women, would throw themselves at him in matinées and that was always pleasant. And some producers would risk an understudy's squeak if it was a matinée and not doing too well anyway. And the idea of a baby could be daunting.

And then there'd been the question of some guilt albatross hanging round Clive's neck. You could know people so well, and still know so little.

And whatever Xandra thought and felt she just sat there, looking pretty and happy in Clive's apparent adoration.

## A Reason For Everything

[Writers' Huddle: 'Do we really want all this next stuff, Gwinny? Sounds a bit obsessional. As if you're trying to prove that it's unprotected sex makes women irresponsible. Isn't it enough to wear them down with all your patronising anti-Millennial blather – for that's what it amounts to.']

Xandra, reflected Gwinny, ordered doctors and nurses around with no problem but when it came to her husband it was a different matter. It could only be a matter of too much unprotected sex. The male ejaculate, so Marco had told her (and in Gwinny's reading of the *New Scientist* she saw the theory repeated), contains a cocktail of tranquillising and bonding hormones – serotonin, oxytocin (the 'love hormone', making a girl snuggly and affectionate), endorphins, oestrone, prolactin, etc. – a mere 3 per cent of it being actual sperm.

It is unprotected sex that makes women love so unreservedly. It's why battered women – be it sexual or emotional battering – keep coming back for more: all the serotonin, oxytocin, endorphins, oestrone, prolactin, etc. that addict her to her testosterone-ridden partner. *Can't wait, can't wait!* It's why there's love at first sight (or rather, first fuck), why the arranged marriage so often works (ditto), why the longer you're married the worse your divorce feels, why the use of condoms is advisable in any relationship if a woman wants to keep a level head.

Xandra hadn't been using condoms. She'd been trying for years to have a baby. She had all the symptoms of an ejaculate-addicted woman: *'Yes sir, no sir, three bags full, sir.'* Some men's ejaculate is particularly potent, some men's less so, being too weak to lead to addiction, but pleasurable enough in its own right at least until the morning, when she'll want to get busy with more important matters.

Meantime, while the old-fashioned girl through the ages (it may be rather different for Millennials, this being the Digital-Anthropocene Age) waited for true love to descend from the heavens in some variety or other of the male prehistoric anthropoidal ape, and for the insensate urge to procreate seize her, there's always other survival work that must be done! From the Palaeolithic Age, grubbing for insects, to the Iron

Age, digging for metals, to the Digital-Anthropocene Age, tapping away on the computer, there's always work to be done. And forget your duty to procreation: a day's work can wear you out!

And certainly Xandra's unnatural frequent night shifts wore her out, and might have caused a few fertility issues, while still addicting her to what turned out to be Clive's spermless but super-oxytocined, serotonin-friendly embraces.

How lucky, then, the super-oxytocined, testosterone-rich men, whose addicted loved ones are in and out of women's refuges like yo-yos. Girls will always cluster round them while friends and family despair. Clive never hit, and his emotional abuse was subtle, but on a bad day Gwinny would see him as just such a brute, only, like Xandra, to go into forgive-understand-forget mode pretty quickly.

## The Art Of Forgetfulness

Perhaps the folk singer at the back of the theatre, sixty-eight years ago, was just such a 'strong sperm' person. Gwinny understood and forgave, but just never forgot. Perhaps she saw him as Apollo in the guise of a folk singer, coming down from the summit of Primrose Hill on that memorable day all those years ago. *'I have conversed with the spiritual sun. I saw him on Primrose Hill'*! If it happened to William Blake it could happen to Gwinny. She's nutty enough. Perhaps Apollo saw her and fancied her and followed her down from the top of the hill and took the shape of the folk singer. (I shan't say stranger things could happen, because probably not.)

Sometimes Gwinny dreams of the folk singer. He comes through the door to where she sleeps, says he still loves her and will make everything all right. It's a junkie's dream, an addict's dream, if ever there was one. Gwinny still yearns for what ruined her. And Clive? Aphrodite must have been really addicted to Zeus if she put up with so much hurt from him. And wasn't she, Gwinny, like Xandra, guilty of putting up with a lot from Clive? That unfortunate possible incident of the lost virginity had been far more recent a one-night stand than the occasion in Drury Lane.

Oh, be gone, false thought, false memory!

## Facing The Facts

Plop, plop, plop, dripped the leaking glass roof of No. 24's new conservatory on the evening that matters maternal came to a head. That wasn't until October 1998 (when Hurricane Mitch made landfall in Central America, killing an estimated 18,000 people). Boreas, God of the North Wind, was howling and the rain got in between two slipped glass panes. The drips began to fall unusually fast, plop-plop-plop-plop-plop-plop now, so everyone was a bit tense in spite of the good hashish Clive had just brought back from one of his slightly mysterious visits to Soho.

My fault. I had made a burnt offering to Boreas in the hope he'd go easy on Nos. 23 and 24 and he hadn't responded in any useful way; on the contrary. I was suing the building contractors, whom I had paid; there was a law suit under weigh and Mr Ipswich had recommended the slipped panes were used as evidence, but these things tend to go on and on.

My plea to Boreas, I could see, was along lateral-thinking lines – if you can't raise the bridge, lower the river – and that might have been why he overlooked the petition – 'get up a stepladder and do the bloody thing yourself' – but the sacrifice should have included horse hair and mugwort, but I had substituted a clipping of Simkins Two's cat hair and sage, so it wasn't really fit for purpose and all I had done was annoy the God. All that winter the North Wind in London blew and blew and blew.

Getting pregnant was all just a matter of time perhaps, I thought, but time did go on and on: not necessarily wasted time, of course, and the Smithsons had twenty more years' worth of time than me. But they didn't have as much as they thought, or certainly Clive thought. Because suddenly instead of being in her thirties Xandra was nearly forty and the drip, drip, dripping of her untried womb became a matter of urgency. The best babies were born if you were in your mid-twenties, everyone knew, and after that it was downhill all the way.

Well, everyone knew except Clive, who was wilfully ignorant when it came to anything to do with the working of the human body. Odd in someone who verged on having a hypochondriacal personality disorder. Marco had described Lord Petrie as such as we lay on the deck of *Gwyneth* and tanned in the Mediterranean sun. It was a very kind and diplomatic way of describing any hypochondriac, paranoid schizophrenic, OCD nutter, a bank robber – whatever. At least it suggested a cure was available. But Marco also suggested that I had a profound 'dependent personality disorder, namely sex addiction, triggered by early trauma' – well, take your pick of them! – which was why I put up with the dying likes of Bunny and his Lordship when others didn't. Sex addiction didn't bother me – a very useful trait in the profession in which I found myself – but I found 'dependent personality' a real turnoff and Marco and I drifted apart.

Anyway, whatever personality disorder afflicted Clive, it made him quite difficult to deal with, especially when it came to bodily matters – fond of him as I was. It was as if he had handed all the responsibility for his physical being over to others simply in order to be able to blame them.

But the time came when even Clive noticed that Xandra was becoming edgy and disconsolate. It was a Thursday. We were waiting for Clive to come back to No. 24 with curry from the Indian takeaway. When it was curry we usually ate at my place because I didn't mind if my long wooden table ended up with turmeric stains – I saw them as stains of honour. Xandra, far more particular than me, would spend hours scrubbing away at hers. And Clive did tend to swing the bag rather boldly on the way home, so the lids were messy when you took them off, and some of the contents would overflow, and the chicken korma end up with the lamb passanda. But the power had gone off at my place, and Clive had promised not to swing the bags.

Xandra had had a particularly bad day at work. A six-year-old had had to have her life support taken away and Xandra had been removing a couple of IVs and the breathing tube when the poor mother changed her mind so blows were exchanged and it had ended up in a general fracas in a ward which was meant to be calm and quiet.

'All the top brass were there to witness,' she said. 'It's quite a thing when you have to withdraw life support, and it's grim and I hate doing it. I don't like to tell Clive because all he'll say is I shouldn't be doing the job in the first place if I want to get pregnant.'

'Poor Xandra,' I said, and she just burst into tears. She put down her healthy freshly squeezed orange juice and she said, 'Sod this. I need spirits.' She seized the vodka bottle from the table – I was having a Bloody Mary – and filled her glass to the top before I could stop her, and swigged it back.

'Sod the baby,' she said 'Fuck everything. If this is what it takes to get pregnant I give up! Sorry, Gwinny. You want it, Clive wants it, but I'm sore and swollen for him trying, and I've had it!'

At which moment Clive let himself into the room singing '*The last rose of summer, 'tis blooming alone,*' his voice only squeaking when he got to '*faded and gone*'.

Clive was in one of his exuberant moods and they were wonderful to behold. He was like Zeus himself, all munificent grandeur, benign and beautiful, radiating all the world's energy and goodwill – though it could switch all too quickly into bad mood Zeus, with thunderous brow, lightning darting round his temples, hand raised to throw his thunderbolts.

On top of the foil containers was a perfect long-stemmed white rose, which he handed to Xandra. I knew it was a sign from Flora.

'For you, my darling,' he said. 'To all three of us, soon to be four of us!'

'Where did you get that from?' I asked.

'The railings of No. 14,' he said. 'The last rose of summer, blooming alone, I couldn't resist it. She's a horrid old bat, anyway.'

More trouble down the road to be sorted out, but I would have to leave it alone for now. I was so immensely cheered by this sign from Flora. I could feel expectation pricking in my thumbs.

'I can't do it, Clive,' Xandra was saying. 'We'll adopt. I'll do anything, I'll live childless all my life. Look at Gwinny. She's perfectly happy. But I will not sacrifice my life for a baby who is not going to happen.'

Happy Zeus was turning into dangerous Zeus. I doled out the curry onto waiting plates. I knew what everyone wanted. Xandra automatically used the paper roll to clear up what I had spilled.

'That's a bit rich, Xandra,' he said, 'after what we've been through together. It can't be your decision alone.'

And he told her what a natural mother she would make, generous, loving and intelligent, a born looker-afterer. She had the baby blues, that was all and perfectly natural. He'd been reading the baby books. He would be there when she went back to work and there'd be Gwinny to help; the first weeks might be sleepless, but she had maternity leave. 'The world is moving into the e-twenty-first century (should we all survive the Millennium Bug, *inshallah*). There's no disgrace in it for me. Lots of women these days go out to work and earn more than their husbands.'

'You mean you'd be a house-husband?'

'So far as my writing would allow. I quite look forward to the young mummies at the school gate.'

'They'll adore you,' said Xandra, quite cheering up.

Which was true enough. To the love-hungry mothers of North London with high incomes and boring husbands Clive would seem a dream come true. No-one would notice his little squeak of a voice, so long as he paid them some attention and was not under stress. There was no further protest from Clive.

'Promise you won't be jealous of the young mummies. You know my heart belongs to you.'

'Don't worry,' she said, 'I'm not the jealous type.'

In my experience this was more often said than meant. 'My wife won't mind' is often said just before she turns up at the bedroom door, hammering and yelping in rage. I have a couple of bald patches in my head.

## Nature Or Zature

How cunning evolution is, so to make a woman docile and loving, not wanting to hurl father and his irritating offspring into the nearest ditch, but to stay around and love, love, love him and all who goes with him. But oh! The anxiety that single bonding event brings with it! It is the root of all jealousy. *Dear God, let him not leave me! Let him not be off with someone else sowing the seed, the selfish gene!* Then when he's back and she has the baby it's all double-bind stuff: *Please, please show your love again, now, now! I need my oxytocin fix! But what's that? The baby's squalling; what do I do? I know he'll starve, I have to go, now, now!*

Mother Nature doesn't care one whit for mother's happiness. Nature is merciless. I don't know why women put so much trust in her. She's the one who sets father off to distribute his genes to the next womb offered, the minute mother and baby seem to be able to look after themselves. Break your heart, what does Mother Nature care! So long as grief doesn't sour the milk, but baby's usually just about weaned by now.

If your partner 'won't commit' that's Nature's doing. She's a real bitch. He just doesn't feel like it? Nature's whispering in his ear – she can look after herself, why should he bother? He's really only into helpless women he can look after, and where, nowadays, can he find one?

'Lie Nature on her side and call her Zature,' says Gwinny. 'She's your enemy, not your friend. All Zature does, when you're past procreating age and have served evolution's purpose, is cast you off like an old glove, dry you up and wither you up, so you go on wanting others but no-one goes on wanting you. Zature has no intention of keeping you happy: all she needs from you is to die so she can use you as fertiliser.'

Gwinny says all this to anyone who will notice, and that's certainly no-one in her Readers' Group, let alone the Writers' Huddle she goes to now she's writing the story of the Smithsons, Rozzie and herself. (Don't worry, we'll get to Rozzie soon enough. As I've pointed out to you wedding guests – *'the Wedding-Guest here beat his breast For he heard the loud bassoon'* – we're still on the detail of how Rozzie came to be born at all.) Both groups have suggested she cut all these tedious sequences out; they will only bore the reader, but Gwinny finds herself as insistent and annoying as the Ancient Mariner with whom she identifies.

The Readers' Group is mostly composed of singletons – well-educated, successful, ambitious and attractive young women in their thirties who spent their twenties tossing their glossy heads, and spurning their suitors while they waited for Mr Right to come along. He didn't, her standards being so high – earn more than me, be nicer than me, more fun than my girlfriends, drive a Ferrari to my little pink VW, have more status than me (all more of Zature's idiotic tricks – she's so A-list herself where was she going to find such a paragon?). Nor is he likely to turn up now. All the Mr Rights seem to be off with silly girls in their twenties.

The grey hairs bent together in the Writers' Huddle are no less distraught. Twenty-three years into the new Millennium people talk faster, walk faster and think faster. Reality itself has gone upside down. Only the young, standing on their heads, seem to understand it. But they're good at points of grammar and structure and what to do if you want to get published. I don't always follow their advice but I feel amongst friends and keep going. Get back to the story.

## Some External Intervention Is Needed

Xandra, Clive and I were seated round the table eating a Christmas dinner for three from M&S (£15.00 with trimmings) and drank red wine and smoked Afghan Gold. On special occasions, which seemed to get more and more frequent with the years, Gwinny gave up her No Alcohol rule, and Clive and Xandra their No Smoking. Xandra was wearing high heels, a smart if tight white skirt, a navy shirt and clunky pink ethnic beads brought back from a holiday in Morocco, much enjoyed. The year was 1998.

It was a special day so we were eating in the new glass conservatory at the back of the house rather than the kitchen and rather wishing we weren't, it being a little chilly and draughty. Boreas the North Wind was having a field day, rattling the glass and pelting it with sleet as if this new structure had no business being where it was. Clive was reciting the *Rime of the Ancient Mariner* as his Christmas gift to us. Xandra had given him a new 26-inch TV to replace the small one which used to be in the nursery. I had given him a very nice old edition of the complete works of Samuel Taylor Coleridge, though he left it by his plate and got gravy on it almost at once. I might as well have given him a Penguin mass market paperback and saved myself sixty quid. But at least when he was reading poetry his voice seldom squeaked and his voice was quite lovely; light yet powerful.

The new extension was under a glass roof, and the builders had gone bankrupt before they could come back to make good, so two panes of glass needed to be re-puttied. It was a small job which Clive would get round to in time, but a saucepan in the corner did well enough to collect the drips when it was raining and the wind came from the North. Clive needed to get down to writing his play in such time as he had free. Xandra and I both hated going up ladders and Gwinny drew the line at paying more for the conservatory. It was only a small leak anyway and a householder can get used to anything. The saucepan remained in place for a year. Time does pass even if you're not having fun, as Xandra wasn't.

Christmas pudding. While we were sprinkling the caster sugar, finishing off the brandy sauce (never enough), Xandra stood up to replenish the double cream (these blow-outs only once a year can surely do very little harm), gave a little cry and ran from the room calling 'Bathroom' over her shoulder as she left. Clive did not stop in his rendering of the *Rime of the Ancient Mariner* (interesting, that spelling. Like 'rime of frost around the rim': but did Coleridge do it on purpose, an old usage, or just opium sloppiness? One will never know) but I thought there was a slight sense of good cheer, almost relief, in his voice. But one must beware the paranoiac tendency; the schizotypal personality disorder might be breaking through.

> 'And now the storm-blast came, and he
> Was tyrannous and strong:
> He struck with his o'ertaking wings,
> And chased us south along.
>
> With sloping masts and dipping prow,
> As who pursued with yell and blow
> Still treads the shadow of his foe,
> And forward bends his head,
> The ship drove fast, loud roared the blast,
> And southward aye we fled.'

Xandra came back in ten minutes wearing a navy skirt and a white shirt and her warm dark hospital coat (Clive hated it) over both, and that was the end of the biscuits and stilton (and just as well). She smiled bravely but she was trembling.

'Oh poor Xandra,' I said. 'Not again!'

'Again,' she said. 'Twelve years of bloody agains. Twelve twelves are one hundred and forty-four. That's more than enough. Clive, we're giving this up. We're going to adopt.' And she burst into great gulping tears. Dinner was forgotten.

Clive folded Xandra into his arms and said, 'Darling Xandra, don't cry!' and exhorted her not to give up. And she didn't, whether thanks to Flora, the entities in the Bardo Thodol, or Clive's frequent cocktail of good cheer and confidence who is to say?

'It's the speed with which time goes,' said Xandra. 'I hadn't realised. I thought we'd just got married but now it seems to be twelve years ago and I'm nearly forty.'

'It's that stupid job of yours,' Clive said. 'It's fucking your life up – no time for living.'

'It's not that,' said Xandra. 'It's the job that keeps me sane.' Clive's fingers clenched.

'It might be time for IVF clinic,' I said. 'Just to keep Xandra cheerful. The stress is getting her down.' 'Stress' had just been discovered as the source of all mental and physical infirmities: in fashion and out like a yo-yo ever since. 'Just a little investigation. Lots of women are in the same boat.'

'I suppose there could be something wrong with my internal workings,' admitted Xandra, 'but that means going private. You have to be under thirty-five for the NHS to do it.'

'Mean bastards,' said guess-who, automatically.

Clive hated all doctors on principle, though what principle was never made clear. They were all stupid, Clive claimed, knew nothing and typically had to sit their exams seven times over until they passed. Xandra told me she knew they had four chances, not seven, but did not like to correct him. It would be seen as disloyalty.

'I was cycling back from the British Museum the other day,' I said casually, 'and I passed a new IVF clinic on Harley Street. The Woolland Brilliant Baby Clinic – "*Meeting Every Newborn's Needs*". Ridiculous cutesy slogan.'

'Charge you the earth,' said Clive, 'and deliver mud. Private medicine. Shysters and con-men. Ever read Cronin's *The Citadel*?'

'Fifty years ago,' said Xandra. She was weakening.

'Almost as old as you, darling,' said Clive. He was not weakening. Indeed, he was switching from funny Clive, life and soul of the party, to mean-and-nasty, self-righteous, know-it-all Clive. The jaw set, the beautiful eyes glazed. Too much food, I thought, too much drink, too much smoke, and Boreas swirling round the room. The speed of the drips was still increasing. I tactfully went to fetch my coat and when I came back the situation had worsened.

'Please don't shout, Clive. It's every woman's right to have a baby. I need to realise my potential and procreate. I find myself looking into other people's prams.' Xandra was snivelling for mercy. How easily strong women are reduced, traduced.

'What feminist tripe are you spouting now?' He was getting angry, as he did when threatened. Time to intervene.

I had passed a shop earlier, which had the new BlackBerry 830s before their official release, and bought one. You could talk to the world. I could see it was the future, though not sure even then that the future was all that desirable. It cost £200, a great deal of money. Now I took it out of my pocket.

'Look at this, Clive,' I said, and spoke to him as if he were a child. And I simply bribed him. I would pay for Xandra's visit to the Woolland Brilliant Baby Clinic and he would drive her down and I would buy him a BlackBerry. Almost nobody had one. It was one of the very first on the market. It worked a treat. A little more conversation, Xandra had dried her tears, and Clive was saying: 'When a new life is at stake money is immaterial, darling. Money can always be found.'

Now it was Xandra's turn to be difficult.

'But I'm an NHS worker. It would feel like disloyalty.' And 'It's not fair on Gwinny. She's not made of money,' and 'Can we really afford it? We live up to the limit. We've only got my wages.'

Clive said nothing. The question of who supported whom was a sore point. After the first initial promise of fame and fortune when he was seventeen and cast as Joseph in the West End and then on Broadway the young couple's financial future had seemed assured enough.

Clive had been snatched out of drama school to become a temporary star, tall and testosterone-charged, gentle-looking and with a voice as powerful as Tom Jones. Sandra, now Xandra, the steady girlfriend, given the small part of Benjamin's wife as a kindness, lurked in the background, piping away valiantly, trying not to feel envious, but also proud. And then disaster had happened and now Xandra was a nurse and before technology made lip-synching a frowned-upon possibility, Clive was never going to make much money and now they were dependent on his occasional earnings, her salary and the fortune Clive was going to make with *Let's Get Out of Here!*, which one day he would finish if only he got enough peace and quiet.

The drip in the corner is so annoying I know I'll end up having to fork out for it, and bother Mr Ipswich, whose wife was having another baby, and the law suit over a possible £190, less than she paid for just one BlackBerry. Now it was two. Boreas has let me down.

## Many A Slip

The appointment at the Woolland Brilliant Baby Clinic was for Friday January 15th 1999. The Sun and Venus both in the first house: an excellent omen! For the wider world 1998 meant the Kosovo war, inflation at 2.72 per cent, Lewinsky and Clinton high jinks: *Armageddon* at the cinema. Microsoft the biggest company in the world. The Millennium approaching and first alarming news of the dreaded Bug. But forget all that. This was important.

The appointment had to be made three weeks in advance but they were 'very busy', they said – or 'pretending to be', as Clive said. I was nervous; Clive might change his mind. Suspicious that he too would end up being tested – and he would not spill his seed Onan-like as easily as young Sebastian had done a full twenty years ago – he might easily see this as an indignity and find something more important to do.

Sure enough, on Thursday January 14th Xandra called them in her lunch break (10.30–11.00 a.m., early shift) to check time and date and came back with some alarming news. She broke it to us when we were in No. 24, having fish and chips and onion rings from the chippie in King Edward's Street. (If Xandra went to the bathroom to get rid of some of it nobody liked to comment. I cycled a lot and Clive never seemed to put on weight no matter what he ate. But Xandra needed to keep trim.)

These days the chippie is proud to serve a vegan fish and chips, the fish made with banana blossom, seaweed and samphire, as well as normal breaded sole, mushy peas and low-calorie unsalted chips, and is doing perfectly well – the inhabitants of Standard Road having suffered a sea change too. It's all progress.

The Woolland Clinic let it be known that they assumed Xandra was bringing in her partner for testing, and Xandra rashly mentioned this to Clive. Clive stopped shaking the tomato sauce, and misquoted as was his custom, '*Shake oh shake the ketchup bottle, first none'll come and then a lot'll*,' and then said, 'Sorry darling. Not me, not into a test tube. Sex is all about love not science. Looking at some rude girlie magazine and squirting into a test tube is too hideous a way to start a baby.'

I marvelled at how innocent Clive seemed to be. Girlie magazines were already a thing of the past. They watched computer porn at the office. These days it took more than some tame girlie magazine to get a man going. But of course he might be pretending innocence. I daresay he watched porn quite a lot when Xandra was on shift. He wouldn't let on. Xandra would have been horrified. She belonged to the WAP group. Women Against Pornography, still vainly trying for a better world. Young girls feel unshaven pussies are unhygienic. [Writers' Huddle: 'Delete the last two sentences. Unhelpful and unnecessary, albeit true.']

'I'm not being difficult, darling,' went on Clive, 'but it is so often the women's fault. They have such complicated insides. Men are out in the open in their workings; there's very little to go wrong.'

Either Clive shut his eyes and ears to everything he didn't want to see or hear, or actually he just didn't notice in the first place, so utterly solipsistic was he. Beautiful women can become so self-centred they lose touch with all reality; I have lived amongst them and know how often this can happen, have hysterics if a minion hasn't taken the brown M&Ms from the box, while taking a botched eye-lift quite calmly. No doubt it could happen to very good-looking, over-adulated men too.

Marco had accused me once of having a depersonalisation disorder – once during sex I had described myself as floating above myself – perhaps Clive had it too. He was so beautiful he just could not get down to earth.

If you equated beauty with power you could see the same thing going on in politicians' heads. Overdose them with power and they'd believe any old thing that suited them. Out of touch, above people's heads, unable to get down to earth. Mad, mad! ['Unnecessary,' says the Writers' Huddle. 'What's got into you? Delete!']

Clive finished his chips and went on to the packet of 'Posh Profiteroles' which I'd bought back from the Camden Town Sainsbury's. Xandra shook her head and declined.

'Darling,' said Clive. 'Honestly, if there is some kind of delay in conceiving this baby you have no-one to blame but yourself. Nursing is a low-paid, practically manual profession and simple secretarial will earn you twice as much and has social hours. So at least I'll get to see you sometimes. Go to this clinic of yours tomorrow, but that's all they'll tell you. I'm all for it, but don't ask me to come with you. Gwinny will take you, I'm sure. People make far too much fuss. Childbirth is a natural process. African women go behind a bush, put it in a sling and go straight back to work in the fields.'

'And then they die,' I said, under my breath, but he wasn't listening anyway, busy pointing out that in any case he had an important audition in the afternoon and though it was a noon appointment, these places loved to keep you hanging about. Xandra looked tearful and Clive said, 'Not the tears again!' Sometimes he was a hard man to love.

'I was in John Lewis's this morning,' I said, when I had recovered, 'and they had such a cute deal on these new iMacs.'

'What sort?' he asked. 'I suppose I could change over to the Apple system. Though one's used to the devil one knows.'

'A 2-for-1 offer,' I said. 'How about it?'

'Okay,' he said, and we got a taxi to Oxford Street. The 2-for-1 offer was no longer available. I bought two.

Really this baby was causing endless expense. I checked out the *I Ching*, threw the three coins and got Hexagram No. 3. *'Difficulty at the beginning works complete success.'* That made me feel better.

## A Pact With The Knowledgeable

Xandra was on early shift on the 15th. [Writers' Huddle says it's okay to shift to her voice. You know her well enough.] She was on Ward 8 up at Hampstead Hospital, where she was the very competent Intensive Care ward sister – annual salary £21,750 – it ended at 11 a.m. and the appointment with Dr Vellum at the Brilliant Baby Clinic was at noon. That gave Xandra just time enough to pick up Clive at No. 24 and Gwinny as witness to the life at No. 23. She drove in her darling little 2CV (£3,000 almost new) and could be in Harley Street by ten to twelve. She almost didn't go. She got cold feet.

Wanting a baby had become a way of life, a habit, tearing her apart. Had it been so long she no longer knew who she was? What about her job? Supposing she had a baby and then couldn't bear to leave it? How would they live? Clive was more ornamental than useful when it came to earning money.

She'd seen women when they came back to work after having a baby, and a weeping, sleepless, exhausted lot they were, unable even to read vitals properly, a danger to the ward: whining, too, always asking for time off for no real reason, and a nuisance to everyone else. But how could she change her mind now?

And supposing it hurt? She'd got away with never working in Maternity, but she'd been in a ward down the corridor once and had heard terrible screams. Most likely hysteria, she supposed, pain relief being so much improved these days, but even so.

But she would not think like this. She was a strong, independent, powerful, self-reliant person. She was an intelligent woman. A feminist. It was every woman's right to choose to have a baby, just as it was her right to choose not to. Whatever happened, she would cope. She could have it all. She would.

But today could be hard. Going out with Clive, especially if it was somewhere he didn't want to go, was often extremely hard. If there was a No Smoking sign he would smoke under it. If he was treated with less respect than he believed he warranted, faced with what he perceived as passive aggression, he would take loud and expletive-filled offence.

He hated everything to do with doctors and now she had dragged him off to sit in a waiting room to discuss a particularly sensitive medical topic. She could cope, but could he?

Poor Clive: he had had such a dreadful beginning. The bullying car salesman father, the over-passive mother, the initial too-early sexual experience – introduced to sex by a prostitute – underage too, and that can wreak such emotional damage, according to all the books. That woman should go to prison. Then the car crash, leaving him an orphan. The sudden rise to fame hadn't helped

*'Whom the Gods wish to destroy, they first call promising'*, as Cyril Connolly had observed. Clive was always quoting him, and Gwinny next door was a real fan. But it was true. When she met him at drama school he'd won the 'most promising' annual award; they were already a couple – Clive and Sandra turning into Clive and Xandra, and they'd been like that all their lives. Clive had been picked up at once and snatched away to play the lead in *Dreamcoat*. He'd insisted on taking her with him and she'd been given a small part, to keep her quiet, she supposed.

There'd been rave notices, management was delighted, offers were pouring in, agents were on the phone (well, at least one or two). Girls were all over him, but then they always had been. She'd had to draw him out of the embraces of her best friend in a dressing-room where some actor had a high pile of cocaine on a marble table and a glass full of straws. Clive had just grabbed one and sniffed quickly and deeply – and there and then damaged his nasal septum so that it later perforated. Perhaps it had been cut with bi-carb, which can be very corrosive. I don't know, she thought. Nobody knew much, back in the seventies, but it was all her fault for being jealous and mean minded. She tried not to be.

We loved each other then, we love each other now, she thought: it was love at first sight and would be at last sight. Love is all, as they say. That, and nursing. Helping other people. Making a difference.

She can have it all: the baby, the career, the family. She will. Too late now anyway. She couldn't just call it off, as if it was a wedding. She would look too silly. It was only a visit to an IVF clinic. Clive would rejoice but Gwinny would never forgive her if she backed out. She would stop brooding and making herself late and go and fetch the others.

If only it didn't all end in some dreadful scene where Clive loudly cursed all doctors as fools and shysters and in public too. She must love him, otherwise why was she still with him?


## Trio Con Brio

Me again, Gwinny. [Shut up, Writers' Huddle. Readers can stand sudden switches in voice, so long as you tell them what's going on. They are not fools.]

I prayed for a parking space so there was one, just outside the clinic – *Hail Mary, full of grace, let me find a parking space*. I'd been to a convent school in my childhood years. The nuns' habitual sharp rapping of knuckles might have driven any formal religion out of me, but had left me with useful survival skills.

The Brilliant Baby Clinic took up only one floor of the building: the waiting room served another dozen doctors. It was something of an anti-climax. We must have looked an odd trio, coming in together.

Xandra, a small, neat, even-featured blonde person, was in a smart white shirt, a straight black knee-length skirt and bold silver chain round her neck with matching shell-shaped earrings and conventional enough. Long ago gone were the tribal print skirts and low-cut peasant blouses of her youth.

Clive, good-looking as ever, wore jeans and black polo neck and a fashionable stubble. Since the unforgettable floral wedding on Hampstead Heath twelve years back he had grown from sinewy youth into very acceptable, craggy, broad-shouldered manhood. The hair was not thinning at all, which was just as well for a man who still hoped to make his living on stage and screen.

Gwinny was a mere 5ft 2in and at first glance seemed a skinny child, dressed in navy jeans and pink cotton sweater, with streaks down the front where she had wiped Chrome Yellow and Venetian Brown from her hands. She had been so lost in her art when Xandra called to collect her she had just run from the house in paint-splashed black trainers and the Basque beret she was seldom seen without. Everyone could see she was a painter, a noble bohemian wedded to her art, not just a childless lady living alone in a dull little house. Only if you looked more closely did you notice the wild hair that burst from the confines of the hat was iron grey and see that the lustrous dark eyes that looked up at you should you say hello were lined with crow's feet. Gwinny saw clothes as functional, there to keep you warm and decent, and stop mosquitoes biting. Some women are like that.

Xandra, who never left the house in disarray, marvelled, and perhaps envied just a little. She found spontaneity difficult, though she tried.

## More Waiting

Xandra was whisked away at once, swept away by silent, impatient forces as soon as she went in – we were ten minutes late: Xandra having got herself into quite a tizz about something or other before we left, unusually for her. Fortunately she was a quick form filler and had all the extras with her – specimens, X-rays etc. She might not be super bright but her efficiency made up for it.

The two of us were in the waiting room for what seemed hours, so it was just as well, Clive joked, that parking wardens were in such short supply a car could still stay where it was for as long as needed. There was no television, and it was too early in the world's history for any of the i's, be it Pods, Phones or Pads. The presence of others in the waiting room inhibited conversation. We sat on stiff upholstered armchairs, the backs still with antimacassars for quick laundering.

There was a big oval table in polished mahogany, copies of *Country Life* and *Punch*, and a scattering of fee-paying patients, as silent and reverent as NHS users are not: a group of decrepit old ladies in wheelchairs with their minders, a couple of white-robed Arabs with their niqabed womenfolk, and an oppressive silence. Time passed. Only the air quivered, Gwinny thought, with a hundred years' worth of expected bad news.

Gwinny quietly leafed through *Country Life* but Clive grew increasingly restless.

'I'm not going to wait much longer,' he murmured into Gwinny's ear, when the hands of the clock reached half past one. There was a rustle of disapproval round the room. All eyes turned to them.

'You pay all this money and they treat you like this!' The more his indignation swelled, so did the squeak. Someone suppressed a giggle. It came from one of the niqabed wives. The sound inflamed Clive the more.

'I'm off!' and he rose to go. Gwinny pulled him back into his chair.

'There's no way I'm going to miss this audition.' While he

whispered he didn't squeak. 'It's a turning point. They're looking for a new 007. My agent said go along; they have new technology that evens out sound. My voice will be just fine.'

He had stopped whispering. Everyone was listening. They had no option. The fog-horn changed to a violin squeak with every second word.

'I know, Clive,' she said. 'But this is important too.'

She refrained from saying that Clive didn't have a snowball's chance in hell of getting the part. Pierce Brosnan was auditioning. Management might in theory find it possible to dub his voice – the script itself demanding little complex chatter, just a few quotable phrases – but why would they bother? More fish in the sea all dying for the part.

More, an initial nasal twang suggesting a cocaine dependency had worried producers in the first place. Jobs had turned up less and less. Unfair, since Clive hadn't touched the stuff for ages, but these days truth was becoming less important than perception. And then there had been a scandal or two: 'Joseph and his multi-coloured threesome' in the Daily Mail. (All lies of course – my brothers again, spreading rumours – Xandra stood by him – Mr Ipswich saved our bacon and the Mail paid up.) But mud stuck. And then the squeak-over had developed into the kind of thing that could make audiences laugh. Like the niqabed girl just now. No wonder Clive was easily upset.

'There's no point in me just waiting. She can tell me when she gets home. It's just she won't like being told she has to give up her job. You can take her home. Or she can drive herself. You pay all this money and they treat you like this!' he repeated, squeaking even louder. Gwinny did not remind him. Another of the niqabed wives stifled a giggle. The sound inflamed Clive the more.

'I'm off!' and he got up and left. Gwinny followed him out into the reception area.

'I'm not missing this audition. It's make or break.'

'I know, Clive,' she said, 'But isn't this important too?'

'God, you're an interfering bitch!'

Clive shook himself and apologised at once. 'I'm sorry. This is very nervy-making. I didn't mean it at all. *My words fly up, my thoughts remain below*: Hamlet.'

'But Clive, I think you're in next. They said they wanted to see you too.'

'You're joking! What, for me to wank into some test tube? We've been through all this. I'm only here to keep my wife company. I'd no idea she'd take as long as this.'

'But it's so important to find out if either of you are infertile.' It came out more head-on than Gwinny hoped. She rued the day. Though at least those in the waiting room couldn't hear.

'Infertile? Me? I'm as fertile as the next man, more so. What are you insinuating?'

Clive slipped, as he tended to do if agued with or criticised in any way, into a different personality, an alternative Clive, someone who didn't recognise you, blink or look agreeable but stared with glassy hate-filled eyes and swore readily. Gwinny reflected that husbands and hospitals seldom brought out the best in each other. Though when he was in a real rage, she'd noticed, the voice changed pitch and became less squeaky, just uncomfortably loud.

He calmed a little. 'Gwinny, you know as well as I do that Xandra just doesn't like it when things don't go to plan. She can't complain I don't fuck her enough.' [Writers' Huddle: 'Not again! Far too many already. Every fuck's a lost reader. Try "do it".'] 'She knows I love her to bits. No, I'm off. Sorry and all that,' and he shouldered the bag that carried the audition brief and added veracity to his claim of an appointment, and prepared to go. Gwinny could only hope he hadn't taken Xandra's earlier 'I'm not the jealous type' too literally. In Gwinny's eyes Xandra was very definitely the jealous type. A proper bunny boiler. In Clive's eyes, she was a self-described loving and complaisant wife.

But the 'God, you're an interfering bitch!' still rankled. As if her motive, born out of simple friendship, were somehow suspect. And now James Bond? He was absurd.

It was just as well that Xandra came into the waiting room

just then to say they had to come back in two days' time. They'd done some tests and had to wait for the results to come through.

'Typical! Bloody incompetents,' said Clive, as they hurried out of the building, loud enough for the receptionist to hear. When he got home later that evening it was to say the audition had run over time so he needed to go again in a couple of days.

## A Scene Better Forgotten

After yesterday's dramas at the fertility clinic Gwinny thought she had best leave the Smithsons for a while: for Clive to calm down and Xandra to see reason. But after Xandra had been home from work for an hour or so No. 24 knocked loudly twice on the upstairs party wall, followed by seven little knocks, the code for 'come round for a meal at seven'. (Well, take yourself back in time to 1999: phone calls from a landline were expensive, so why call when you could knock?)

Gwinny had spent the day at her easel on not exactly a portrait but a half-way step towards a landscape, after Arcimboldo. This one was called *Landscape of the Heart*: and instead of vegetables or flowers the face was filled with draped baby blankets, rattles, soft toys, locks of golden baby hair and only the occasional hideous imp peeking out. The thought of a baby next door fed her creativity in some way. It would need to be a girl of course, friend not enemy. If she herself could do some of the rearing while Xandra worked – and she could see that with

Clive as a house-husband it might end up quite a lot – Gwinny reasoned she might get it right this time round, do better than she had with her horrid little brothers. She'd be more patient, she wouldn't slap so much.

She'd waited for a girl when she was small, but out they'd popped, boy, boy, boy, boy. Gwinny didn't want her perfect girl to come out with a temper like Clive's. Or a loser like Clive, come to that. Because that was what Clive was, with his vanity and nasal cocaine voice and the play that would never be finished, let alone performed, leaving Xandra to earn the living. No. She just didn't want the baby to turn out at all male.

When Gwinny tapped on the door of No. 24 at seven o'clock that evening it was Clive, not Xandra, who opened it to her. He looked square and bold and surprisingly cheerful. He wore black cords and a black vest showing beneath a black denim shirt and some startling black and white Black Indigo trainers, as befitted a famous actor. His teeth seemed very white and his smile was wide and seemed quite genuine. His brown hair had been streaked with blond, and was silky, thick and bouncy as ever. Enough to make anyone want to run their fingers through it. He looked a good ten years younger than his years.

Today, Gwinny could certainly see what Xandra saw in him: Xandra was pushing forty and looked it: perfectly neat and tidy like any office worker, any dweller in one of Pete Seeger's *Little Boxes*. Today, Clive looked as if he lived in a mansion in Beverly Hills, still blessed with the inviting bloom of sexual possibility.

Xandra would have to look out. Clive was devoted, if naturally indolent, but might not stay so for ever.

For all she had been to RADA, Xandra had turned out to be something of a bureaucrat at heart. Very different from Gwinny, who had left home at fifteen – albeit almost sixteen, but still underage – and even into her sixties, for all she lived in a little box, at least kept her eccentricities in dress and behaviour. She was a born artist and as such kept a certain allure as creative artists do.

(Gwinny still regrets the time she'd been with Sebastian outside Cheyne Walk. She should have bought that house when she could – they'd thrown out a really good easel and various odd lots nobody wanted of stubby oil brushes and random half-empty pots of good-quality paints, though mostly in sombre colours of brown and purple and so lasted for ever. She should have run off with those rather than the old purple velvet sofa with broken springs. Gwinny had always felt these things brought her luck.)

But this evening Clive had opened the door of No. 24 not with the usual accepting grunt, but by flinging his arms round her, kissing her, not just twice but three times and not just mwah-mwah-mwahing but actual soft lips against cheek. Very continental, and even a suggestion of sexual interest in his hug, of which Gwinny had never before been aware. But then for once she was wearing a dress which showed her figure – still good, and certainly better than Xandra's – not her usual dungarees, and she had washed her hair and taken care with doing so, and then smudged her eyelids with kohl so her eyes looked sultry and large. She'd felt there was something different in the air tonight and had dressed for it.

Even disregarding his looks, Clive seemed twice the man he'd been in Dr Vellum's waiting room, and certainly a lot more amiable. But why? No-one surely would have been mad enough to actually give him the James Bond part, even if he had got to the audition in time, which Gwinny doubted. The voice was hopeless. There would have been at least fifty actors with noticeable star qualities applying. A lead in a musical twenty years back and little of any note since would hardly have been a recommendation. Yet here he was, suddenly exuding star quality and good cheer?

Clive could suddenly have been released from a bi-polar cluster personality disorder – the new word for manic depressive – but Gwinny dismissed the thought. Marco had explained that the switch from depressive to manic happened over weeks: this was too abrupt; but split personality, though rarer than anyone thought, was a distinct possibility. Certainly no fit father for a child. Just as well mumps had struck in his teenage years. It might well have to be a donor.

'So what's up?' I asked, when Clive opened the door to me. The light in the bedroom was on. Xandra was upstairs.

'I'll tell you later. But just listen,' and still on the doorstep he opened his mouth and sang: *'The Hills are Alive with the Sound of Music.'*

The voice that came out of the strong frame and the soft lips was no longer fog-horn, or violin-squeaky and laughable, but deep and profound. Almost an Elvis Presley sound. It was a shock. It was a marvel. And also, one of my first thoughts, rather worrying for Xandra. Instead of one or two hard-of-hearing school-gate mothers after her husband, which she could manage, no squeak meant dozens. An observable catch. Knickers thrown on stage time.

These thoughts raced round my mind as Clive shared the pleasure of his saccharine song – fortunately he thought one verse was enough – bellowing the improving words down the street for all the neighbours to hear, proudly declaring his new identity as King of the Castle. Gwinny was thinking furiously as she did from time to time: thoughts without words, a kind of non-verbal gibber, especially when she had been to the chemist and bought some Pro Plus wake-up pills, which she often did before she went round to the Smithsons. She must try and cut down.

'No, tell me now,' I said. 'What happened?'

'What a story!' he said. 'But you'll have to wait.'

And he burst into further song, there upon the doorstep. It was ridiculous. But oh, the voice was thrilling! Like the deep Welsh voices of my childhood in the Midland Railway Choir which annoyed my mother. Gwen always preferred Aidan safely at home. Now, in the glow of the street lights, Clive was singing, Mario Lanza-like, someone's terrible version of *Trees*, an even worse poem when set to music than on the page.

I could see Xandra's shadow silhouetted in the upstairs window as now she patiently and methodically changed from uniform to cooking and cleaning wear. She'd put the light on, by accident or perhaps not, as I sometimes thought, being something of an exhibitionist, and encouraging the neighbours to see what they could, which, considering our neighbours, was not exactly wise.

I think it was almost to stop Clive singing *Trees* that I let him kiss me and pull-me-push-me round to the side of the house, when the kisses slipped from cheek to mouth, and press me against the wall standing up, and I cannot remember what happened, we are now in 2023 and that was back in 1999, and it was only a few minutes but I had to arrange my dress: for once, fortunately, I had not been in my jeans. Clive was singing *Trees* again as we went back into the house – where Xandra was now in the kitchen cooking supper. But the acting profession is like that. They need sex to lubricate their voices. It means nothing. I'm sure he forgot it. I never mentioned it.

## An Explanation

Gwinny had followed Clive into the conservatory of No. 24 where the table was already laid and there were flute glasses for champagne on the coffee table, which Gwinny always thought rather vulgar. What was wrong with French café glasses? Flutes were thin and easy to spill and tended to break in the washing machine. But at least Xandra had dinner in the oven. Gwinny could smell it. Beef, onions, garlic. Clive's favourite. If Xandra had her way it would be M&S's fish pie. But then she was a working woman.

Xandra came in to vacuum the conservatory with her new Dyson vacuum cleaner. Gwinny was still happy with her old Hoover Constellation though its capacity for picking up dust was limited. Xandra seemed to have noticed nothing untoward. She was wearing an overall over her dress while she worked – there was no denying she was a fantastic housekeeper: 'An orderly mind needs an orderly house to keep it company,' Xandra would say.

She vacuumed with one hand while tidying with the other, emptying Clive's ashtray into the path of the new machine, bending and reaching to push away Clive's many screwed-up handwritten pages and a few bloodstained tissues as it approached them. She seemed tireless and a touch fanatical. Clive stood and watched, grinning like a maniac.

The Dyson was put away, a few cushions plumped, then into the kitchen where the papers were binned, the dishwasher cleared and the things put away ready for the next batch, and her overall removed. Only then did she turn and welcome Gwinny.

'Darling, you're so early.'

'No,' said Gwinny firmly. 'I'm punctual.'

'Then it's me. My fault. But one way and another it's been such a day! Clive has his voice back. Didn't you hear it?'

'I thought it was someone's radio.'

'I'll tell her in good time, darling,' Clive warned Xandra in his new rich voice, or perhaps it was just his old one suddenly back again, finally recovered from the too many high notes and cocaine parties of the past. Xandra's fault. Hitler, historians say, was blind for a full year from shell shock, and was cured overnight by a simple trick. The affliction was psychosomatic. Perhaps Clive had had some kind of Bond shock?

'Is that why the champagne?'

'Wait till we're all sitting down and relaxed, darling Gwinny.'

Both Clive and Xandra were rather over-free and generous with their darlings, Gwinny had always noticed, but she liked it. It made her feel secure in her welcome, which was not the case with everyone. So though intensely curious, she did relax. All three toasted 'the future' in Bollinger, and sat down to dinner. More, Clive and Xandra seemed to have given up their Atkins high-fat low-carb diet overnight; not an undressed salad leaf in sight along with the beef and onion stew, just piles of mashed potato. There was a block of butter on the table with an elegant little horn-handled butter knife stuck into it. No. 23 had never seen a butter knife in all its existence. The brothers would have laughed themselves silly.

Only when plates were half empty did Clive explain. Then he talked and talked, animatedly and with many actorly gestures, in the new persuasive crooner's voice. Clive acknowledged that mumps in fucking adolescence could in a few cases affect a man's fertility – he'd assumed just the vocal cords could be affected, as if that wasn't crap enough. Xandra should have stuck to the National Health if she was really worried, which he personally wasn't. If Xandra would only take time off work and rest: then it would be simply a matter of time.

'Anyway,' Clive said, his assertive new voice dropping a pitch to one that wooed and seduced, 'I shouldn't have been such a grumpy bear at breakfast, I'm sorry.' No, he hadn't been offered the James Bond job though he had been offered a small part which he'd turned down. A figure of fun in James Bond Jr, an animated TV spinoff, as Oddjob the minder, hilarious, because a big man with a squeaky voice always is.

'And then this peculiar thing happened, you darling dears.'

'Seconds, anyone?' asked Xandra, adding a dollop of mashed potato to Clive's plate, to sop up the gravy. Far from Atkins, but she loved him, and this was a special day.

'Not now, darling. I'm telling Gwinny what happened. Isn't the voice marvellous?'

And he tried it out there and then, a scale from bottom to top, bass to tenor and even a hint of counter-tenor so a glass clock on the mantelpiece shook and made a vague pinging sound.

'Oh please darling, treat the voice gently. It's so new! The high notes—'

'Fuck the high notes. It's the voice of my fathers but safer now I'm older. It does what I tell it to. The power of Tom Jones, the thrill of Richard Burton, all mine, returned. Oh, rejoice!' How he did talk, but at least the squeak was silenced.

'Oh please,' said Gwinny, 'please, just tell. What was the peculiar thing?'

'Hear me out,' said Clive. 'I haven't finished. Wait till I get to the end of my sentence. It's impolite to interrupt, and surely, at such a juncture!'

'Yes,' cried Xandra, reproaching, doling out slices of Waitrose Apple Pie, and bringing out the cream jug. 'Let Clive do it his way, Gwinny.'

'A simple blow to the side of the bloody head, darling,' said Clive, the lure of invective getting the better of the joys of declamation. 'That's all it took, Gwinny. All those crap procedures, all those stupid fucking medicos, curse them all. The NHS ruined my career when all that was needed was a little tap on the head.'

'That was BUPA,' said Xandra.

'Don't spoil a good story,' Clive rebuked her. She shut up. I don't know why I felt victorious. I suppose it was the incident on the step. Women are so competitive with each other. She was twenty years younger than me and still I'd had him. [Writers' Huddle says the switch to first person would have been okay here had I put it in brackets.] Forget that it was already out of Clive's head, washed away in a tide of animation and song.

That morning, it seemed, Clive had decided to cheer himself up by dyeing his hair to get rid of some errant grey – which had been toning down the golden brown – and an idiot of an arsehole of a producer had made some comment. He was just unwrapping the silver foil when he'd slipped and fallen and hit the side of his head on the edge of the bath and passed out.

He'd bled a bit but not much. It was more shock than cut. He'd been all alone in the house because Xandra was out to work. He'd come to and said shit, fuck, and cursed the bath as one does, and had felt his own voice vibrating in his chest. It was different, deeper.

'The blow had cured it, Gwinny. Rearranged some flip in the brain's wiring. It happens. If a sudden blow can make the blind see, the deaf hear, why not the dumb speak?'

He'd re-read his play and decided it was crap. He'd deleted it. One click of a mouse and it was gone. All gone.

'Eight years' work at least!' said Gwinny. 'First there, then not there. Awesome!'

'Clive is so decisive,' said Xandra. She is not exactly a fool, thought Gwinny, but she has to survive somehow and how else but by being in love? All that sex had worked its hormonal power. And some kind of mother-love must have worked on her, Gwinny, too, to have rendered her so forgiving all those years. And now she had had another one. Madness.

She felt guilty and excited at once, the lure of the forbidden. But she must act on principle, forget all that had happened. Women should not betray one another or all feminist ideals were in vain. Clive was a victim of his own male drives and must be excused. She was still uncomfortable 'down there' as Gwen had trained her to say, in the days when sex was a mystery and parts never named, but she rather liked it. The sensation was rather comforting.

Tomorrow they would go to the clinic again. Clive would be declared as infertile. What then? A donor? Anyone to father the longed-for baby, when it came to it, and at least it wouldn't be Clive.

## Possibilities Occur

The next day the three of them were back at the clinic. Clive was cheerful and in full voice. The waiting room was emptier than before, more like a mausoleum than ever but with only two immobile old ladies sitting next to one another on the upright chairs. Xandra had been whisked away at once and very shortly a white-coated man of some foreign ethnicity appeared and fell into the normal small-male trope of worshipping deference to men taller, younger and better-looking than themselves, humbly apologising for interrupting, all of which suited Clive very well, and asking Mr Smithson to accompany him.

Mr Smithson was to see Dr Vellum's senior colleague. Clive went without demur, other than looking back to Gwinny, and saying, 'Better than the bastard NHS, innit?' Gwinny saw the white-coated shoulders stiffen.

Gwinny looked through the magazines on the big central polished mahogany table and noticed an expensively produced brochure for the Woolland Brilliant Baby Sperm Bank. On the back cover was a quote from Kahlil Gibran's *The Prophet*, Clive's favourite philosopher-poet:

> *Your children are not your children.*
> *They are the sons and daughters of Life's longing for itself.*
> *They come through you but not from you,*
> *And though they are with you, yet they belong not to you.*

It was possible, thought Gwinny, that even if Clive did turn out to be fertile, he was not necessarily the best father around for Xandra's baby. He was too impetuous, too actorly. Clive at twenty, perhaps, with his *Dreamcoat* just behind him, but not now, at thirty-six. Bitterness had entered into his soul, along with idleness, and if you had any belief in the new evidence that acquired characteristics could affect DNA and therefore sperm, Clive's might not be the best in the world. Though *New Scientist* could have it all wrong or herself misremembered.

Xandra, of course, might still be thinking otherwise, seeing no further than that Clive was the best lover, forget the best husband, if only because opposites attract – but how easily are women not blinded to a man's true nature? Xandra, with her twelve years of frequent unprotected sex while hoping to get pregnant, every act sealing her fate. As a result she had been tranquillised, oxytocinased to moral death. No wonder, fucked stupid, she traipsed up to the hospital every day meekly and obediently, just to serve an unfaithful and ungrateful husband while spouting feminist doctrine with the best. Clive and Xandra, Gwinny realised, were so in the habit of believing they were in love with each other that not even the passage of time could break the bonds. But it was a delusion, a *folie à deux*, a mwah-mwah habit. Time for it to stop. Truth and reality must out.

And here on these glossy expensive pages she found list after list of other possibilities.

Gwinny flicked through page after page of potential donors, 2,000 of them, drawn silhouettes with features blanked out, each with a few brief lines of description printed between their ears – *blond hair, blue-eyed* (meaning white, one supposed, in the same way as *black hair, brown-eyed* suggested 'otherly ethnic'), alleged profession (*medical student, accountant, engineer, explorer* seemed to be favourites, each with a clumsy attempt to describe a lifestyle (*family guy, physics whiz, guitar supremo, life and soul of the party*) – strict anonymity and HFEA registration observed and required, rigorous screening checks performed, healthy sperm guaranteed and '*quested by our talented medical staff*' (one did rather hope not 'provided by': wasn't there an elderly IVF doctor in London who went to prison for fraudulently fathering eighty-four children?) and '*a great family-building option no matter what your circumstances*'. Heights were in there too – ranging from 5ft

10in – the shortest any donor would admit to – to 6ft 2in. Lots of those. Her eye fell upon '*6ft 1in, blue eyes, blond hair: BA (Oxon), action man, aristocrat*'. She rather fancied that. She had to peel off an 'old stock half price' sticker to see it properly. She dropped it into the waste bin. Frozen donor sperm was meant to last for ever. The Brilliant Baby Clinic was being over-cautious.

It was a great and tempting offering, thought Gwinny. She slipped the brochure into her bag. A whole new race of children conceived without love, perhaps, born not of the attraction which drew couples together, but with any luck into a loving family. A lucky dip, since free choice so often ended up a failure. And any baby was better than no baby. Life was getting boring as her years advanced; there were no more brothers at hand to rail against, and the chance of new sexual encounters less common.

Even Gwinny's ginger cat Simkins Two was slowing down; these days just a vast shapeless mass curled up on a cushion, no longer a skinny, manic leaper-up the dusky velvet curtains, hanging there by its claws in a mad-eyed effort to entertain. And without an infusion of new life into the Smithsons' next-door existence, it was all going to be pretty much the same. Entropy. On the other hand an infant off-shoot of Clive, eaten up by narcissism and vanity, crawling round and declaiming his woes, did seem a trifle off-putting. The lucky dip of a sperm bank would be preferable.

And then the peace of the waiting room was broken by Xandra running in, click, click on polished floor, flushed and looking wonderfully young and happy as she had been on her wedding day, before time and life had worn her down.

Gwinny's heart melted. It always did. And for poor Clive of the many mishaps as well. He was a wounded Apollo, and Achilles with a sore foot.

'Oh Gwinny,' Xandra cried, 'Dr Vellum is such a lovely, lovely man, adorable! There is nothing wrong with my innards, nothing wrong with me at all. I am as fertile as can be!' And Xandra approached Gwinny as if to hug her, but since Gwinny had been brought up in an era where people did not hug one another easily and if they told someone they loved them it was with a love that included sex, she drew back from the embrace – to the relief of the two motionless old ladies who still remained in the waiting room.

'Of course he's adorable. He's paid to be adorable. He's a snake oil merchant. They're all adorable,' said Gwinny, rather crossly. Her own voice could be quite piercing but Gwinny had concluded that the immobile ladies were too deaf to hear, if indeed they were human at all and not just holograms.

Even as she spoke one was called for and then the other. Both were in wheelchairs but one seemed to be in charge of the other, and directed a malevolent look at Gwinny as she pushed by. Gwinny thought she heard 'Some people just don't know how to behave,' but may have imagined it, the old paranoiac cluster personality disorder surfacing. It had been quite a stressful time.

'No, no,' cried Xandra, who seldom noticed what was going on if it did not concern her directly. 'Dr Vellum really cares. He's a truly great guy, and his colleague is the best in London, or Clive wouldn't have seen him in the first place. So courteous and polite and wise, all of them here. Dr Vellum says it's all because of Clive, not me. Clive's sperm are missing or immobile. Pre-pubertal mumps with complications.'

'Can't the immobile ones be speeded up?' The implication of sterility was fearful, though the satisfaction of being right was great.

'You don't understand. It's medical. No. And certainly not at this stage of genetic technology,' said Xandra. She sounded rather relieved. 'We may have to adopt.'

It was at this point Clive strode into the waiting room with his beautiful face like Zeus in a bad mood, and his eyes as when Lord Krishna hurls his thunderbolt (I see nothing wrong with veering between Hellenism and Buddhism), glassy and staring.

'Bloody incompetent cunt of a quack,' he squeaked. [Writers' Huddle: 'No! The c-word never gets forgiven. Yet on the other hand "cunt of a quack" does have quite a ring to it.'] 'Stupid idiot. No idea of what he's talking about. And now I'm going to be late. This is disastrous.'

Yesterday's melodious voice had been forgotten, washed away in a tide of vitriol. It was as if every wrong, major or minor, that he had ever suffered burst from him like a pus-filled boil. Poor

Clive, so vainly and desperately trying to hide self-knowledge from himself, blaming everything and everyone, never himself. It must be really exhausting.

Clive took the car keys from Xandra's pocket, jingled them briefly in front of her, and said, 'I'm already late, darling. I'll take the car,' and went off into gathering gloom and cold, leaving Xandra and me to find a taxi, which at this time of day in Harley Street was not the easiest thing in the world.

## A Wake-Up Call

Xandra speaking. [Writers' Huddle: 'Okay, great, Gwinny, at last, for once! You haven't given Xandra much of a chance to speak for herself, poor lovesick loon.']

So now I had another set of problems. Dr Vellum had certainly seemed to think yesterday that I was in denial of some kind. He was a pleasant friendly man, lean and bespectacled in a dark grey suit – expensive, I thought. So it was more like talking to a close friend rather than a doctor.

'You mean it's never even occurred to you that it might be your husband's fault, not in all these years? Handsome girl like you, Xandra – I may call you Xandra? – and at it all the time, to all accounts and no contraception? That's very strange for the obviously bright medical professional you are. Perhaps you're just in denial of what you very reasonably suspect?'

'I love my husband, if that's what you mean by *at it*,' I said, without thinking. And he laughed; brown warm crinkly eyes and such a crisp white coat now over the elegant suit. Our hospital laundry just squashes instead of irons.

'Of course you love him. And so you should. Anyone would. I take it he's *the* Clive Smithson who was Joseph in that glorious production of *The Amazing Technicolor Dreamcoat* how long ago? Ten, twenty years back?'

It was so long ago but still people remembered. The future had seemed so assured. Clive's success as the great singer, dancer was a blissful certainty. That and the whole world's future, come to that. *We shall overcome, some day.* Mind you, even back then the IRA was planting bombs all over the place, though nothing compared to what was to come from other quarters.

'More like twenty,' I said, sadly. 'We were all so young then.'

'And never sired a child himself?'

'Not that I know of.'

'So my colleague tells me. The news is not good, I'm afraid. Your husband developed pre-pubertal epididymo-orchitis as a child.'

It was probably his way of breaking news gracefully but I knew what that meant. A child with salmonella had actually died from it when under my care.

Clive was indeed infertile. It was good to be right about something.

'Time to think of donor sperm,' he said.

## Marriage Can Be Difficult

I'd dragged Clive along to the Brilliant Baby Clinic more from nervousness than anything else, and to keep Gwinny from nagging away at me to get pregnant. We do need to keep on the right side of Gwinny; I can afford the mortgage all right but not the expensive electronic gear Clive needs on my salary. Sex is so much better without contraception! So never getting pregnant really quite suited me for ages, until the baby urge cut in. But now my cover's been blown and I have to rethink everything.

Don't mistake me; I really do love Clive. When we were in our teens we joined together like magnetised iron filings – clunk! – and never thereafter wanted to be parted. But he can be quite difficult. If you asked me whether I loved my job or Clive most I wouldn't know how to answer. I'd certainly been rather nervous that when he did come face to face with the good doctor, and perhaps didn't hear the news he wanted, Clive would not be his normal polite and charming self. He saw himself as a very successful virile man. And so he was, he just didn't have all those swimming, diving little homunculi spurting out of his cock that other men do. [Writers' Huddle: 'Ouch! Yuk! No!']

Clive had had bad news. I had had good. I was fertile, he was not. I hadn't thought through the consequences when I broke my unspoken bond with the NHS and went private. Clive was my Knight in Shining Armour, I was the Princess he'd deigned to rescue and would bear the brunt if anything went wrong with our shared happy-ever-after vision of ourselves. I would stand by his side.

Marriage can be very difficult, as I daresay it is for many wives, nervous in case their husbands behave badly in public, understanding only too well, as strangers don't, the tensions and troubles that drive them to behave as they do. Loveable little boys, if never quite grown up, to their wives. To strangers, outrageous. I knew what Dr Vellum had said to me because I was there. I knew only what Clive thought – that Dr Vellum's colleague was (squeak) a 'cunt of a quack', or was it 'a quack of a cunt'? – and could only hope that he had not said as much to the good doctor and so had compromised any further dealings I would have with the Brilliant Baby Clinic. I decided I would not ask Clive for too much detail when I got home that night, and would take good care not to look too cheerful through supper. Simple tact demanded it. Compared to home, work is a piece of cake.

## Time For Reflection

'So what are you going to do?' asked Gwinny. 'At least you know there's no point in trying.' They were walking down Harley Street towards Kentish Town. Clive had taken the car.

Taxis whizzed by with their lights off. Shops and businesses were closing: it was the rush hour. Rain was beginning to fall. 'Go down the nearest pub and pick up someone who looks like Clive? That's what I would do.'

Xandra looked quite shocked.

'I could never do that,' she said. 'I'm surprised at you. We might adopt, I suppose. A baby from Africa or Thailand perhaps. The world is over-populated as it is. But I don't think Clive would allow that.' She was shivering from emotion, shock, damp and cold. The streets seemed hostile and merciless. 'Poor Clive. Such a shock to him. I love him. I would rather die than be unfaithful.'

If only the same could be said of Clive, thought Gwinny. Forget herself, what went on at all these auditions. No wonder actresses insisted they all be called actors. But actors weren't all that different. [Writers' Huddle: 'Very unwise to insult a whole profession. They'll take offence, never see the joke.'] But she held her tongue. They had reached the Mason's Arms, and still no taxi: inside the pub all seemed cosy and warm.

'We need a drink and a warm fire,' said Gwinny. 'We can wait here until the traffic dies down.'

'Certainly not,' said Xandra loftily. 'I don't drink. Or only in exceptional circumstances.'

'These may well be them,' suggested Gwinny. 'Clive need never know. Just make sure the lucky guy doesn't have red hair, or paternity might be suspect.'

'This is no joking matter,' said Xandra. 'Whatever we do will be with Clive's knowledge, consent and understanding. I'm really rather shocked at you, Gwinny.'

Gwinny had to remind herself how much of a younger generation Xandra was. Now almost sixty, Gwinny was a survivalist, a wartime baby reared on black market meat and fancies fallen off the back of a lorry and no questions asked. Clive was a moralist (failed). Xandra was a real moralist and foolishly assumed Clive was the same. Gwinny thought at the time that this propriety augured no good for the future of her country, which would sink under a population of Mrs Grundys, male and female, so cautious and approval seeking were they. She had yet, of course, to encounter a new race of female Millennials, who see love and sex as a reactionary folly.

'Clive does take a little time to adjust to new circumstances,' said Xandra, ever conciliatory. (You can say that again, thought Gwinny.)

'I just hope he gets to be James Bond. With his lovely new voice he could reapply. It would make all the difference.'

But of course Clive didn't. Karma had caught up with him, carried along in the vitriol flow. '*Many are called but few chosen*': motto of Equity, the actors' union – it isn't but it should be. Especially if the manly lips open and a little tinny squeak emerges.

After a drink in the pub Xandra and Gwinny took the bus home and arrived there, damp, cold and hungry, at a quarter to seven, by which time the 2CV was parked outside No. 24 (1999: not yet any double yellow lines in Standard Road, or even single ones) and Clive was already home.

Gwinny, always a quick thinker, shoved the clinic's glossy donor brochure into Xandra's bag as they parted ways, Gwinny into No. 23, Xandra into No. 24. Xandra did not refuse it but covered it up with her nurse's blue scrub cap, which she just so happened, and probably illegitimately, to have with her, in case she ever found she'd left her petrol cap behind in a garage as she'd been known to do, the scrub cap being good enough as a replacement. She took the brochure indoors.

Clive had gone to bed, so Xandra assumed because he had not got the job and, more, his virility had been insulted. She realised men could be very stubborn when it came to their own bodies and did get virility and fertility confused – well, the words are similar. But she assumed Dr Vellum was right: pre-pubertal mumps could be disastrous. So she heated up some fish pie in the microwave and shook out a bag of mixed salad leaves for supper and went to bed next to her beloved. He had taken sleeping pills so she did the same. It had been a very tiring day, starting with the two crash calls and one death, and Gwinny, much as she loved her, could be quite a tiring companion, as well as looking rather extraordinary, and people tended to stare. She was so practical and sensible but when it came to feelings could be rather insensitive. She took sex lightly. Xandra didn't want any old baby, she wanted

Clive's baby, and if it turned out she couldn't have that then she'd adopt, or go without. Which would be the right thing to do in an overcrowded world.

## Xandra At Work

Xandra got home from her shift in a very good mood. To find that she was fertile was more of a relief than she had expected. To find out that Clive was not and she and Gwinny had been right was somehow cheering. Clive himself had been not too bad over breakfast. He seemed not to have noticed that the squeak was back and had other things to think about than the state of his sperm. He had managed to recover the text of the novel or the play, whichever it was.

True, it had been another tiring day on Intensive Care – she'd been one junior short, and had to put another on reprimand for panicking and dialling 217 for the crash team unnecessarily and now 'lessons would have to be learned'. But then in her lunch break she'd been down to her post cubby (thanks to her intervention as head of the Stakeholders' Contributory Team all senior staff had them now) and there found an official letter from Jan Eyres, Nursing Superintendent, to say she had passed her Associate of Science Degree, and could from now on call herself a nursing consultant. This would mean a whopping rise in salary, though she'd have to wait to the end of the month to find out exactly how much. Jan, the dear, had added a handwritten note to say there was a vacancy on the Risk Assessment Legal Team and suggesting Xandra apply, which of course she would. After a year or two in the post she'd be able to move to the private sector and get some senior job in medical insurance and never have to wear scrubs again. She could kick off her flats and wear high heels for the rest of her life.

Xandra made sure such letters went into her post cubby in the hospital and never reached home. She kept her work life away from Clive as much as she could. In his view, and indeed in Gwinny's, all of life must be a battle against mediocrity, entropy, ordinariness, the dreaded *Little Boxes* of the Pete Seeger song. That was why Clive was so against her employment with the NHS, or National Death Service, as he liked to call it, seeing it as a descent into bourgeoisity, a betrayal of his own creative aspirations, which of course it was not, just the cruel necessity – which Clive was so reluctant to face – of making a living for both of them. That she actually enjoyed it made the matter worse. That she might strive for promotion in the desert of bureaucratic unreason would be seen at home as almost satanic.

At least Clive thought she was doing a properly female job, seeing her in his mind's eye in a frilly apron and cap, like some parlourmaid whose job was to bring people cups of tea. He just wasn't interested, and assumed hospitals and doctors were for the weak and helpless, whom he despised.

She and Clive's ways had really parted right back when he became Joseph of the *Dreamcoat* and she got Wife of Benjamin, abandoned her own hopes of stardom and got a proper job. If no longer as a doctor (she'd given up medical school to follow Clive to drama school) at least as a trained nurse she could get a good job at a moment's notice. Wherever Clive's star went she could follow.

But a baby! By a donor? The great welling up of instinctive longing as she neared the end of her procreative life might be natural and normal, but was hardly rational. And at such an inconvenient time, even if she could somehow square the matter of paternity with Clive. It really was at a turning point in her career. Clive of course saw nursing as just any old job: Xandra saw it as patiently climbing up the ladder of excellence to reach a point where – in the language of the King's Fund, a charity that supports the NHS – *'passion, commitment and enthusiasm for change and the practical realities of making things happen within the constraints of prevailing system priorities'* were hers to bring about.

Clive would have laughed himself sick if she'd given that as a reason. At least Gwinny seemed to understand. The previous night, as they'd tried to get home in one piece, and when Gwinny had said 'Go down the nearest pub and pick up someone who looks like Clive?' it had seemed like a sensible enough suggestion, though she'd pretended to be shocked.

One needed the right kind of clothes to pick up men and she looked a sight, but Clive had asserted his fertility so couldn't grumble if his wife was suddenly pregnant. She'd been wearing her comfy knickers straight from work. If in desperation she did such a thing Clive need never know. But the truth was she needed sex, she liked sex, perhaps even more than babies. It's what Clive and she had in common. And what would happen if Clive turned out to be one of those Mother-Madonna-Whore men, the sort who go off their wives as soon as they turn into mothers, seeing them as Madonnas, too sacred to fuck any more, and go off to whores instead? His father used prostitutes, apparently.

## Going Private

But nothing is to be gained by subterfuge; not for nothing had the King's Fund instructed me as I studied for my certificate: '*Leaders need to work on the quality of their inner game, or their capacity to tune into and regulate their emotional and mental states, before they can hope to develop their outer game, or what it is they need to actually do.*' Well, I'd have to do some rather quick work on tuning my inner game. Though first I'd have to find out what it was.

The neat solution was not to have a baby at all. I knew I'd made a real fuss about wanting one, even weeping and wailing in a lamentably unregulated emotional and mental state, but one does rather look round for something in life to explain a perpetual vague dissatisfaction and plumps for the 'I am childless, therefore I am unhappy' option, the better to nail it. But supposing it didn't work? Supposing the unhappiness, the disaffection, that was inherent in all human beings simply returned after the birth?

Perhaps it did, which was why women went on having baby after baby, like Gwinny's mum, trying to plug the stream of unhappiness and never managing. And if it did work, and you had a baby, think of the horror of having to breastfeed it in public. Breasts were erogenous zones, so far as I was concerned, and Clive would not like them abused, especially by some rug rat not even his own. Though of course he wouldn't know that.

No, I decided as I drove home in my little Citroën *deux-chevaux*, my umbrella on wheels as Gwinny unkindly called it (I loved that car, and she'd have been glad enough of it last night if only Clive hadn't taken it), that the outer game must be to agree with Clive that Dr Vellum was an idiot and didn't know what he was talking about, just go on having sex, lots of it, knowing it wouldn't work, and get on with the career.

No baby.

But then what about the inner game? The search for the real me? It was a toss-up whether I'd ever find her.

## Taking The Plunge

It was Clive who found the brochure in Xandra's nurse's cap and decided his wife must have a baby by a sperm donor. He now had other fish to fry. Dreams of house-husbanding were out the window. Xandra was too exhausted to argue.

Clive called the clinic and apologised to everyone: to the receptionist, the Asian man and both doctors, explaining he had been under extreme stress, and they sent him the required sample. They warned him it was old stock, being anonymous, which had legal implications. It had been brought in when the Your Beautiful Baby Clinic went belly up in 1981. It was half price.

'Suits me,' said Clive as I wrote out a cheque for the required £2,000.

I'd warned Xandra that it was old stock and though the clinic said it would probably work they couldn't guarantee it. She looked at me as if she was startled and then asked me for a coin. I gave her a two-pound piece – they're rather pretty, I always think. My thumbs were pricking away for some reason. It had started when I wrote the cheque. (It hadn't happened for ages and was so severe I thought perhaps it was carpal tunnel syndrome but it cleared up after she'd thrown the coin so I didn't go to the doctor.) She used the back of her hand. It came out heads.

'So that's settled,' I said, 'whatever it is?'

'No, it isn't,' she said rather sharply, 'I'll do it three times.' She did it two times more and all three were heads. She did it another three times and they too came up heads.

'In *I Ching* hexagram terms,' I said, 'in the Chinese Book of Oracles, that's extremely lucky.'

'Well, I think it's spooky,' she said crossly. 'But oh well.'

And that is how I ended up plunging in the turkey baster that produced Rozzie.

# PART FOUR

# Rozzie As A Child

The date of impregnation was March 18th 1999, almost thirteen laggardly years after the Smithsons got married. Rozzie was born in the Whittington Hospital in Archway, on the last stroke of midnight on January 1st 2000. But Flora had at last come through. I can see now she had her reasons. The new century!

The *Daily Mail* was waiting. First babies of the New Millennium. I have the yellowed press cutting in my files: doctors and nurses raise a celebratory glass to the baby, and no doubt to the fact that the predicted Bug, the Y2K, has not struck and caused digital chaos throughout the land, so at least their premature cots are still working.

The mother is out for the count – it was a long labour (it had to be, to get the January 1st date, not December 31st) and I, Gwinny, as per usual, am the one holding the baby. The father is not to be seen.

For when it came to it Xandra, aged thirty-nine, and in medical terms an 'elderly primigravida', had not been as strong and powerful in childbirth as she had hoped to be, indeed expected to be. The 'natural' childbirth she had organised for herself did not happen. Xandra had never worked in a labour ward, but had done stints in A&E, where the first 'ow' gets a knock-out by a jab, and had yet to realise to what degree the female body ruled the female mind. The pride of feminist theory, alas, came before a biological fall.

Xandra found herself as outraged, weepy, howling, drugged-up and dependent as many new mothers are when the body takes over the mind and there is no mind left, just a convulsing mass of muscles you had no idea existed, shrieking in pain, abusing the staff, demanding the despised epidural, grabbing for the gas-and-air and furious. So furious when asked to push she actually pulled against all the forces of nature.

Though all this may have been, as she later alleged, because when the first severe pains had started Clive had unexpectedly parked outside the hospital steps not the car park, and just dropped Xandra and me off, which was not at all how Xandra had envisaged the birth scenario, in which Clive sat by her birth bed and mopped her brow while she peacefully laboured with controlled contractions coming at regular intervals, holding her hand and marvelling how well his darling was 'doing this'.

But it clearly wasn't to be like this at all. What was happening in front of the hospital steps was that Clive was letting the engine run and opening the door for Xandra and me to get out.

'I'm not actually coming inside, darling. What, did you expect me to? Surely not. A maternity ward is no place for a man. And I can hardly pretend to be the father when I'm not,' Clive had protested on the hospital steps; he was holding traffic up.

'Fatherhood is a social rather than a genetic description,' Xandra had wailed. '*A baby belongs to whoever looks after it.*' Brecht said so in *The Caucasian Chalk Circle*. Nurture always wins over Nature. We agreed! Please, please!'

I did (mostly) so love this couple. Even *in extremis* they would theorise. And they both adored Brecht. Honk, honk, went the cars behind.

'*We are not meant to resolve all contradictions but to live with them,*' quoted Clive, switching to William Blake. 'You're a feminist, you asked for a doula, a woman companion. Apparently a man isn't good enough any more.'

Some two months ago and still working and Xandra, knowing Clive, had murmured that she would like me to be her doula, her female 'birth companion' and saying things like: 'I so look forward to the birth! How strong and powerful I will be!' He had said nothing at the time but evidently held this lack of trust against her.

Now I had watched my mother horribly give birth to four, and the fifth one carried her off. Marie Stopes had claimed back in the old days that with every birth, a mother's risk of death rose by 50 per cent. I realised times were very different now but feeling at the time that Xandra was perhaps being over-optimistic, suckered by the National Childbirth Trust who so like to emphasise the joy of the process rather than the pain, so I had said, 'Yes, of course I'll be your doula. Whatever.'

'But your doula won't leave you, will you, Gwinny?'

I too had assumed Clive would come in with us. I helped Xandra out of her bright little yellow car. Xandra could hardly stand without toppling over.

'Of course I won't leave her,' I said, grabbing her. She smelt of blood, sweat and tears.

Xandra had looked forward to the culmination of the pregnancy. She had sailed through life so far, why should luck desert her now? Birth was a natural, normal thing, and so long as you breathed and visualised properly, surely medication of any kind would be unnecessary. Only wusses fussed.

'Try and understand, darling. You and Gwinny chose another father. It just doesn't feel right for me to be there at the birth,' pleaded Clive, the lovely black-fringed eyes opened wide and beseeching, as they always would be when he felt under attack; his Liberty of London cravat (not cheap) perfectly tied, his pale grey jacket (Armani from the look of it) suave and smooth, his brow unruffled. Hoot, hoot, all around. Still he went on.

'Let the turkey look after his own. You're a big healthy girl, and childbirth is a natural process, not a medical condition. You've kept telling me so.'

'I didn't know I'd be so frightened.'

But now he heard the blaring horns.

'I must go. I'm holding people up. It's a very important audition by the way, but of course that means nothing to you,' and he slammed the car door between us and zoomed off towards Soho, where indeed his agent had a penthouse, or towards wherever it is that men go in their very best clean clothes when their wife is having a baby.

I helped Xandra up the steps. She was enormous, and already shuddering, and wondering why she had embarked on this in the first place. There being no father in sight, it was me she shouted at and hit and scratched while giving birth, screaming 'I hate you!'

## A Much-Filmed Child

Rozzie was filmed as she was born; as the determined little head eased into the world and her mouth took its first breath, a camcorder watched (wielded by me, I know, I know! Who else?). Even earlier, her very heartbeat – biddy-de-de-boom, biddy-de-de-boom, very strong and fast – could be heard and was credited by name – *baby Rosalind Smithson, HBM135, female, 8 months 16 days* – also starred in a training video for aspiring midwives, though one understandably never shown – it was not a well-managed birth, and the mother tore quite spectacularly, though baby Smithson's HBM maintained a steady 140 even throughout labour.

Even as Rozzie left the hospital two weeks later in my arms – Xandra didn't trust herself with the burden – a CCTV camera watched us. That was for our own safety. New mothers have been known to break away and run to the nearest high-rise car park and throw themselves off.

And as the tiny, perfect baby grew, the world came to Rozzie through the TV in the room: everything the film makers thought worthy of the public's attention – mainly shock horror, war, violence, sex, crime, both 'real' and fictional if that failed. Criminals, terrorists and sexual perverts have very little imagination, unlike writers, but now the writers are at hand to add their own rich fantasies to the brew, and female death by broken bottle, once seen, becomes quite normal on our BBC. ['Cut,' says the Writers' Huddle, 'one of your rants coming up.']

But it's what Millennials have been brought up with for years. Rozzie is just as an example; once the nasty person could only be as nasty as his neighbour, now thanks to the internet he can be as nasty as the nastiest person in the world. Who wants One Man and His Dog (surely sexist anyway?) and the Naked Chef (likewise), when there are richer, sexier serial murderer drama series to be found? Argument flares up for a while: can children be influenced by what they see on the screen, but the answer from trade research always comes back 'oh no'. But what could anyone even mildly cynical suppose the result would be?

So could it have been scenes of slaughtered babies in the Congo, starving ones in Somalia or Queer as Folk on the telly that turned Xandra's milk sour as she failed to bond with Rozzie? Well, something did. The birth itself had been fairly traumatic, and I daresay it's difficult to pin down any particular source of blame. Nevertheless, how the tiny Rozzie cried and wailed in distaste for her first two months! Not that breastfeeding went on for long, only six weeks. Xandra couldn't wait to get back to work, to leave pain and shame behind. It had to be bottle, not nipple, no matter how wave after wave of 'bloody Breast Nazis' (Clive) from the National Childbirth Trust argued '*Breast was Best*' to make you feel bad when you couldn't, it hurt so much.

## Naming The Child

Against the noise of the battles on TV Clive and Xandra argued about the baby's name. They couldn't go on calling it 'it' for ever. Clive wanted Rex, which Xandra argued was a good name for a puppy but she'd given birth to a human not a dog, in spite of what Clive had probably hoped.

Xandra was not in a good place. Rozzie was five weeks old and Xandra had not yet forgiven Clive for deserting her on the hospital steps and going off God knew where – he'd said it was an audition, but was it? – and she was having trouble feeding and everything about her still chafed or dripped or hurt.

They were great theorists, the pair of them; Xandra had always been a Bertolt Brecht enthusiast – having once had a small part in *The Caucasian Chalk Circle* – and chose Michael for the baby's name after Grusha's baby. Determined that there was no real difference between male and female, she had added the 'a' to the name only after much persuasion from Clive and myself. It was to be Michaela, not Rex.

'A girl called Michael is going to go through hell at school,' he'd argued. 'Don't do it to her.'

'Then people should learn not to be so sexist,' snapped Xandra. 'Surely the sooner gender nomenclature is reformed the better.'

'Such a little thing, an *a* at the end of a name.' I, Gwinny, ever the peace-maker, mediated. Xandra had been going through a thoroughly feminist phase since the baby had been born, though battered, bruised and traumatised as she was. She had not quite yet abandoned feminist theory in the face of reality.

'It's not in the least little, it is enormous,' Xandra reproached me. 'It's like acknowledging that Eve was created out of one of Adam's ribs. It's symptomatic of female acceptance of male superiority.' But not having the strength to pursue the argument she had relented in the end. When I suggested Rosalind she simply accepted it. I like to think Xandra acknowledged that while she was good at theory I was good at practicalities.

I am a fraction too early for the boomer generation of post-war decades, being conceived in 1938 and only born in 1939, and so have the remnants of the survivalist instinct, as well as seeing common sense as a virtue. Clive and Xandra are late arrivals of the X generation – energetic, confident, non-compliant – but regard common sense as expendable, a rejection of right thinking. They are relativists.

Much as I loved the Smithsons, both Xandra and Clive tended

to see the world as their own construction and political correctness went deep into its foundations: even as Clive railed against it, he was conscious of it. I saw transitional demands as ephemeral; wishful thinking drifting here and there, not solid at all. Make Poverty History. Make Love not War. Might as well be Apple Pie for Everyone. Nice work if you could get it. Unachievable. That was the point.

[Writers' Huddle: 'Do you think this is the right group for you, Gwinny? These days you don't seem willing to take our advice. Can we recommend the Hampstead Huddle? It's much more experimental!']

I once listened to Clive rehearsing for an audition as a voice-over for some TV commercial company, when the squeak was only occasional and technology could get rid of it. More or less. You can get good money as a voice-over. Clive was reciting Kipling's poem *The Gods of the Copybook Headings*.

Alas, Clive's voice simply wasn't up to it: the poem needs a kind of throaty roar and Clive was offering a plaintive squeak. At this stage he was still in denial about his vocal cords.

'*And that after this is accomplished,*' he squeaked, '*And the brave new world begins, When all men are paid for existing and no man must pay for his sins, As surely as Water will wet us, as surely as Fire will burn, The Gods of the Copybook Headings with terror and slaughter return!*' Xandra had interrupted, but objecting apparently not to the voice but to the message of the poem.

'Oh, the cynicism! You can't possibly use that piece, Clive. There's such a thing as progress, you must admit!'

So Clive chose another poem: on my recommendation, Joyce Kilmer's *Trees*, which could offend no-one and which happened to be Xandra's favourite, and for once he actually got the job. They didn't seem to mind the squeaky voice but then it's always seemed to me to be a rather soppy idiocy of a poem. Droopy and feeble. But then I do have ultra-sensitive ears, as had been pointed put to me by the dirty-toed folk singer when I was a stage door groupie. I wonder if Anthea has inherited perfect pitch, and if so was it from dirty-toes or from me?

*'I think that I shall never see'* – it goes – *'A poem lovely as a tree. A tree whose hungry mouth is prest, Against the sweet earth's flowing breast, A tree that looks at God all day, And lifts her leafy arms to pray.'*

But that was before his voice had got really bad.

## The Good Neighbour

Xandra, usually so small, neat and contained, had in late pregnancy seemed to somehow overflow. I had thought it rather unwise of her to snap at Clive, when in the seventh month she found her libido increased to such an extent that Clive was staying out of the marital bedroom for fear of harming the unborn baby. 'Why do you care?' she had complained, she who normally never complained. 'It's not your baby anyway. If you want to find someone "normal" find someone else. I'm not a jealous person. Sexual exclusivity is against my principles.'

How little people know themselves. It could have been me in my wild-child days but was not sensible for someone like Xandra, nearing forty and on the brink of the twenty-first century. It was a time when fidelity was all the rage and broken marriage vows tended to end in divorce and swift remarriage. Men sought the 'authenticity of their feelings' – however transitory those feelings turned out to be – weekend or holiday and set out by bus or train to locate their latest step family. In which case little Rozzie would have had yet a third father to deal with. Birth father, legal father, stepfather.

If Clive had taken Xandra at her word and found someone less energetic than his wife, at least on a temporary basis, that might well have been the end. I did not doubt his love for her, just its exclusivity. Xandra and Clive did not mind being overheard. They never seemed aware, during our many long and lovely candlelit dinners in No. 24, just to what extent their love and lust for each other could be heard through the walls of No. 23. Our bedrooms were adjacent, and the walls rather thin and ticky-tacky, having been built for the Victorian lower orders, who were known to put no premium on privacy.

I was the good mother neither of them had ever had. They trusted me, and if they were a tad exhibitionist – well, both did have a theatrical background. All art, I used to think, circled at a distance from the central act; the eye of the storm, as it were, the swirling centre of the hurricane, once too dangerous to approach, or only if you were the Marquis de Sade and had quite a literary following.

Now the act is on everyone's iPhone, I fear there is no more art, or only shadows of what went before, and few are interested anyway. Sex? A good dinner with selfies is more absorbing. ['Okay,' say the Writers' Huddle. 'You can probably get away with that.' They too suffer.]

## Getting By With A Baby

The once longed-for motherhood had more problems than Xandra had anticipated. There were so many other considerations to worry about. Her duty to her patients: they depended on her, needed her, deserved more, surely, than did the ungrateful pain-monster in the IKEA cradle. The baby would be better off without her, they were both so un-bonded. She'd thought all mothers bonded with their babies; well, she just didn't. It was a two-way street. Perhaps this happened because it was a turkey-baster baby, a stranger to the household, and not a real one born out of love and familiarity?

Clive even seemed fonder of the baby than she did. He didn't seem to mind whose it was. He carried it round and cooed at it even when it was squalling, which was most of the time. And called her Rozzie, a name she hated. Rosalind sounded civilised but Rozzie was too like rozzer, an old-fashioned stupid policeman. All Gwinny's fault.

Clive had even volunteered to be a house-husband, at least when he was resting, and said there was Gwinny next door to understudy him should need arise, and that the TV in the corner was the best baby sitter imaginable. The baby stared at the screen all the time, the only thing that seemed to stop it crying. As soon as Xandra was back at work she would be able to afford a new 32-inch screen. At least the telly didn't teach you to swear all the time, unlike Gwinny and Clive, fuck, fuck, fuck and the occasional cunt. [Writers' Huddle: 'No! What about audio sales? They'll choose another to avoid argument.']

In the meantime Rozzie imbibed TV with her formula: no longer breast milk, no cuddling and gazing into one another's eyes, no 'one-step-two-step-tickle-you-under-there' nonsense, and she was right off sex.

Clive found the baby more interesting than he found Xandra. And next to the baby was TV. He liked to have it on as a background to life.

## The Big Break

Hope, Bacon's *'good breakfast but a bad supper'*, lives eternal in an actor's heart. The big break was bound to come. Clive still believed it. Xandra, though, had long ago accepted that such a thing was unlikely, faced the truth that she herself was only chorus material, not lead singer, and her legs were nowhere long enough for show-girl status. She would have to be the bread-winner so would do better to train for a proper job with opportunities for promotion. It was too late for medicine: she would try nursing.

Clive could keep his dreams but their future lay in her steady job and a bourgeois life, and that, surely, would include a baby. Or even two, though it was getting rather late for a third. Somehow she would survive.

So now the Smithsons had been living mostly on Xandra's wages up at the hospital – a good thing she kept on passing exams, working hard and getting promotion but all the more tragic if she didn't get back to work soon; she would spend quality time with Rozzie, and children benefited from the social life in the crèche and the nursery, as everyone knew. And Clive's multimedia stage opus, a tragicomedy called *Let's Get out of Here!*, in which a dumb (orally not intellectually) hero accomplished deeds of great valour which won him the respect of a threatened community. A bit like *Jaws*. The play would succeed and they would all be rich and famous again.

## Out Of The Dark Age And Into The Light

All that time, while Xandra and Clive tried in vain to conceive – well, at least Clive did; Xandra was caught up in her nursing career – his Lordship's seed stayed in the freezer. '*Action man, aristocrat*' appealed to no-one else until the fickle finger of fate, in the form of Gwinny's finger, fell upon it in January 1999. Twenty years unclaimed! Put in the archive freezer when the

Your Beautiful Baby Clinic went out of business to be taken over by the Woolland Clinic and its Brilliant Baby division.

Aristocrats must have been rather out of favour in the interim as a breeding opportunity, perhaps because of a growing radicalism in the nation at the time: the feeling that an elected House of Lords was preferable to one that depended upon inheritance. Rozzie, of course, meant to change all that.

A conclusion that the US Senate came to a hundred years earlier. One of Rozzie's earliest ambitions, when she could barely walk, was to be a cheerleader in an American presidential election. The TV, that excellent baby sitter, was kept on in Rozzie's crèche and later nursery and of course when she was at home, where it was never switched off – for ease of viewing by day, to ward off robbers at night, and to save Clive from the terror of silence.

These days far more sophisticated devices are available for self-fertilisation than a turkey baster. But this particular vaginal basting was done in 1999 which was practically in the dark ages so far as the HFEA, the Human Fertilisation and Embryology Authority, was concerned, as later a bitter Rozzie was frequently to remark, once she realised her anonymous origins.

## A World Of Cameras

Clive remarked in 2015 that there was one CCTV camera for every eleven people. These days there are far more. Every sensible householder has one over their front door. We have them over Nos. 23 and 24. Rozzie did not want her properties, as she prudently waited for them to go up in value, to be robbed or vandalised. We old people, Xandra, Clive and myself, were allowed to live here in our lifetime or until she chose to sell, whichever was soonest – Rozzie had very good lawyers – when we would be out in the cold and on welfare. There would be precious little left of my bequests; I'd spent prodigiously and carelessly when I could, much of it on Rozzie.

'*How sharper than a serpent's tooth it is to have a thankless child!* Act One, Scene Four, *King Lear*,' as Clive would say. I am more tolerant of his irritating quotes than I used to be. Sometimes life is so puzzling one is driven back to the poetry and wisdom of the past. I find myself reading the concluding, rather sour verses of FitzGerald's version of Omar Khayyam: *With them the Seed of Wisdom did I sow, And with my own hand labour'd it to grow: And this was all the Harvest that I reap'd – I came like Water, and like Wind I go.* And even Gibran: *Let these be your desires: To melt and be like a running brook That sings its melody to the night. To know the pain of too much tenderness. To be wounded by your own understanding of love; And to bleed willingly and joyfully.* All very well for Clive to gain comfort from them, I suppose, but too airy fairy to be any help for me.

I have to remember that Rozzie is a Millennial. She had been born into a world of cameras, to be the observed, not the observer. She had been filmed and recorded since birth: the most observed generation since technology began, and the most self-conscious and the most riddled with anxiety.

Our forefathers ground glass in order to see through spectacles as they aged and eyesight dimmed: for Rozzie and her young friends the lens turns the other way, the better to magnify imperfections. The girl in her selfie, all too anxious about her looks, lowers her head in a gesture of submission, drops her chin and widens her goggle eyes and presents herself to her friends as helpless – *poor little victim seductive me: love me, help me, be my boyfriend, do!* she cries in her heart even while her mouth utters *MeToo. MeToo!*

Not that Rozzie ever bothered about her looks; she didn't have to, she was more or less perfect anyway, and at least knew all about the curvature of the camera lens from a very early age, so was in no danger, as are so many of her daft generation, of going off to the plastic surgeon to get her nose made smaller.

Does this make her behaviour any more excusable? Well, perhaps – her main terror being of homelessness, with which her generation is cursed. So now she owned the freeholds of both 23 and 24. We'd handed them over freely while Mr Ipswich had hysterics. We were no help; we did nothing to foresee the cataclysm coming, or perhaps we didn't want to. We are the guilty pre-digitals and the post-digitals are the victims. No wonder they despise us, can't wait to get rid of us.

## Screen After Screen

Clive still never bothered to turn the TV off, so blood, death and destruction poured out of the corner of the kitchen all day.

We did nothing to develop a sense of compassion in the poor child.

In the years after she got back to her gainful employment, saving lives not ruining her own, screen size rose from 32-inch to 40-inch. Xandra would turn the thing off automatically when she came back from work, but Clive would turn it on again, claiming the higher moral ground – she had saved a life or two that day, true, but had he not borne the humiliation of house-husbanding, rocking a cradle that was none of his own? (Old Irish folk song; Clive's favourite; the young wife goes out partying: the auld feller is left with the child: – *'Perhaps your own daddy might never be known, I'm sitting and sighing and rocking the cradle, And nursin' the baby that's none of my own.'*)

'Please don't sing that!' Gwinny heard Xandra say. 'Suppose little Rozzie puts two and two together.'

'But I'm only joking, darling!' Clive replied. 'She's too young to add up. No worries. Intensive Care is hardly partying, I quite realise, and none as virtuous as you. *The wicked are wicked, no doubt, and they go astray and they fall, and they come by their deserts; but who can tell the mischief which the very virtuous do?* William Makepeace Thackeray, *Vanity Fair*. I had a hard day too.'

It was the equivalent, Gwinny used to think, of the husband who defies fate by leaving lipstick on the collar, a note in the pocket, bound to be discovered, anything, anything, to relieve the strain of secrecy. The TV stayed on and the screen size got bigger, and 'Rocking the Cradle' got more frequent. At least it was a nice tune. The dirty-toed folk singer had sung it the night she lost her virtue in the alley behind the Drury Lane theatre.

Rozzie had a tablet when she was two – a great baby sitter even in its primitive pre-app form – and played *Grand Theft Auto* at two and a half (when Tommy Vercetti left Liberty City for Vice City); she could read, write and add up when she was three – but that didn't stop Clive singing the none-of-my-own song – losing interest in video games only when she came across chess at the age of five.

Clive assumed all children were like Rozzie, never having been to the baby clinic – Gwinny would take her – and having no idea about developmental milestones, and so forth. But chess worried him a little. 'We don't want her to grow up into some kind of female nerd. Though I suppose it's rather like horses, a girl gives up chess when she meets her first boy.'

Clive began to call her his Little Major General and would sing her to sleep at night with tongue twisters from *The Pirates of Penzance*, in a bid, Gwinny reckoned, to mock Rozzie out of too much learning.

'*I am the very model of a modern Major General,*' he'd sing, and Rozzie would stare at him with her large dark eyes – such a contrast to the blonde curls – with puzzled admiration mixed with embarrassment – '*I've information vegetable, animal, and mineral, I know the kings of England, and I quote the fights historical, From Marathon to Waterloo, in order categorical; I'm very well acquainted, too, with matters mathematical, I understand equations, both the simple and quadratical, About binomial theorem I'm teeming with a lot o' news With many cheerful facts about the square of the hypotenuse.'* But you don't want to grow up into some whiskery old general, do you, Rozzie, you're going to be a real little princess.'

But you had to admire him. Clive managed the tongue twister without hesitation or doubt in his powerful tenor voice, with the occasional squeak. The squeak was what still kept producers from hiring him – they'd risk him as an understudy because he'd recover so quickly and carry on unabashed and energetic but audiences would giggle and lose concentration. And he demanded star money and though he looked like a star and behaved like a star he was not a star. But heard through a stud wall from No. 23 he was pretty good, and Gwinny was not above putting an ear to the wall.

In the dull days before Flora relented and gave them Rozzie – it was she, surely, who had guided Gwinny's finger when she selected aristocratic action man as the one who had provided Rozzie with such excellent genes, and who held Gwinny's hand steady while she pressed down the pump – both households had built loft extensions (Gwinny paid). She had saved money by soundproofing between Nos. 22 and 23, but not between 23 and 24, not because she wanted to spy on the Smithsons but it was as well to have a vague idea of what was going on with Rozzie; Clive thought nothing of leaving her alone in the house even before she was twelve, at which a normal child is regarded mature enough to be left. And even though Rozzie was not exactly normal, just super normal, it still worried Gwinny.

Rozzie was so sensible and rational nothing was likely to go wrong but she liked to keep an eye on things.

Which meant that Gwinny too, along with Rozzie, heard the wars, and realised that peace never came. As one war rolled by, another took its place. Landscapes, if you were watching, changed, or at least the backdrop did, thus giving useful variety to the cameraman, as did different languages to the sound man, though the screams and moans, the bangs and crashes of explosions, Rozzie too noted from the youngest of ages, always sounded much the same, whatever the ethnicity of those involved. The Somali wave of whimpers and screams gave way to the Kosovo conflict when Rozzie was in the womb – 'conflict' sounding more rational and controllable a word than actual 'war', though it looked and sounded pretty much the same on the screen. In swift succession in Rozzie's life there came the Philippines, Horn of Africa, the Congo, Darfur, Afghanistan, Iran, Iraq, and the Twin Towers – how everyone crowded round the telly for that. A great day for burying other news, that one! Then the War on Terror – great news for the US arms industry and the faltering trade in UK torture devices – and offering years of teary telly opportunities for so many, in Lebanon, Iraq, Libya, Gaza, Pakistan, Syria, Nigeria, Sudan – one after another all blaring out from the TV. Gwinny used ear plugs.

It never occurred to Clive to switch the thing off and he did so like the volume up high, as if blocking out the possibility of disagreeable thought. He saw war and violence as something happening somewhere else and far away. He took the haunted eyes of starving children for granted, the whimpers as they died, the blood and terror as shells crashed and tanks crushed, the snapping of bones and howls of maternal anguish as he lovingly spread Marmite, her favourite spread, on his almost-child's toast. All that stuff, nothing to do with him or his family.

Buried in many a mind – not least Clive's, as Gwinny came to realise – is the memory of some terrible fall from grace, too painful to surface. Some distant disaster, small or great, which changes our lives and alters us for ever. In Gwinny's mind it was her brother Geraint saying she was not family but her mother's by-blow, a bastard, and her father was not her father. For Clive it was when he was seventeen and saw on the evening news a clip of the car crash in which his parents died, and his mother's white leg sticking out of the wreckage. It shouldn't have been screened but these things happen.

What Clive went on not remembering, Gwinny was relieved to find out, was any connection between the girl from Madame Clothilde and the person who became his next-door neighbour.

Xandra put up with Clive's TV addiction – and addiction it was – from a mixture of love and compassion. Gwinny just kept her ear plugs handy. Rozzie looked and listened and made what sense she could of it. Real life seemed pale and wan to all by comparison to the attractions on a screen which had grown to 60 inches by the time of her thirteenth birthday. Clive liked to own the newest and best, while retaining his vision of himself as a bohemian creator, and Xandra, maternal guilt by now well established, worked overtime to make sure he had the newest and best to hand. If reality ever ran out of death and destruction there was always drama on the telly. A murdered girl here, a raped one there – always young and nubile – as plot fodder for the thriller; blood and gore and open-heart surgery if it had to be doctors-and-nurses, not serial-killers-and-cops.

## A Very Clever Little Girl

Rozzie, asked by Gwinny when she was ten why she wasn't watching *Downton Abbey* like everyone else, told Gwinny she was 'fictioned out'. She didn't like 'made-up stories'. They weren't true. They were childish – her favourite term of opprobrium at the time.

'Don't you like beginnings, middles and ends?' asked Gwinny cautiously. 'The good being rewarded, the bad being punished?'

'No,' said Rozzie calmly, 'because that's not what happens in real life. Mum's good, so she gets shit pay for important work; Dad's bad but he gets to sit on a sofa all day and watch telly and leaves Mum to earn. Where's the justice in that?'

Gwinny could see that this was a fair assessment of the situation, if rather an alarming one, and asked whether she, Gwinny, was in Rozzie's opinion good or bad.

'Mixed,' said Rozzie,' but at least you do what you say you will. If I was ruler of the world I'd ban all fiction. It's bad for people, it gives them a false view of the world.'

Gwinny did not pursue the matter. Rozzie seldom said more than a sentence at a time but when she did it was, well, awesome. The child saw too much and knew too much and expressed herself too well for any normal ten-year-old. Miss Wessler, headmistress of the local primary school, had Rozzie's IQ tested when she was eight and it came out at 140 on the adult intelligence scales, which was as far as it could go, so they reckoned the test was faulty, and tried another test instead which goes up to 160, but there Rozzie rated only 135, so the (part-time) school psychologist abandoned any real attempt to define her abilities. If she finished a two-hour exam in ten minutes, well, Nature threw up these sports from time to time.

Rozzie, Gwinny concluded, had deliberately messed up the second paper, seeing the benefit of pretending to be more like other people if she wanted to be liked. To be bright, but not too bright, was advisable. But pretence could be maintained for only so long. By the time she was ten Rozzie was losing her friends – one bored, withering look would do it – and worse, the goodwill of the teachers as she corrected their spelling and gasped at their ignorance.

Tact was not necessarily Rozzie's strong point. The perfectly modulated words which came out of the pretty little mouth when she was small were not always kind, just told the truth of what she was thinking and feeling. But as she grew older she realised, perhaps in response to Clive's quote from T. S. Eliot – one of his favourites – that 'humankind cannot bear too much reality', moderated her behaviour, and she soon learned how to flatter and charm. But it was a learning process, rather than one which sprang from her heart.

Gwinny could see Rozzie would have to be found some special school for gifted children before reasons were found to get rid of her as 'difficult', and said so. Clive protested vigorously. Rozzie did not need any kind of 'special school', she must stay in the mainstream and learn to get on with other children and not be rude to her teachers. Xandra disagreed and thought Rozzie should leave before she got into any trouble and it went onto her school record. The important thing was always to have a clean record.

*'I'm very good at integral and differential calculus, I know the scientific names of beings animalculous. In short, in matters vegetable, animal and mineral, I am the very model of a modern Major General,'* Clive sang to Rozzie over tea, over the rattle of gunfire and exploding IEDs in Afghanistan, and without a flicker of a squeak. 'That's all very well but if you're not going to grow into that leathery old nerd of a major general what you have to learn is how to be kind to others.'

'Daddy,' said Rozzie, carefully scraping the icing off a bun before she ate it, butter-less. She had no intention of getting fat. 'You sang that so perfectly I think you must be superman. But what you need to learn is to be kind to me. If I stay where I am I will get bored and go to the bad and you wouldn't want that.' She turned her lovely liquid eyes to her father and smiled in adoration – she was good at that – and his resolve melted. She must go wherever she wanted.

So that was that. They turned to Gwinny in expectation, and Gwinny found a private school, St Katherine's Anglican School for Gifted Girls, who said they only had room for near geniuses, child prodigies, in fact, but offered her an interview. 'They'll say that to all the parents,' explained Rozzie, and went along alone. They let her in. It was not cheap but Gwinny paid the fees. She realised that her wealth was not endless, but there was still more than enough to go round and she could see how much Rozzie needed her.

Neither Xandra nor Clive seemed to have noticed just how extraordinary a child they were raising. They took it for granted: Xandra because she was so busy with her nursing career, and Clive because he was too worried about the state of his vocal cords to pay much attention to anything else going on in the world. And how they did justify themselves!

In the early days Xandra attributed Rozzie's brightness to the fact that she, Xandra, was a working mother. 'A year old and already walking and talking! You see, far better for a baby to be in a crèche than cooped up with just one person. It develops sociability and brain power! A stay at home mother is no good for a child. And anyway, Clive's at home.'

Clive attributed Rozzie's intelligence to his own influence. He would forget it could hardly be an inherited trait; enough that she was brought up with him at home. He might not have been to college, but drama school provided a better training in empathy and the arts than any Russell Group university could provide.

He was not the best stay-at-home dad in the world. 'I'm just no good as an early riser,' Clive maintained. 'I need my beauty sleep if I'm to find employment. I'm an actor, after all. You're an early riser, aren't you, Gwinny.' And Gwinny was, so she did a lot of what was necessary in collecting and delivering from crèche to nursery to primary school.

'See!' Xandra would say, when the girl was at primary school. 'Rozzie's doing so well at school! Passing all her exams and good as gold. They say that's what happens if you have a working mother – you grow up self-reliant and IQ points ahead of the rest. I love her so much. If I'd been a stay at home mother I'd only have smothered her individuality. I've been doing Jung for my psychiatric qualification and know all about the devouring mother.'

'It's nurture not nature that counts,' Clive would say. 'She sees a lot of me: of course she's bright and beautiful. Cute. And a lovely little voice. No sign of migraines, unlike her poor dad. Anyway, so long as she's happy. She'll be a beauty when she grows up. She'll be an actress. It's in the blood.'

'Actor,' Xandra said automatically, and Clive quickly corrected himself. He was rhetorically more of a feminist than even his wife. Though Xandra would be saying how nurses knew more than doctors when it came to keeping people alive, it was left to Gwinny to talk about being a writer, a director, a producer, not just an actress, a doctor not a nurse, running the world. Aim high. Rozzie would just look at Gwinny with a faintly amused air.

Ministers for Education came and went before Rozzie was eleven. David Blunkett, Estelle Morris, Charles Clarke, Ruth Kelly, Alan Johnson, Ed Balls and Michael Gove. Rozzie could name them all, and give a brief résumé of their intentions and achievements, flattering and otherwise. Gwinny liked to think it was her habit of condemning educational theorists, as Ministers of Education tend to be, that promoted Rozzie's interest in world affairs. It couldn't be the Smithsons. Xandra was too busy saving lives to notice, Clive too fascinated by bangs and bombs on the TV to wonder why they were going off, and fully occupied learning poetry by heart and preserving his voice against over-strain – the doctors said he had to be careful, the less he used it, the less the squeak – to take much notice. Rozzie said the squeak was the equivalent of a stammer: most people stuttered when they were stressed and spoke. Her father stuttered when he sang, because for him, song, not speech, was the source of stress.

## Ignorance Is Bliss

They somehow managed to overlook the intervention into Rozzie's existence of the sperm bank; the fact that Rozzie had a biological unknown, un-named father other than Clive. There was certainly never any mention of it. Mind you, it's an awk- ward and embarrassing conversation to have with any child. The man you think is your Daddy is not your Daddy never goes down well. And the mere existence of Rozzie, so pretty and clever and good, reflected a certain glory on Clive, who longed for glory but found it so elusive.

Gwinny told them keeping Rozzie in ignorance was unwise, but they took no notice. Why would Rozzie ever need to know? The law changed in 2005 so donation ceased to be anonymous and a donor child had the legal right to know who had fathered it, but the law, thank God, was too late for Rozzie. The law was an ass anyway. Just as they referred to the police as 'the pigs' (a leftover from their hippie days), they treated all institutions with blanket derision, from the State, the Police, to the Law, and peppered their conversations with the occasional 'bloody' and 'fucking' when searching for an elusive adjective. Gwinny would ask them not to. When she was eighteen months old Rozzie startled the crèche nurse by asking her for the 'fucking dummy'. Quite an incident, at the time, as 'uses foul language' nearly went on little Rozzie's school record.

A terrible thought for Gwinny: suppose it was Clive who managed to impregnate Xandra the same month as she was turkey basted; supposing he still had a few slow-swimming sperm left in his balls when it happened? Supposing Rozzie was Clive's child, after all, not Sebastian, Lord Dilberne's? Perhaps the out-of-date, half price, frozen sperm had failed after all, and one of Clive's rare laggards had finally speeded up and just got where it was meant to go, even after thirteen years of Clive trying and failing. Just one was all it took. Perhaps Rozzie was just a cooler, brighter, better version of Clive?

Perhaps Flora had responded okay to Gwinny's imprecations but got the timing wrong? Perhaps there had been a power cut during the twenty years in the freezer, so the sperm didn't 'take'. The Gods were a tricky bunch. Then the beautiful Rozzie would not have Dilberne genes at all.

What, and all this fuss for nothing? Never! She wiped the very possibility from her mind.

So it was resolved, almost by default, that Rozzie could be kept in ignorance of her true parentage.

'Yet ah! why should they know their fate? Since sorrow never comes too late, And happiness too swiftly flies. Thought would destroy their paradise. No more; where ignorance is bliss, 'Tis folly to be wise,' quoted Clive once again from Thomas Gray's Ode.

'Silence can be ominous when delivered as a mortal blow to the psyche, heart or the soul,' quoted Gwinny in defiance, but for once they took no notice of her Gibran.

'So long as Rozzie's happy,' was Xandra's attitude, when her primary school entered her for a Camden Junior Chess Championship.

'Who needs her to be clever?' said Clive.

## The Wrong Time

The Smithsons' 'your-father-is-a-turkey-baster' conversation happened on New Year's Eve, Thursday December 31$^{st}$ 2015. It was the day before Rozzie's sixteenth birthday. We were having her party a day early, because on New Year's Day Xandra had a triple-pay shift up at the hospital which she could not afford to lose, Clive claimed he had an audition and I had a sitting with a client from the old days.

Rozzie was due home from the All London Champion Chess Club in Hendon at around five. She loved chess, and why would she not? She was better than most at it, barring a few grand-masters. A child chess prodigy. The *Ham & High* filmed her as she played – the pretty little blonde head bowed in concentration over the board. At primary school she played against a visiting grandmaster, and the game ended as a stalemate. And it wasn't only chess. She had an eidetic memory, was as good at the sciences as the humanities – and as for Maths! – well, she took her GCSE three years earlier than was normal even at St Katherine's Anglican School for Gifted Girls.

When she was small all went well. Rozzie was obedient, sweet and kind. And she could sing. She was quiet, tidy, and seemed possessed of sufficient empathy not to be fully on the autistic spectrum. She could not only out-quote Clive from the age of six, looking up everything he quoted on Google and coming back at him going one better, but doing so tactfully. Xandra and Clive could see she was bright, but resolutely denied that she was anything special. Why would Clive want to admit that this brilliant paragon of sweetness and light derived from loins other than his own? Why would Xandra want to risk any further disturbance to domestic harmony than she absolutely had to? They loved her; that was surely enough.

It was 5.30 on New Year's Eve, 2015. Rozzie was due home from the chess club around now. At fifteen a girl is old enough to get home safely from Hendon, though perhaps too many will already be rolling around drunk. It's only five stops on the Underground – Hendon to Chalk Farm on the Northern Line. She was an independent girl and already a karate junior black belt.

## A Dreadful Row

Xandra herself was just back from a long shift on the Intensive Care ward up at Hampstead, where she was now a Band 7 practice instructor. The secret of managing both home and family, achieving a successful work/life balance, Xandra knew, lay in organisation and she was a great organiser. But sometimes you would just like to kick your shoes off your swollen feet and sit down. She did love Rozzie, even though she was sometimes if not exactly frightened but a little awed by her, and it was nearly her birthday, and like any other mother she too wanted to celebrate. So within five minutes Xandra had washed her hands and changed out of her uniform (in the last sixteen years she'd speeded up) and was already preparing the white bread (a special treat) Marmite sandwiches for Rozzie's birthday party, with insufficiently softened butter. Clive had forgotten to take it from the fridge early as she'd reminded him to do.

Clive had his feet up on the sofa. He was back home from a matinée performance of *Phantom of the Opera*, which had run for two hours and forty-five minutes instead of the usual two hours thirty. Nobody takes matinées seriously and Clive was understudying the understudy who that afternoon was taking Hugh Panchetti's place as the lead, and though Clive was for once earning he felt generally bored and humiliated. Not surprising; when Clive played Joseph, Panchetti had been the one to understudy him. That had been thirty-eight years ago.

Well, that's life; some rise, some fall; in showbiz sometimes meteorically. But resentment and fury can make a man really tired.

'Good day?' Xandra asked Clive, as she trimmed the bread for the sandwiches. It was a half-way house between tea and supper to suit Rozzie's convenience. Hard-boiled eggs with tuna dip to follow, and a spectacular iced birthday cake from Waitrose Xandra had picked up on the way home.

'Idiotic question,' growled Clive from the sofa. Few men look good when they lounge on a sofa drinking beer in front of the TV. But Clive managed, even at fifty-two, albeit by now a little grey jowled. He had kept his excellent matinée-idol looks – the narrow face, straight nose, firm chin, the bright blue piercing eyes, the lean, graceful body of the man Xandra had married twenty-nine years ago.

Xandra, now fifty-five, seemed both shorter and wider than the slim, dancing creature she had been at the wedding. Employment and motherhood had aged her. Now she carefully softened the butter with the same methodical efficiency with which she administered life-critical injections. Two seconds in the microwave and you had spreadable butter. Three, and you were left with a yellow pool of grease.

'Boring as hell if you want to know. The Phantom was even flatter than usual in *Music of the Night*. Giggling in the front rows didn't help. Calls himself a tenor and can't even hit an A flat. Sleazy little worm. Okay? What other details do you require?'

Xandra said that was more than enough and cut the crusts off the sandwiches, filled half of them with Marmite, and half with a soft crab pâté, then arranged them on paper doilies. She laid the table as prettily as possible and put the cake in pride of place, while Clive went on contemplating in graphic detail with whom the Phantom's understudy could have slept on his race to the bottom of the singing world.

At 6.50 Clive had exhausted his daily wrath, pulled himself together and by seven was washed, shaved and smartened up to be the usual charming self he liked to be in front of Rozzie, though with a bit of tissue sticking to the shaving cut on his chin.

All he wanted to do was relax and watch the thriller on BBC and wait for Rozzie to turn up at the door. He was watching a group of male detectives and one female – Gillian Anderson of the *X files*, now in *The Fall* – huddling over the broken body of a young, naked girl. She lay on a slab in the corner of the Smithsons' living room, limp hand dripping blood from her fingertips, neck slit. But forget the dead girl. A truly charming and good-looking serial killer was at work, and the lady senior detective seemed to have a yen for rough trade. Clive was smoking weed, and didn't want to miss a frame. And Xandra, who annoyingly never smoked, was prattling on.

'Sometime, Clive, we do have to tell her. Perhaps today would be a good time? She's on the brink of womanhood, all that.'

'Tell her what?'

'You know.'

'No I don't know. What are you talking about?'

'The sperm bank. All that.'

'There's no reason whatsoever to tell her "all that". She's doing very nicely as she is. Why do you want to upset her? Children belong to those who look after them, not those who donored them. Ha-ha. Joke. We have it on Brecht's authority. Anyway it was an anonymous donor. There's no point in her knowing. She looks like me, she thinks like me, leave it at that.'

'But supposing she ever finds out? You're meant to tell them.'

'Meant, by whom? Why? Not like today when you can check medical records. Rozzie can't. What good would it be for Rozzie to find out her dad's a paranoid schizophrenic? And for all we know that's what he is, with any luck dead by now. Bless him.'

By which he meant 'curse him'. Clive was smoking, going into rant mode. He must have had a very bad afternoon at the theatre. Xandra's hadn't been too good, either. She was back on Intensive Care and had lost one newborn, and a twenty-year-old lad who'd been hovering for three weeks, and came out of a coma only to promptly die. She wanted to cry but had been trained not to, and Clive would just suggest she changed her job to something better paid.

'I only meant—' she started, and then gave up. He was rolling another and Rozzie would be back soon. Clive believed he never smoked in front of Rozzie, but the sudden movements, the rapid stubbing out and the emptying of the ashtray, as he deleted the traces of illegality and dependence, were obvious to friends, family, and anyone with half a brain. And Rozzie noticed everything. But what could Xandra do? She too had smoked in her time. She understood Clive's necessity. He had smoked so much and so long.

'Meant, meant!' he scorned. 'Just because some stupid corrupt politicians in hock to the NHS fiddle with the law, doesn't mean we have to take any fucking notice. Just another way of making our children miserable. Satanic. *The child is innocence and forgetting, a new beginning, a game, a self-rolling wheel, a first movement, a sacred Yes.* Friedrich Nietzsche, *Thus Spoke Zarathustra.* But what do they care? So let's just forget, shall we?'

Xandra sighed. It was time for a diversion. She could open the window and put on the fan as soon as he left the room. He needed protection from himself.

In the meantime she was worried. New Year's Eve and already pictures on the telly of drunken crowds rollicking round.

Xandra moved the hands of the clock on twenty minutes so Clive would think it was later than it really was. Clive stared at the next naked girl choking and dying nastily.

'I'm worried. Where has Rozzie got to?' said Xandra.

'The child doesn't need mollycoddling,' said Clive. 'She'll be perfectly fine. It was her choice to go. She needs to learn to hurry home. You're not nearly strict enough. *He that spareth the rod hateth the child: but he that loveth her chasteneth her betimes.* Proverbs 13:24,' he misquoted.

'Do just take the car and go and find her, Clive,' she begged. 'It's New Year's Eve. Everyone will be drunk.'

'Calm down,' he said. 'You're being menopausal. The streets are safe enough. One CCTV camera for every eleven citizens in London. The *Daily Mail* says so. If you're really worried you can always go and fetch her from the chess club.'

'You just don't want to get off the sofa. I know you've had a hard day's work and you're tired,' said Xandra. 'Well, actually, so am I.' Which was true enough.

'I wish you had a normal job,' said Clive. 'Do something different. I daresay Rozzie would like a bit of attention from her mother for once.' *The Fall* had come to an end; there was lots more to come but you had to wait a week for the next episode. He switched off *iPlayer*, and rolled another cigarette, signalling how hard done by he was. 'Toothache has started up again. I need to stay as still as I can. I don't dare set it off again. That shit of a dentist, curse him. I hope he dies in front of his children, in great pain. Don't look so shocked. It's the same shit he inflicts on me. Am I what you call ranting again?'

'Yes,' said Xandra. She was crying.

'And you'll blame it on the weed, I suppose. Which it is not. I will not be censored in my own home. Go on making your dainty little sandwiches; Rozzie still won't love you. You're never here to love. Why would she? And I'm sure you're tired. You're always tired. Watching people die is a tiring business. No wonder you're crying at me. If you're really worried about your poor neglected child and too tired to get her, try Gwinny next door.'

So Xandra did, though rather red eyed, and Gwinny went in search of Rozzie straight away. And that was the end of the attempt at the important conversation.

Clive was very sensitive on the subject, and it had been foolish of Xandra to raise it. Few of their rows were quite as awful as this one.

## Chess Foster Mother

So it was Gwinny who'd had to act as chess mother and fetch Rozzie. She'd done so from the beginning, borrowing Xandra's little yellow 2CV, ferrying the child here and there, getting her from this tournament to that, soothing the anxious brow (though Rozzie scarcely ever scowled. She did not intend to develop frown lines in later life). Not that Gwinny resented it – someone had to do it – but the Smithsons did sometimes seem to take advantage.

It wasn't that they were stupid – or only when compared to their daughter – they just had a tendency to believe what it was convenient to believe, to blind themselves to what was obvious to others.

Gwinny found Rozzie walking up the Chalk Farm Road. CCTV cameras followed her all the way so she had adjusted her behaviour accordingly, striding gracefully, not slouching; smiling for the omnipresent lens. She got into the car in a not very good mood. Gwinny could tell from the way the girl tapped her deft little fingers, half adult, and half child, on the dashboard of the little yellow *deux-chevaux*. Others were picked up from the club, or indeed from St Katherine's Anglican School for Gifted Girls, in Rolls-Royces, at the very least Mercedes. Standard Road was still a somewhat down-market area but other grander, richer streets were all around. Rozzie was in danger of turning into a little snob, Gwinny feared.

It seemed Rozzie had been in the running for the FIDE English

Youth Grand Prix, but today, she complained: she had actually been beaten by a twenty-five-year-old Russian by the name of Igor, who had not had the courtesy of letting a schoolgirl win, not even one as prettily seductive as this one, and one who was surely deserving of some respect, having taken her Maths GCSE three years earlier than normal and had, she reminded me, rubbished a grandmaster while still at primary school.

'You must learn to take defeat gracefully.'

'I don't see why. It doesn't happen all that often.'

Gwinny could see that a likeness to Clive, if not nature, was certainly nurture.

They drove in silence a little. Gwinny tried to make the silence seem disapproving but it didn't work, for the next thing Rozzie did was to ask how much her house was worth.

'Your parents bought it for a song in 1986. Now it's worth £600,000 and rising fast.'

'I suppose it's some kind of security.'

'I would have thought so. Mine is worth more because of my studio.'

'Peanuts,' she said. I was really glad to get her home. Fortunately she beamed such a charming smile at me, and thanked me for picking her up and apologised for being grumpy but she had a few things to work out in her head, that I forgave her at once. She had a kind of Aphrodite smile she could switch on or off at will. She had learned it at nursery, given it up in primary school, rediscovered it at St Katherine's, where the girls were both posh and clever. I had seen her use it once on one of the fathers, a Minister of State, no less. She only went for the top. I don't know what happened and I don't suppose much, but the daughter no longer spoke to her.

'There, told you, Xandra,' said Clive when we came in. 'No need to worry about our Rozzie. But thank you, Gwinny.' He was always on his best behaviour when Rozzie was around, but I felt she was not fooled. Xandra, though tear stained, was smiling bravely. High tea was served in the conservatory.

The cake, the talking point, was iced in pink and decorated with especially crafted mini-make-up – miniature lipsticks, eyebrow brushes, mascara wands, discs of rouge, all blended tastefully into the icing – and in spun sugar the message 'Welcoming our very special girl to the world of grown-ups'.

'I wasn't sure it was suitable,' said Xandra, 'but the girl in Waitrose said it was the season's bestseller so I placed an order.'

'Absolutely lovely, Mum,' said Rozzie, 'Waitrose always gets it right and so you do too. It's high time I started to use make-up, isn't it?' She was using her dutiful daughter smile, demure and obedient. Rozzie had a range of very effective smiles for every occasion. Earnest scholar, good friend, responsible daughter, sleepy girl, hungry girl and dieting girl: I'd met them all: the full-blast Aphrodite one I'd had just now, only occasionally used – I think I only got it because she was preoccupied. I wasn't particularly useful to her.

'Shall we all just sit round the table and eat the cake,' she suggested. Obediently, we all did. She had her patient girl smile, the one she used when talking to the particularly stupid. She waited until all our mouths were full of a quite dense Madeira cake.

'I want you all to listen very carefully. It's obvious to me, Clive, that you're not my real father. Somewhere, somehow, I have another one. Two brown-eyed parents, if both are heterozygous, can have a blue-eyed baby. Mine are hazel, which comes into the brown cluster. By these rules it would seem that two blue-eyed parents cannot have a hazel-eyed baby. However, eye colour is polygenic, and several other genes exert their effects as well. So yes, while it's unusual, it is possible for blue-eyed parents to have a hazel-eyed child. But there is other evidence.'

Alerted by eye colour, she told us, she'd had a DNA test done – fifteen Y-chromosome samples in all – and it had come back to prove negative for Clive as father, positive for Xandra as mother. She'd used hair from both their combs. Rather disgusting. Clive should take care to clean the teeth of his from time to time, preferably in the dishwasher which sterilised things properly. She had concluded she must be a donor child. Clive was not her father.

'I'll have something to say about that,' said Clive feebly,

spluttering cake crumbs across the table, but was too shocked to say what it was. He turned to me and said, 'And you stop laughing,' which I suppose I was, but none of it seemed very funny. Cake was dripping out of Xandra's open mouth.

'Just as well for you, Mum,' said Rozzie, 'that I share many genes with you.' Such a neat little mouth, such a sweet little face. 'Otherwise I'd have thought you'd got out like Simkins Two one night and come back with kittens, and Pa wouldn't have liked that one bit.'

She helped herself to a nibble of hard-boiled egg. The tuna dip she found too messy to undertake.

'I told you so,' said Xandra to Clive. 'Now see what you've done.'

Clive turned to Rozzie. 'After all I've done for you.'

'You did a fucking good Modern Major General,' she said generously. 'I'll say that for you. But that was about all. You were home all day and Mum was out all day.'

Clive wandered over to the TV and turned it on. He was unsteady and stumbling. He had drunk nothing, but had probably smoked quite a lot.

'*O monstrous beast, how like a swine she lies!*' he declaimed. '*Taming of the Shrew*, Shakespeare. You'll hear more of this, young lady,' he muttered from back on the sofa. 'How dare you speak to your mother like that!'

On the screen the New Year revelry in Trafalgar Square was beginning. Clive turned the volume up. Xandra had always thought perhaps he was a little deaf, but no. This is what he had spent decades training for; never to hear anything he didn't want to.

Rozzie raised her clear bell-like voice just a little. She enunciated beautifully. St Katherine's had trained her well.

'Except there was always you, Grandma Gwinny. But you're no relative at all. What goes on? I know what the neighbours say but I don't think so.'

'It is certainly not so.'

'I don't know what we would have done without you. However, here we are, me a sperm bank baby, fathered by a turkey baster. Bet you had to do it, Gwinny. He wouldn't have had the nerve. But you should have told me early on, not left me to find out for myself.'

I realised she was not as friendly to me as I had hoped. Between us we, representatives of the pre-digital age, had created a monster Frankenstein would be proud of.

Xandra pulled herself together, crossed to the sofa, switched off the TV and even pulled the plugs out. Clive looked bewildered and rolled another joint. Xandra shared it with him. A gesture of solidarity, I thought.

I could not deny that Rozzie was very much my own creation. I was the one who selected her father, warmed his frozen sperm in the microwave – and Rozzie was right. Clive, suddenly squeamish, having bought the baster in the first place from Woolworth's (remember Woolworth's?), lost his nerve and left it to me. And me, I'd had to act before the stuff got cold. Xandra was fretting and Clive was quoting: '*Let not lust's winter come ere summer half be done*: Shakespeare: *Venus and Adonis*' – although doing what I did did seem at the time something of an unwarranted intimacy – impregnation was a man's job, not a woman's. But Clive was like that. As impetuous as Xandra was steady.

Little, villainous, child prodigy Rozzie, always with an eye for drama, was thus able to emerge triumphant, unscathed and perfect from her mother's battered womb, like Aphrodite from the foam.

But she hadn't finished with us yet. She named her father as Sebastian, Lord Dilberne. *6ft 1in, blue eyes, blond hair: BA (Oxon), action man, aristocrat*. It was my turn to be shocked. The previous Lord Dilberne had been a friend of Lord Petrie; as his nurse I had manoeuvred the latter's wheelchair up the broad steps of 3 Belgrave Square many a time; as his wife I had spent weekends at lovely Dilberne Court in Sussex. I knew the family – not well; I was not of their class – but enough. Nor did I suggest by as much as a blink of an eye that the name meant anything to me.

But how, how?

'Easy enough,' she said, 'if you put your trust in lateral thinking. Millennial thinking, indeed.'

## *I Ching*: Hexagram 61. 'Inner Truth.' Pigs And Fishes

She'd discovered the envelope in which the sperm, labelled no. 116349, had arrived hidden in Xandra's knickers drawer – kept for sentimental reasons, Rozzie hoped. Perhaps her mother had some residual feelings for her, after all.

Xandra puffed away at another joint, snuggled up to Clive and tried not to hear. They would sit this outbreak of teenage hysteria out. She switched the TV on again. New Year fireworks filled the old 26-inch screen, popping and screeching and sending a range of coloured shadows racing through the conservatory. The North Wind got up. People on the screen screamed and ran for cover. The leak in the glass roof opened up. Plop, plop, plop.

Good old Boreas. I knew someone from Olympia would surface. But perhaps it was he who'd blown a chill through Rozzie's heart? I shouldn't have been mean. I should have got the roof mended. Should, should, should.

Rozzie had peeled off the Brilliant Baby Clinic sticker and found an older label for the Your Beautiful Baby Clinic underneath. Since the sperm was half price she had realised her parents had been offered old stock. Google told her where the Your Beautiful Baby archives were kept, in Hatfield, for some reason.

She had gone there posing as a journalist (Young Reporter of the Year Prize, age group 16–17) and been welcomed by a bored archivist, had reckoned back to the date of her probable conception, and looked through the files to find one which tallied with the date that sample 116349 had left the refrigerated warehouse. She'd found *6ft 1in, blue eyes, blond hair: BA (Oxon), action man, aristocrat* to be the one.

That was when she'd had her stroke of luck. There'd been a pencilled note at the bottom of the form with the date of an Oxford v. Cambridge cricket match, 1979, presumably written by the sperm bank technician, no doubt a cricket fan. Sebastian had been enthusing. It was then just a matter of interviewing such cricketers as were still alive to see if they could identify which of their number was likely to have donated sperm anonymously. It had been tedious but not difficult. She had friends.

Five instantly named young Sebastian, in particular a Lord Monty of Castlehaven. Monty remembered the incident well. He even spoke of Sebastian's poetic genius. 'Oh the spinning, the spilling, the spurning, the spurting of the spunk!' After that it was peanuts.

'I don't believe a word of it, silly girl' said Xandra. 'Where would you find the time?'

'If you'd ever bothered to visit the chess club you might have found I wasn't there. They allow five hours a match. I take one.'

'Off to bed, you little minx,' said Clive affectionately. He was almost asleep. Rozzie took a phone out from beneath her bra. It was an old Galaxy which Clive had discarded for a newer and better version, but no doubt still had enough surplus recording energy in its guts. The one good thing we had done for her, I could see, was not let her have a smartphone, thus saving her from social media. Or so we had thought.

'I've recorded all this,' said Rozzie. 'I'll send you a copy.'

There was a tap on the front door. I went to answer it. It was a very good-looking young man come in search of Rozzie. I had not seen him before but to my reeling brain he looked very like Mercury. All kinds of disordered personality functions were no doubt clustering. Rozzie came out and flashed her Aphrodite smile at him. They went upstairs and came down with suitcases, already packed.

'Where are you going?' I asked. 'You're underage.' But of course she wasn't any more. She was sixteen. She could leave home.

'Off to claim my heritage,' she said. 'I'm his Lordship's oldest child.'

# PART FIVE

# Time For Reflection

I thought back to so many things. I remembered how much younger we'd seemed the day we all sat round sniffing cocaine and Clive had been so happy. His voice had come back loud and clear, after the brief squeaking patch at the clinic when so stressed. Mind you, I'd not been at all sure I liked this new cheerful version of Clive: the familiar old misery with the squeaky voice might have been preferable. Sudden change was always upsetting. But at least neither version of Clive would be able to father Xandra's baby. Mumps presumably would have happened to both old and new.

Such a vivid scene, the day we'd gone through the brochure together when Clive discovered it in Xandra's nurse's cap. It had seemed the obvious answer. A donor. The new Clive was even less likely to believe Dr Vellum's diagnosis than had the former – how could such a paragon of vocal, broad-shouldered maleness be infertile? It had suited Clive to forget such unpleasantness altogether. And it was important for me that one way and another Xandra must have a baby and soon. The window of opportunity was closing. The clinic could deliver the frozen phial to No. 23. Everyone needed a daughter when you grew older, to go shopping with and keep you company and look after you when you were old.

'*A son is a son till he gets a wife, but a daughter is a daughter the rest of your life.*' Wasn't that so true! I assumed Xandra would have a girl. I was just lucky, I suppose, that it was, not Flora's doing. Though I was still well into Hellenism at the time, up and down on my bike to West Hampstead with goodness knows what in the basket.

Clive had even apologised because he'd changed *Let's Get Out of Here!* from a stage show back into a novel. As if I cared. We were in the conservatory, eating fish fingers and chips, in rollicking, rolling mode. For once the TV was not on.

'I'm sorry, Gwinny, I know you did lots of work on it, read it and so forth and were sweet about it and your reaction kept me going but you missed the point. Action beats alone don't make a stage play. A film perhaps but not stage. I realised that watching the James Bond films. I might have said a few imprudent words to those oafs which I shouldn't. I think perhaps I did, but I was stressed. But never mind. Everything has changed. The future is mine.'

And he broke into song again with Joseph's closing number, *Any Dream Will Do*, while avoiding the very high notes, I noticed. Clive was never lost to all prudence.

When the table was cleared Clive collected a razor blade from the bathroom, took Xandra's bag and extracted a ten-pound note and her round make-up mirror, onto which he then shook a little plastic packet of white chunky powder, put it on the glass side table and used the razor blade to cut it to sniffable dust. He did all this with style and ceremony.

'Oh really, Clive,' said Xandra. 'That stuff is so dangerous. And I won't, if you don't mind. I have to think in the morning.'

'Expensive, too,' I said, 'and no thanks, I have to keep my wits about me.'

'Sorry about you two misery guts, but I think I deserve a little celebration in the circumstances,' said Clive, cheerfully enough. He'd met an old mate at the audition and they'd shared some good stuff before they went on – and afterwards they'd bought some: 'Only a couple of grams and a just couple of hundred quid.' I winced and Xandra looked at me nervously. She'd be down on the mortgage.

He became more eloquent still as he told Xandra he wouldn't stand in her way; he knew how badly she needed a baby and he thought she should do it, and soon. He'd do what he could in the way of house-husbanding until his career took off again and Xandra could afford to give up her job and with Gwinny-next-door's help no doubt they would cope. But Xandra must realise he needed to travel where the work took him, the big musicals, Broadway, Tokyo, Berlin. He might even try serious opera. He'd always wanted to try *Turandot*. No, it wouldn't be fair to stand in her way. Their love was a fixed thing, a never wand'ring star. And he'd seen the Brilliant Baby catalogue in her bag earlier (he'd been looking everywhere in her bag for a mirror – more likely the ten-pound note, thought Gwinny – so he knew which way her mind was going) and probably what with the mumps and all it was best. And though Clive would be horribly jealous at least it was a test tube stranger and not his best friend or the kind of sneaky thing a lot of women did in similar circumstances.

*Sniff.*

I'd succumbed and taken some too.

*Snort.*

So we all looked through the catalogue of potential fathers together and wondered at the marvels of modern science and new worlds now opening up for us, and Xandra succumbed and sniffed what was left, and all three together were in this state when we ended up choosing the donor who was to be Sebastian, Lord Dilberne. And so we produced Rozzie and got what we deserved.

But it was mostly me. The other two were too busy giggling. And now I knew who the donor is, Lord Sebastian, I can only wonder and worry. I do not worry about Rozzie at all. She is young in years but certainly not in competence and can look after herself all too well. Xandra of course is beside herself with worry, and Clive has phoned a grief therapist for a consultation. But they will get over it.

I worry about Sebastian, wandering about the vastness of 3 Belgrave Square not knowing what's going to hit him. Should I warn him or should I not? He is a nice man; a family man in his late fifties, quiet and gentle, a touch neurasthenic, with something of a reputation as a violinist, busy with various charities. He has an unmarried son, Dennis, twenty-five, heir to the title and estate, and a daughter, Victoria Hedleigh, aged twenty-eight, a powerful and forthright person, currently campaigning to get the Succession to the Throne Act, 2013 changed to include the nobility as well as royalty, so gender is irrelevant when it comes to inheritance.

I remember my trust in lateral thinking. 'Don't raise the bridge, lower the river'. 'Don't go to prison, change the law'. She might have it in her mind to go one further, so that babies conceived by sperm had equal rights to those naturally born. In which case heaven help Victoria. But she would be a formidable foe.

And heaven help Sebastian too. The nobility may be richer and snobbier than the rest of us, but in their youth are not necessarily more sensible. The legal and personal ramifications that might possibly ensue were far from his Lordship's mind. Donation was still anonymous in 1999, but it was not so difficult, if only by claiming a false identity, for his daughter to discover from whose loins she came and play it to her advantage. As her legal father Clive Smithson, writer and house-husband – the two so often go together – now frequently observed, Rozzie was not one to let legality, let alone common decency, stand in her way.

Sebastian was to tell me at one stage that he saw Rozzie, his eldest daughter, as a direct re-run of his own great-great-grandmother, Adela Ripple. Adela, as described to him by his great-aunt Mallory, still going strong (well, as strong as you can be when in your late nineties) in the Dower House of Dilberne Court, had been a monster. Fetching and charming though

Adela was, she was an inveterate seductress, an unrivalled social climber, and a born liar, doing great damage to all around with the sweetest of Aphrodite smiles. She had even tried to claim the great-aunts as her own, bypassing their real mother, the saintly Vivien, of whom much has been written. Even as nonagenarians, Mallory and Stella, twins, did not forget or forgive. And as Sebastian says to me sadly from time to time, echoing Gwinny, 'genes will out'.

But that's to come. [Writers' Huddle: 'Gwinny, are you sure about all these timeline changes? You may think it's too late in the novel for readers to close the book, but it never is. Just be careful! Signed Consuela, Group Convenor.']


## Rozzie The Dutiful Daughter

To all outward appearances Rozzie remained a dutiful daughter. She did not blot her copybook. She visited once a month, no doubt having future court appearances in mind. She gave us news of where she was living and what she was doing. She showed her concern for our health and well-being, offered to take Simkins Two to the vet to be put down. But there was always a satirical undertone to everything she did or said.

The first time she came, mid-February, Xandra stopped worrying and Clive cancelled his grief therapist appointment, Rozzie was so affectionate and fond. And I tried to quell my paranoiac disorder cluster, though just because you think everyone is out to get you doesn't mean they're not.

But somehow she had managed to make us feel guilty, so when she suggested we gift the freeholds of Nos. 23 and 24 to her we happily did so. You can do this to your children so long as you stay alive for seven years after doing it. But in the meanwhile you are in your children's power. They can evict you, make you homeless if they want to sell, and leave you helpless in your dotage: but you loved them and you trusted them so what could go wrong? Rozzie had all the necessary documentation with her and sent for Mr Ipswich to witness. He came round like a shot to tell us not to do it.

'But Rozzie's our child,' we said. 'We trust her implicitly. She'd never harm us in any way.'

'You'd be surprised what children can do,' Mr Ipswich said, and regaled us with tales of treachery and woe and how sibling rivalry was as nothing compared to suppressed filial rage.

Rozzie listened patiently and sweetly and said, 'But you've known me from birth, dear Mr Ipswich, and I'm not like that. I love the old dears to bits. I've left home but I can manage on my own. I'd just feel so much more secure if I had some assets behind me. If I needed a bank loan, or backing for a start-up – I have a few ideas.'

And Mr Ipswich just gave up – I reckon she gave him an Aphrodite smile – and we signed and after that were in her power and reluctant to cause her any trouble in case our paragon of sweetness, light and brilliance turned nasty.

I realised I could not in all conscience (well, self-interest) go to poor Sebastian and warn him.

## From Out Of The Bardo Thodol

[Writers' Huddle: 'This will put many readers off. *Do* rethink. Too many are averse to supra-natural speculation, and you've already had a fair go at them – warn them, perhaps, to skip this section and go to the next?']

If I were a superstitious kind of person, which I am not, being a thoroughly rational person, just a believer in many overlapping universes – I could see karma at work, what we all deserved, or at least some wild plan hatched in the Buddhist Bardo Thodol, where time as we know it does not exist.

*'Used loosely, the term "Bardo" refers to the state of existence intermediate between two lives on earth. According to Tibetan tradition, after death and before one's next birth, when the soul is not connected with a physical body, the consciousness experiences a variety of phenomena.'* [Maurice, deputy Group Convenor of the Writers' Huddle: 'Thank you Wikipedia – tell them you'll give them a bit of money, Gwinny!']

It may well be that the soul of Adela, born 1884, niece of Isobel, Countess Dilberne, born 1860, came into existence again as Rozzie Smithson, born in the year 2000, perhaps with a chance of getting it better this time round. And also, of course, of getting the title. Greed is imbedded in the human soul, and even as a child Rozzie always asked for more.

No coincidence perhaps, just more Bardo Thodol stuff, that it was I, Gwinny, who just so happened to choose the 9th Earl's sperm. When I came to visit old Great-Aunt Mallory in the Dower House, I showed her a very much mended silver-rimmed glass bowl that Xandra had given me on my birthday, reputedly valuable, which had come down to her through the generations of her more humble lineage. Mallory recognised it as one apparently given by Adela to Elsie.

And I was two Welsh cousins removed, via my Welsh father Aidan, a genealogist I employed had discovered, via my Welsh father Aidan, to Xandra, Elsie's descendant. Elsie, Mallory reckoned, must have been born around 1879, and was the parlourmaid up at Dilberne Court. Elsie had been given the bowl to keep her quiet about a family scandal concerning Adela's daughter Vivvie. Vivvie had become pregnant out of wedlock by a thriller writer called Sherwyn, giving birth to Mallory and her twin Stella in 1923. Adela, in love with Sherwyn (by then her own son-in-law), had tried to claim the twins as her own. And here was I, Gwinny Rhyss, child of the nineteen forties, wielding the turkey baster in 1999 for Xandra, a family relative, however distant. (DNA gets everywhere, so long as it's through the female line, as is well understood in the Jewish religion.) Myself, Gwinny, always the serving maid, toiling away as I had done for my mother Gwen, and Xandra parlourmaid, low in the hierarchy of servants. The Bardo Thodol, it seems, likes to keep one in one's place.

Perhaps even Xandra could claim distant lineage with the Dilberne family, through some vague Chicago connection, albeit illegitimate. The original Viscount Arthur Hedleigh, who had ended up as a car manufacturer in the States, had also when young rather put his sperm about, if rather less rashly than had his descendant Sebastian. Mallory suggested that some might well have drifted Elsie's way. The dance that goes on between upstairs and downstairs in these great English country houses seems to go on for ever. Mind you, Mallory herself can be quite mischievous, perceiving nonsense and stirring the pot.

## Who Is Sent Where?

[Writers' Huddle: 'Half the world believes in reincarnation, Gwinny, so it can't all be absurd. Carry on. Our members just agreed by a vote of seventeen to fourteen that there is no proof that there's no such thing, and it's certainly more fun to contemplate than is the sudden shock of blankness, non-existence, total annihilation which the atheists insist on. "The Calvinist tendency in spiritual terms," as one of our most successful best-selling members observed. What a waste that finality would be! Nature abhors waste. And by the way, apologies for suggesting the Hampstead group. Some of our more vociferous members have resigned from the group. Let's just get on with the fantasy, the fictional stuff. All success to your elbow. email from Felicity X, the new Group Convenor.']

So, anyway, I, Gwinny Rhyss, who likes to think she's Elsie's descendant, found herself wielding the turkey baster – these days you can find a rather less crude purpose-built fertility pipette from Boots – in the service of Xandra. I wonder what jeers and cheers there were in the Bardo Thodol when the plunger sent the pale slightly sweetish stuff, the source of human life, shooting out. But as I say, I am a practical kind of person, not given to fanciful belief or speculation, just the reliable if inquisitive next-door neighbour, witness to the Smithson life. I live at No. 23 where I was born. The Smithsons live next door at end-of-terrace property, No. 24, and moved in thirty years ago. That's all. And when Rozzie owned us I was not as wealthy as I had been and feared eviction. I had as Mr Ipswich tells me, spent money like water.

For the next few months when Adela – sorry, Rozzie – came to visit us she was living with Facebook friends, she said, and doing a degree in law. A model of respectability. She had a thousand blog followers. She was sweet and helpful.

I caught a glimpse of her down the sidebar of the *MailOnline* one Sunday. It was admiring her 'enviable curves and pert bottom' at an A-list celebrity party. With any luck, I thought, Rozzie would have forgotten all about Sebastian, and decided, along with Brecht, that nurture triumphed over nature and we were her true family. She had merely left home rather early after a row with the parents. But teenagers would be teenagers.

At least the *MailOnline* wasn't talking about wardrobe malfunctions and boob slippages, and the other guests were quite respectable. Indeed, I noticed that Monty Castlehaven was one of the guests and Rozzie looked more like granddaughter than daughter, but no Sebastian in sight.

I took it she was just getting on with her life. So were we all. Xandra was now a member of the local Clinical Commissioning Group, and saving hard, and Clive's voice was reasonably good, though never quite as steady as it had been on that remarkable evening on the doorstep of No. 24 – how long ago it seemed – and he even had a steady job in our local Repertory Light Opera Society. I was painting away furiously for a new client; we were all trying to adapt to a vegan diet.

Time passed. Rozzie's visits were not so frequent. Then one day she phoned and said she was coming the next day, so we did the cleaning and tidying one does before a landlady arrives, expecting to see her perhaps with an engagement or even a wedding ring on her finger. But no.

She congratulated us on our vegan carrot and caraway crackers and then said she had good news. She had a well-paid new job as an archivist. I asked her where and she said at 3 Belgrave Square, working on a private collection of ancient books and music scores. It was a live-in job.

I tried not to show any alarm, thinking she might be trying me out, and paranoiac clusters rising all over the place. I decided if I just happened to call by Belgrave Square, since she had mentioned the address, I could now do so without raising suspicion. She ate all the vegan crackers. They're not all that filling.

## Oh The Spurning And The Spurting!

I was in luck. When I knocked upon the door and asked for Miss Smithson the door was opened by Sebastian himself. He was in his slippers and rather casually dressed, in jeans and an old sweater but looked relaxed and cheerful and even young for his age, though his blond hair was quite sparse and thin. He had blue eyes. He told me that Miss Smithson was out shopping. I told him I was Rozzie's grandmother, that not being far from the truth.

'Oh, lucky you!' he exclaimed. I feared the worst. He told me she would be back in half an hour, if I cared to wait. I said I would and sat down on one of the stiff brocaded chairs in the hall. I thought it could do with a good dust and a bit of a polish, but servants are in short supply and old retainers long ago died off.

'Oh, wait in the library,' he said, and I followed him into the magnificent oak-panelled, book-lined room. 'Rozzie works here. She's our very skilled archivist. We're so lucky to have her here. We've even persuaded her to live in, and she's no trouble, no trouble at all.' Bet she isn't, I thought. Wait until she shows her claws. He brought me a glass of very pale sherry, and I sipped it. It was so dry it was hard to enjoy. But then I am a Welsh builder's daughter and my plebeian tastes are hard to overcome. I do like a nice dark sweet sherry.

'Don't I know you from somewhere?' he asked suddenly and I explained that in a past life I had been Lady Petrie and had been to a charity event or two in this very house.

'Dear good old Peterloo,' he cried. 'I remember him well,' and insisted he call his mother Lucy and his daughter Victoria down to meet me. His son Dennis was down at Dilberne Court sprucing the place up. It was falling down. I told him I had met Mallory and asked how she was. 'Battling on,' he cried, 'battling on.'

Lucy declined to come down.

'I'm afraid she's rather taken against our Rozzie. You know what mothers are.'

Victoria came down to meet me in full battle-axe mode, and said rather sourly, 'Oh, Rozzie's grandmother. How old is that girl?' I said seventeen or eighteen and I thought Sebastian looked rather annoyed at so unnecessary a question.

Then Rozzie came home from her shopping with bags that did not look as if they contained coffee beans and biscuits but more like stuff from South Molton Street, and at which Victoria looked askance, and the gathering quickly dissolved.

When I was alone with Rozzie we exchanged pleasantries and I explained I had just come by to check out where she was working. She seemed almost pleased to see me and showed me some of the early Baroque music scores she was cataloguing. I said she seemed to know what she was doing, and she flashed me a thank-you smile.

'I feel my natural home is here,' she said as she saw me out. Well, perhaps it was. Interfering would do no good to anyone.

## Truth Will Out

About a week later there was a knock on the door of No. 23 at around seven o'clock in the evening. Clive and Xandra were off at the cinema watching *La La Land*. To my complete surprise it was Sebastian.

'Nice place you have here,' he said. 'Not so large, of course, but a lot cosier. One could relax here.' By which he meant the washing up was piling up in the sink, and all the ironing piled on the chairs. I leave suburban tidiness to Xandra. I asked him how he knew where I lived and he said he'd looked up Lady Petrie on Google.

'And no doubt a whole lot of newspaper cuttings as well,' I said, 'and a lot of old scandals.'

He agreed, but said he remembered me because I'd been so nice to old Peterloo and obviously made him happy. But that was not why he was here, rather because I was Rozzie's grandmother. I knew what it was like for there to be a great age gap between spouses and did I think it would work? Since his wife Veronica had died he'd become increasingly lonely. He was thinking of asking Rozzie to marry him.

Round and round it goes, I thought. There is a certain inevitability in the pattern of our lives. As in *La Ronde*, that old French film of the fifties. I'd seen it at the Everyman when I was pregnant with Anthea, spending my last penny before I moved into the Home for Fallen Girls. The film had quite cheered me up at the time.

Now I could see I had no option.

'I don't think that's such a good idea.'

'But why not?'

I told him he was her father, and gave him chapter and verse. He remembered almost nothing until I quoted his spinning, spilling, spurning, spurting line back to him.

'Good line,' he said, and then he remembered.

He was pale. I thought he might faint. I had to put my arms round him. He reminded me of Peterloo and the way shock had always affected him.

He had already been seduced by Adela – sorry, Rozzie. No doubt she had used her Aphrodite smile. There would have been no way the poor man could have resisted. And yes, he had already given her clothes and jewels – she was so nice when she was nice, so horrid when she was not. Gradually the horror of it sank in.

'But it's incest!' he cried. 'I didn't know. Supposing she tells. The police can drag me through the courts. Someone in my position. The public disgrace, the humiliation. My poor family! Poor me!'

'Exactly,' I said, 'and now you too are in her power. She's merciless. She's a Millennial.'

'But why, why?'

'She wants revenge,' I said. 'Millennials do. They hate the old on principle. We deserve it. The things we shouldn't have done which we did. They find us out in every way.'

'But what can I do?' He was weeping.

'Nothing. Just go on being nice to her. Humour her. Don't upset her.'

He wept some more. I comforted him in the only way I knew.

## The Fight Against Homelessness

The next time Rozzie came to visit us she was very much acting to the manor born. She was wearing a fur coat though the weather was warm. Like Clive she had no taste.

The news was not good. My advice to Sebastian had gone somewhat awry. He had given away the title of Baron of Montewan, as under Henry VIII's charter of 1532 he was entitled to do, along with Dilberne Court and the 5,000 acres remaining of the original estate. When Sebastian died, Rozzie would own it till she wills it away to her oldest child, be it male or female, regardless of the seven-year rule. She would continue in Isobel and Adela's footsteps and go on improving the place to fit the Millennium until it did not recognisably exist at all. And Sebastian, like all his predecessors to the title, would go on believing that *amor vincit omnia,* and chafe and wriggle and do nothing.

Memories of the past will be satisfactorily extinguished. Mallory will die of shock when she has to be transported elsewhere. What would Rozzie care? The old were useless. I blame all those pre-millennial history teachers who saw the past as another country but not that they did things differently there, and so turned the past into the present.

He may think he gives away everything because otherwise she will expose his crime and drag him through the courts and bring the family name into disrepute, but really because he is still 'in love' with Rozzie. He will love her whatever she does. He cannot help himself. He may yet marry her.

Rozzie twirls her pearls – she knows, she knows! I told him and he told her: secrets are impossible to keep. Maybe because I told Sebastian that Rozzie was his daughter, maybe because I comforted him in the only way I knew. But it scarcely matters which, either offence will do. The girl's a Millennial. She puts feelings above facts. She tells us she's really sorry but she feels she has to evict us. She needs Nos. 23 and 24 – now as it happens one house; we finally 'broke through' – for her staff. (Oh, I think: that Cheyne Walk house! The things we regret!) But we have three months before we have to go. She's being very generous, she says. We see her politely out. There is no way to comfort anyone at all.

## A Scandal

The next person to call at my door is Victoria. She is in a great state of agitation. She had her way with the Succession to the Throne Act, 2013 and now she will inherit and not her brother Dennis. 'He's a degenerate anyway,' says Victoria. She has no time for him. But now there's another problem. Rozzie, well known to boast that she's in a relationship with her father, a much older man, is now claiming to be the eldest child and is thus entitled to inherit. Rozzie's case is that her existence should hail from the date the paternal sperm was spent, not her birth. Absurd. But a dreadfully lefty (Victoria's description) Star Chamber is taking Rozzie's plea seriously. The papers call it the Dilberne Spillage Case , and the whole family is the source of abuse and ridicule. Victoria is almost ashamed to leave the house. Does Gwinny know anything about Rozzie's birth that might help her, Victoria? She believes Gwinny is quite close to her father.

Gwinny says she can't help, she doesn't dare to. But she hopes Victoria has done all the required DNA tests and has urged the court not to take them too seriously.

'Why not?'

'Well,' says Gwinny. 'One of Clive's grey hairs looks very like one of Sebastian's grey hairs. It would be a simple thing for Rozzie, knowing Rozzie, to switch them. In the laboratory, if need be.'

'You really think–?' Victoria was incredulous.

'I've no idea,' said Gwinny. 'I've really no idea.' And she didn't.

# PART SIX

## Exodus

Rozzie was found dead in her bed in Belgrave Square the next morning. Police and medical reports suggested dopaminergic neurotoxicity and the coroner confirmed an accidental overdose of amphetamines. A syringe, a box of Ritalin pills and a cut-glass jug engraved with the Dilberne crest – a heart, and a banner claiming *Amor Vincit Omnia* – were found on the little Chippendale bedside table. Strange, because Rozzie was not one for love.

Rozzie had not been down to breakfast and Victoria had gone up to call her, since the maid was waiting to clear. Rozzie had been lying naked on top of the coverlet and had seemed to be breathing but when Victoria had tried to feel her pulse there was none to be found. The family doctor had been called and declared the young woman to be dead and the authorities had been summoned. Or so Victoria described what she thereafter referred to as 'the incident'.

A week later the coroner declared an accidental overdose, but I, Gwinny, doubted that very much, as did many. So many people benefited from her death. Lucy, Dowager Countess of Dilberne, even held a celebratory party; Sebastian, released so suddenly from blackmail, rose from his sickbed and regained his full health. English Heritage, I imagine, refrained from actual cheering – being so well mannered and stiff-upper-lipped – but would have been quietly delighted that their precious Dilberne Court was to be saved, at last, from the succession of titled Dilberne ladies – most recently Isobel and Adela – who had done their best over the previous century to do what the Germans would call *Verschlimmbesserung*: to make worse by improving. Rozzie's way was to simply raze it to the ground.

To my mind it was murder plain and simple, the chief suspect being Victoria. Through history the eldest sons of the nobility often enough die mysteriously so that the second in line can inherit. Since the amendment in 2020 to the Succession to the Throne Act, 2013 which abolished gender discrimination as it related to the peerage, it will no doubt extend to the dangers faced by the eldest daughter. A great deal of money, power and prestige is involved.

Rozzie's suit being discontinued by reason of her sudden death, Victoria was safely now a Viscount and would inherit the property, titles and duties of the Earldom and have a seat in the Lords when Sebastian died. Her wife Amy would then become a Countess and if they had children, provided they were begotten by 'natural means' and not with the assistance of genetic technology, they would in their turn inherit. A lot of wives have murdered a lot of other wives to secure the succession of their children.

Or else Victoria and Amy did it together. Having persuaded Rozzie to join them in some kind of '*let's all be friends*' New Year's Eve drugs party it would have been easy enough for either of them to add a handful of Ritalin tabs to the cut-glass Dilberne water jug for Rozzie then to inject more as midnight struck. Victoria and Amy would have crushed and snorted a smaller dose themselves to keep Rozzie company on her journey to heaven or hell.

But I did not want to add to the complexity of the affair by suggesting any such thing to the authorities. Accidental death would do: better than a suicide verdict any day. If the police started any real investigation they would have turned up far too many stones for comfort.

As it was, the press and associated media had had more than enough of a field day, first with the hilarious scandals associated with the Dilberne Spillage Case, with its 'Oh the spinning, the spilling, the spurning, the spurting of the spunk' quote from his young Lordship back in 1979 as reported to them by his ancient duffer 'friend' Monty. The lovely young girl protagonist Rosalind and her older female antagonist Dicky Vikky (you could tell whose side they were on!). And now the *Daily Mail*'s drone pictures through the open window of 3 Belgrave Square of the body, young, naked and beautiful, a real sleeping beauty with the added attraction of being dead (and on her birthday too, January 1st 2021) which went spectacularly viral on social media. Mr Ipswich tried but said there was no way of stopping it.

The room Rozzie died in had been the then Viscount's bedroom in 1895, which was, if I am to put two and two together, one of the very rooms in which Arthur would have bedded the parlourmaid Elsie and, later, the lady's maid Grace. It had a curtained double bed – and I doubted the mattress had been changed or the curtains washed for a hundred years, that very grunginess being one of the reasons, I expect, that Victoria allocated Rozzie the room in the first place.

Lawyers had advised that having the same address for the appellants would do much to suggest to the court that there was no undue animosity between the appellants. Also, of course, the room was on the second floor at the front and so open to paparazzi drone camera attack. I suppose Rozzie herself might have opened the window to hear the New Year's bells, whistles and sirens, as Victoria suggested, but I don't think that was at all in Rozzie's nature. She hated crowds. I think it was to facilitate such a drone attack.

Rozzie's mother was allowed in to see the body and I went with her. Of course it was dreadfully upsetting for both of us. But now the freehold of the knocked-through 23 and 24 would, with a little of Mr Ipswich's help, revert back to us. And old Mallory, at ninety-eight, would not be driven out of the Dower House to suit Rozzie's stated desire to flood the market with thinking, feeling robots.

I cried a little, Xandra cried a little, but somehow the child Rozzie had switched to the wholly Millennial Rozzie, wholly calm, wholly composed and totally ruthless, stretched out upon the bed, cold and bare, too perfect to be entirely human. We mourned for something long past.

The Millennial had come of an age. The Bardo Thodol had

reached out to claim its own, perhaps alarmed with what it had done. In the House of Lords Rozzie might well have had power enough to have started World War Three.

A flash of the old schizotypal personality disorder it may be – that someone somewhere must be seen to be in charge and know what they're doing – but forgive me. It was only a flash. Since Anthea came back into my life – I have Rozzie to thank for that and I am truly grateful – the personality disorders have faded and gone, following in the footsteps of Clive's last rose of summer.

The Bardo Thodol is a figment of a fevered imagination; the Goddess Flora has nothing at all to do with Rozzie's existence; the fact that Simkins died the day I dismantled Apollo's shrine is a mere coincidence; and if Mother Mary smiled at me last time I was at mass, it was a trick of the light. I have returned to the religion of my childhood. I no longer cast a horoscope or even consult my stars in the evening paper.

Xandra has lost her only daughter, but enjoys the trust and respect of those who work with her. Clive has lost the child he was so determined was his, but seems energised to actually finish the work he started so long ago. He promises to give it to me to read soon, which I rather dread. They are trying to adopt, but fear the adoption people will reject them on grounds of age, both of them being into their sixties. I would add smoking, swearing, drug taking, TV noise, unmodulated *cris de jouissance* (they are still at it) and a degree of political incorrectness to the list, but I daresay social services will figure it all out.

The necessary tale has been told; I have written enough; I will write no more.

I will cycle up to Anthea's and Philip's big house in Hampstead for Sunday lunch. Anthea is sixty-seven and still working as a clinical psychologist, Philip her husband is a Freudian analyst. I tell no-one more than I need, or I think they need to know. They are all very proper. But they make me very welcome; indeed they seem to love me. Anthea's daughter Flora will be there – the name only a coincidence – Anthea tells me she always loved it – and Flora's two little daughters Chloris and Phoebe, my great-granddaughters. So many girls! And on we all go.

Just now I thought I saw a cat's tail whisk round the corner, a flash of white and ginger, brown and black. Simkins Three, the calico cat? But that also can only be imagination.

I, Gwinny, am very happy.

## Postscript

Thanks very much, oh Wedding Guest, for your patience. Understand and forgive them all. And as Coleridge said, waking from some opium dream…

> *Farewell, farewell! but this I tell*
> *To thee, thou Wedding-Guest!*
> *He prayeth well, who loveth well*
> *Both man and bird and beast.*
>
> *He prayeth best, who loveth best*
> *All things both great and small;*
> *For the dear God who loveth us,*
> *He made and loveth all.*
>
> *The Mariner, whose eye is bright,*
> *Whose beard with age is hoar,*
> *Is gone: and now the Wedding-Guest*
> *Turns from the bridegroom's door.*

And as I say, mildly misquoting Coleridge's last verse…

> *He goes like one that hath been stunned,*
> *And is of sense forlorn:*
> *A sadder and a wiser man,*
> *He'll rise the morrow morn.*